PEACHTREE

SABOTAGED

ALSO BY MARGARET PETERSON HADDIX

THE MISSING SERIES
Found
Sent

THE SHADOW CHILDREN SERIES
Among the Hidden
Among the Impostors
Among the Betrayed
Among the Barons
Among the Brave
Among the Enemy
Among the Free

The Girl with 500 Middle Names
Because of Anya
Say What?
Dexter the Tough
Running Out of Time

Claim to Fame
Palace of Mirrors
Uprising
Double Identity
The House on the Gulf
Escape from Memory
Takeoffs and Landings
Turnabout
Just Ella
Leaving Fishers
Don't You Dare Read This, Mrs. Dunphrey

THE MISSING: BOOK 3

SABOTAGED

MARGARET PETERSON
HADDIX

SIMON & SCHUSTER BOOKS FOR YOUNG READERS

NEW YORK   LONDON   TORONTO   SYDNEY

SIMON & SCHUSTER BOOKS FOR YOUNG READERS

An imprint of Simon & Schuster Children's Publishing Division

1230 Avenue of the Americas, New York, New York 10020

For information about special discounts for bulk purchases, please contact Simon & Schuster Special Sales at 1-866-506-1949 or business@simonandschuster.com.

The Simon & Schuster Speakers Bureau can bring authors to your live event. For more information or to book an event, contact the Simon & Schuster Speakers Bureau at 1-866-248-3049 or visit our website at www.simonspeakers.com.

Book design by Tom Daly based on an original design by Drew Willis

The text for this book is set in Weiss.

Manufactured in the United States of America

0710 FFG

2 4 6 8 10 9 7 5 3 1

Library of Congress Cataloging-in-Publication Data

Haddix, Margaret Peterson.

Sabotaged / Margaret Peterson Haddix.

p. cm. – (The missing ; bk. 3)

Summary: Time-travelers Jonah and Katherine are summoned to help another missing child from history, this time Virginia Dare from the Roanoke Colony, but their journey is sabotaged and goes dangerously awry, leaving them in the wrong time period. Includes author's note about the history of Roanoke Colony and Virginia Dare.

ISBN 978-1-4169-5424-8 (hardcover : alk. paper)

1. Dare, Virginia, b. 1587—Juvenile fiction. 2. Roanoke Colony—Juvenile fiction. [1. Dare, Virginia, b. 1587—Fiction. 2. Roanoke Colony—Fiction. 3. Space and time—Fiction. 4. Science fiction.] I. Title.

PZ7. H1164Sab 2010

2009020056

ISBN 978-1-4424-0646-9 (eBook)

For the Westdorps

ACKNOWLEDGMENTS

With thanks to Joy, Eric, Faith, Ethan, Meredith, and Connor for accompanying me during my research, and for listening to all my wild theories. Sorry about the sand!

ONE

Jonah fidgeted in his seat, and his chair fidgeted right along with him. In another mood, Jonah would have been fascinated by this—how was the chair programmed? Did it have a computer chip making it squirm? But right now Jonah was too distracted. He was sitting in a sterile, nearly empty room, waiting to travel back in time to an unknown era and unknown dangers. So all he could do was fidget.

You'd think, with time travel, there wouldn't have to be any waiting, he thought grumpily.

Beside him, his eleven-year-old sister, Katherine, bounced in her chair—making the chair bounce too—and chattered away to Andrea, the third kid who would be going to the past with them. Indeed, Andrea was the most important time traveler that day. She was the reason they were all going.

"Don't worry," Katherine told Andrea. "You don't have to hold your breath or anything to travel through time. It's easy."

"That's good," Andrea said softly. She sat perfectly still, and so did her chair. She had her eyes focused on the blank wall across from her and barely seemed to be paying attention to Katherine. Normally Jonah would have approved of that—he tried to ignore his younger sister as much as possible too. But unlike Katherine and Jonah, Andrea had never traveled to the past before. She didn't know what time period she was going to, or what she'd have to do there. Shouldn't she be asking questions? Shouldn't she at least act like she cared?

"Only, if you get time sick, that's no fun," Katherine rambled on, flipping her blond ponytail over her shoulder. "When we went back to 1483 with Chip and Alex, I thought I was going to throw up for sure. And I felt really dizzy, and—"

"Katherine!" Jonah interrupted, because he could put up with Katherine's babbling for only so long. "Andrea won't get time sick like you did. Remember? She's going back to her proper time. Where she belongs. So she'll feel good."

At that, Andrea's whole face brightened.

Wow, Jonah thought. *She's really pretty*. He honestly

hadn't noticed before. Of course, he barely knew Andrea. The first time he'd met her, there'd been thirty-four other kids around, and four grown-ups fighting about what was going to happen to the kids, and people being Tasered and tied up and zapped back in time . . . Jonah had had a good excuse for not looking closely. All he remembered from that first meeting was that Andrea had worn her long brown hair in two braids, and she hadn't screamed and panicked like a lot of the other kids. And he guessed he knew that—like him and the other kids the grown-ups were fighting over—Andrea was thirteen years old, and she was a missing child from history, one who had been stolen from her proper time and place by baby smugglers. One who had to go back, to save history.

Suddenly Jonah really wanted to remind Andrea that he and Katherine had already proved that they could save history *and* save missing kids, all at once, even when the time experts thought it was impossible. They'd managed to save Chip and Alex from the 1480s, hadn't they? Jonah started to smile back at Andrea and was working up what he wanted to say to her: something suave but casual and not too conceited-sounding . . . . Did, *Don't be scared. I'll take care of you* sound stupid?

Katherine began talking again before Jonah had a chance to say anything.

"Andrea can too get time sick," Katherine argued. "Not the kind from being in the wrong time period, but the kind just from traveling through time. Remember JB thought I had both kinds? And that's why I felt so awful? And . . ."

Katherine broke off because the door opened just then and JB, the very person she'd been talking about, stepped through.

JB was a time traveler from the future, and the main person who was trying to fix time by returning all the stolen kids to history. Tall, with gleaming chestnut-brown hair, JB was so good-looking that Katherine had nicknamed him cute janitor boy before any of them had found out what he really did for a living. For some reason, JB's appearance really annoyed Jonah right now. Depending on how you looked at it, Jonah had known JB for only a few weeks—or for more than five hundred years. (Or, actually, more than a thousand, if you counted the fact that Jonah, Katherine, Chip, and Alex had traveled between the fifteenth and twenty-first centuries in *both* directions.) Regardless, it had taken Jonah a while to figure out whether to trust JB or not. JB had helped Jonah and Katherine and their friends, but Jonah still wasn't sure: If JB had to choose between saving kids and saving history, which would he pick?

I have to make sure that isn't the choice, Jonah told himself grimly. He gazed over at Andrea again, with her clear pale skin and her gray eyes that somehow looked sad again— haunted, even. *I will* protect you, he thought, even though he figured he'd really sound foolish if he said that now. He kicked his foot against the ground, and his chair kicked too.

"Careful," JB warned. "Those are calibrated to a very sensitive level." He seemed to notice Katherine's bouncing for the first time. "They're not really meant for kids."

Katherine stopped mid-bounce. Her chair rose up and caught her.

"Sorry," Katherine said. "Can we go now? There's no chance that we'll hurt your precious chairs if you just send us to the past."

She sounded offended. Jonah wondered if he should warn JB that it wasn't a good idea to offend Katherine.

"Not yet," JB said. "You need to be debriefed first."

Katherine leaned forward in her chair, and her chair leaned with her.

"Really?" she breathed, seeming to forget any hurt feelings. "You'll tell us where we're going this time—before we get there?"

JB laughed.

"You didn't give me much of a chance the last time," he reminded her.

"That wasn't our fault," Jonah argued hotly. "If you

hadn't sent Chip and Alex back without telling them anything, and if you hadn't cheated when I gave you the Elucidator, and if—"

JB held up his hand, cutting Jonah off.

"Hey, hey," JB said. "Calm down. I'm sorry, okay? That's over and done with. Water under the bridge. Haven't you ever heard the expression, 'No need to relive the past'?"

Katherine and Jonah both stared at him blankly.

"Um, isn't it kind of, uh, contradictory, for a time traveler to say that?" Katherine asked.

"Yep." JB beamed at them. "You caught the irony. Time-traveler humor—gotta love it."

He turned toward Andrea, who was still sitting quietly, unaffected.

"As far as I'm concerned, we're all on the same team this time around," JB said. "From the very beginning. No keeping secrets unnecessarily. Deal?" He held out his hand to Andrea.

"Of course," Andrea said calmly. She shook JB's hand, before he moved on to shake Jonah's and Katherine's in turn. Maybe if Jonah hadn't been paying such close attention to Andrea now, he wouldn't have noticed that Andrea hesitated slightly before speaking, before taking JB's hand.

She is *scared,* Jonah thought. *She really does need me to take care of her.*

"So you'll tell Andrea who she really is?" Katherine asked eagerly.

And me? Jonah almost asked, forgetting that he was supposed to be all about protecting Andrea at the moment. Jonah had seen his two friends Chip and Alex learn their original identities in history. And he knew that, ultimately, he would have to return to his original time period, at least briefly—just like all the other missing kids from history. But, as much as he wanted to know his own identity and his own time period . . . maybe he wasn't quite ready to know right now?

The moment when he could have asked was past. JB was answering Katherine.

"I thought I'd just show her," he said.

JB flipped a switch on the wall behind Jonah's chair, and the wall opposite them instantly turned into what appeared to be an incredibly high-definition TV screen. Waves crashed against a sandy beach, and Jonah had no doubt that, if he looked carefully enough, he'd be able to make out each individual grain of sand.

"Just skip to the part she's going to be interested in," JB said.

Jonah wasn't sure if JB was talking directly to the TV screen (or whatever futuristic invention it actually was) or if there was someone in a control room somewhere who was monitoring their entire conversation. Sometimes Jonah just didn't want to think too much about the whole time-travel mess. He knew that JB had already pulled them out of the twenty-first century, and the waiting room they were in was a "time hollow," a place where time didn't really exist. He knew that JB was probably about to show them some scene from Andrea's "real" life, before she'd been kidnapped by unethical time travelers, and before she'd crash-landed (with all the other missing kids) at the very end of the twentieth century. But it made Jonah feel better if he told himself he was just watching a TV with really, really good reception.

The scene before him shifted, seeming to fly across the water to a marshy coastline and then inland a bit to a primitive-looking cluster of houses. Some of the houses were encircled by a wooden fence that was maybe eight or nine feet tall. Both the houses and the fence looked a bit ramshackle, with holes in several spots.

The view shifted again, focusing on a woman rushing out of one of the nicer houses. The woman was wearing what Jonah thought of as old-fashioned clothes: a long skirt, long sleeves, and a funny-looking hat covering her head. The skirt wasn't quite as sweeping as the ones he'd seen in the fifteenth century, but Jonah wasn't sure if that meant that he was looking at a different time period now, or if he was just watching different people. Poorer ones. Not royalty anymore.

"Mistress Dare's baby has arrived!" the woman called, joy overtaking the exhaustion in her face. "A wee girl child, strong and fair!"

Other people began rushing out of the other houses, cheering and calling out, "Huzzah, huzzah!" But Jonah got only a brief glimpse of them before the camera—or whatever perspective he was watching—zoomed in tighter. Through the door, across a clay floor, up to a bed . . . On the bed a woman hugged a tiny baby against her chest.

"My dearest girl," the woman whispered, her face glowing with love, even in the dim candlelight. "My little Virginia."

"NO!" someone screamed.

It took Jonah a moment to realize that the screaming hadn't come from the scene before him. He peered around, annoyed that Katherine would interrupt like that. But Katherine, beside him, was gazing around in befuddlement too.

It was Andrea—quiet, calm, unperturbed Andrea— who had her mouth open, who was even now jumping to her feet, eyes blazing with fury.

"NO!" she screamed again. "That's not me! That's not my mother!"

TWO

The "TV screen" turned back into a blank wall.

"Andrea," JB said soothingly. "I know this is hard to comprehend, but you really are Virginia Dare. The first English child born in the so-called New World. Would you like to see the DNA evidence?"

"That's so great," Katherine interrupted. "I'd love to be Virginia Dare. You're, like, one of the most famous mysteries in American history." She looked up at JB. "So what did happen to Virginia Dare? Or, I mean—what's supposed to happen?"

Jonah wanted to kick his sister. Maybe, if he knew how to work it right, he could get his chair to do that for him. Couldn't Katherine see that Andrea was traumatized by the news of who she really was? Didn't Katherine understand how hard it must be for Andrea, to know that she wasn't really the person she'd always thought she was?

Of course not. Katherine wasn't one of the missing kids from history. She wasn't adopted, like Andrea and Jonah were. She'd always known that Mom and Dad were her parents, in every sense of the word. She'd never had to doubt her own identity.

JB ignored Katherine's question.

"Andrea?" he said again.

Because Jonah was watching very closely, he saw something like a mask fall over Andrea's expression. One moment she looked furious, ready to scream some more. Maybe even ready to attack. The next moment her face was smooth and blank, every emotion erased.

"Sorry," she said softly. She eased back into her chair. "I just—sorry. You can go on."

"Wait," JB said. "I know what to show you. The direct link, maybe?"

This must have served as directions for the TV. An image reappeared on the opposite wall, this time focused in even more tightly on the newborn Virginia Dare, a tiny red-faced infant. It took Jonah a moment to realize that the baby was growing up before his eyes, in a weird sort of time-lapse photography. After a minute or so, the screen went dark for a second. When the image reappeared, it was clearly the same baby, but she was wearing a Mickey Mouse T-shirt now.

The baby grew even more, into a toddler wearing an Elmo sweatshirt, a preschooler carrying a book of fairy tales, a six- or seven-year-old holding a soccer ball . . . the images flew by, one blurring into another. Jonah couldn't have said how old the child was before she was clearly recognizable as Andrea—eight? Nine? She kept growing, changing, maturing. In the last seconds of the flashing images, Andrea's appearance changed again, even more dramatically than the switch from the infant in the old-fashioned nightgown to the baby with the Mickey Mouse T-shirt. In all of the last few images Andrea's expression was plaintive, guarded.

The final image might as well have been pulled from a mirror held up to Andrea exactly as she was now, dressed in a nondescript gray sweatshirt over a T-shirt and shorts (which was a little odd, Jonah thought, since it had been November back home.) In both the image and reality, her hair fell straight and smooth past her shoulders—and she had her lips pursed, her jaw tight, her eyes narrowed.

"Wow!" Katherine exploded, forgetting herself and bouncing in her chair again. "That is so cool! Can you do that for me? Show what I've looked like since birth, I mean?"

"Not right now, Katherine," JB said. He was watching

Andrea. He touched some control on the wall, and the last image of Andrea as Virginia Dare appeared again: a baby in a bonnet and a gown edged with lace. Beside it he pulled up the image of baby Andrea in her Mickey Mouse T-shirt. And then he zoomed out from both images, to show the scene surrounding the different versions of Andrea as a baby. In both, a woman was holding the baby: on the left side, Mistress Dare, thin-faced and haggard now, but still gazing at her daughter adoringly; on the right, a petite muscular, curly-haired woman who was grinning down at the baby cradled in her arms.

In both images, the baby Andrea looked so happy that Jonah could practically hear her gurgling.

"You could have done that with trick photography," Andrea said in a tight voice. "You could have used Photoshop."

"You know we didn't do that," JB said.

A single tear rolled down Andrea's cheek. Almost all of Jonah's experience with girls crying was with Katherine, who was given to big dramatic wails, "Oh, this—is—so—unfair!" In fifth grade Katherine had had some problems with friends being mean, and it had seemed to Jonah as if Katherine had filled the house with her loud sobs every night for weeks: "I can't believe she said that to me! Oh, why—would—anyone—say—that?"

Jonah had gotten really good at tuning out all of that. Somehow, Andrea's single tear affected him more. It seemed sadder. It made him want to help.

Andrea was already brushing the tear away, impatiently, as if she didn't want to acknowledge that it was there.

"Don't do this to me," Andrea said. "Just send us back. Now."

Her voice was hard. She could have been a queen ordering soldiers off to war or calling for an execution.

"Uh, Andrea, that's probably not a good idea," Katherine said. "I mean, you will have Jonah and me there to help and all, but being in a different century . . . it's probably smart if we can find out as much as we can ahead of time."

By this, Jonah knew that even Katherine was scared. Maybe she was also hoping that there was still some way to avoid going back in time.

"JB can tell us what we need to know once we get there, right?" Andrea asked, her expression still rigid.

"I *could*," JB said. "I will be in contact with you through the Elucidator the whole time."

Jonah grimaced a little, remembering how much trouble he and Katherine and their friends had had with an Elucidator in the fifteenth century. Part of his problem was that he still didn't understand it completely—it was a time-travel device from the future, capable of doing much more than Jonah had ever witnessed. But it impersonated common objects from whatever time period it happened to be in. In the twenty-first century, it mostly looked like an iPhone.

In the fifteenth century, it had looked like a rock. It had still managed to translate Middle English, communicate back and forth with JB, turn Jonah and Katherine and their friends invisible, and—oh, yeah—annoy Jonah's friend Chip so much that he'd thrown it across the room.

Jonah tried to figure out how to mention the problems with the Elucidator without sounding cowardly or scaring Andrea. But she was already answering JB.

"Fine," she said. "Then give us an Elucidator and let's go." She sat up straight, and her chair seemed to rearrange itself in a way that made Jonah think of mother birds pushing baby birds out of the nest.

"I don't think that that's the best—" JB began. He stopped, a baffled look coming over his face. He turned slightly, no longer addressing Andrea. "Really? Are you sure?"

He took a few steps away, like someone suddenly interrupted by a call on a wireless headset. Of course, Jonah couldn't see even the slightest trace of a headset near either of JB's ears. By JB's time, Jonah figured, they might be microscopic.

"Yes? Yes? You ran *that* projection? Just now?" JB paused. "Yeah, Sam, I know it's your job to think of everything, but still . . . that was fast." Another pause. "Oh, when Katherine asked, not Andrea. That makes more sense." He waited, then gave a pained chuckle. "No, of course I won't forget the dog."

He looked back at the kids.

"I've been corrected," JB said. "My top projectionist says it *would* be best if we sent you right away and then filled you in on everything once you get there. It seems counterintuitive, but projections often are."

"Projections?" Andrea repeated nervously.

"Predictions," JB said. "Forecasts. Before any time trip, our projectionists run checks on as many variables as they can think of, and as many combinations of variables, to see what would lead to the best outcome."

"But," Jonah began, "you said the projections don't always . . ." He stopped himself before the last word slipped out. It was going to be *work*. *The projections don't always work.* JB *had* told them that. But again, Jonah didn't want to scare Andrea. He finished lamely. "The projections don't always . . . make a lot of sense."

"Exactly," JB said. "Which is why we're sending Andrea

back with two untrained kids. I didn't think I'd ever have to do anything like that again. And you don't need any special clothes this time, but you do need . . ." He opened the door he had used before and whistled out into the hallway. "Here, boy!" he called. "Here, Dare!"

A shaggy English sheepdog came padding into the room.

"Oh!" Andrea said, clearly surprised.

"Didn't JB tell you?" Katherine said. "That was one of the experts' projections, that this was the only combination we could succeed with: you, me, Jonah, and the dog, all going back in time together."

"Um, okay," Andrea said.

JB rolled his eyes.

"Believe me, I've never sent a pet back in time before," he said. "I mean, kids *and* a dog? If it was anyone else giving me that advice, I'd tell them they were crazy. But Sam is the most brilliant projectionist I've ever worked with, so . . . meet Dare. Your fourth traveling companion."

The dog padded right over to Andrea and put his big head in her lap. He gazed up at her sympathetically, as if he knew that she'd been crying a moment ago, and he completely understood and would sacrifice his own life if that would make her feel better.

How do dogs do that? Jonah wondered. He was a little

afraid that the dog gazing at her might make Andrea cry again, but she just buried her face in his fur and gave him a big hug.

"Nice to meet you, Dare," she mumbled. Jonah noticed that she sounded happier than she had meeting him and Katherine. She lifted her face and peered up at JB again. "And the Elucidator?"

JB pulled something small out of his back pocket—it looked like the Elucidator was currently impersonating a very, very compact cell phone. He pressed a few buttons on the "phone," and slid it into a pouch on Dare's collar.

"All set," he said. "I'll talk to you again once you get there. All you have to do is link arms and hold on to Dare's collar."

He waited while the three kids got into position. Jonah was kind of hoping he'd get to stand next to Andrea, but Katherine ended up in the middle. JB reached down and touched something on the Elucidator. "Three, two, one . . . *bon voyage!*"

The room disappeared.

THREE

Does anyone ever get completely used to time travel? Jonah wondered.

He knew, because he'd done it before, that it just *seemed* like he was falling endlessly through nothingness, toward nothingness. He knew that eventually lights would rush up at him, and he'd feel as if his whole body was being torn apart, down to each individual atom. And then he'd land, and he'd sort of feel like himself again. After a while.

He knew all that, but it was still horrifying to fall and fall and fall. . . .

It must be worse for Andrea.

"Are you doing all right?" he yelled across to her, the words ripped from his mouth by the air rushing past.

Still, she nodded. She had a resigned look on her face, as if she was braced for anything.

Or—as if she didn't really think this was that bad, because she'd already gone through something that was much worse?

Jonah reached out to her with his free hand. If he linked his left arm around her elbow the same way he'd linked his right arm around Katherine's, they could travel through time in a circle, with the dog in the middle. When he and Katherine and Chip had traveled back to 1483, they'd formed a circle like that, and it had been comforting, a way to close out at least a little of the void around them.

But Andrea jerked back from Jonah's touch, swinging away from him.

"Hold on—I'm scared the Elucidator is going to fall off," she called.

The pouch on the dog's collar had looked secure to Jonah, but he couldn't really see it clearly now, in the dark nothingness. He sensed, more than saw, that Andrea was leaning in toward the dog's collar.

"The strap's loose," Andrea said. "I'll just hold the Elucidator myself."

Your hand might go numb at the end, Jonah wanted to tell her. *When you land, you may not even be able to be sure that the Elucidator is in your hand. . . .* That's what had happened to him in the fifteenth century.

But some random air current hit Andrea just then, and

she swung even farther away from Jonah. She still had her left arm linked around Katherine's elbow and her left hand clenched around the dog's collar. But the rest of her body flipped almost completely behind Katherine's back.

"Watch out!" Katherine shrieked, just as Jonah called, "Andrea! Hold on!"

He reached over to put his free hand on top of her hand on the dog's collar, to hold her in place. It seemed entirely possible that she could be yanked away. And then what would happen to her?

He jerked his head to the right, trying to see behind Katherine's back. This was kind of like playing three-dimensional Twister—his hand had to stay on Andrea's hand, his arm had to stay linked through Katherine's, and that didn't leave him much room for arcing back, trying to see where Andrea was now. He got a quick glimpse before his head jerked forward again and Katherine's shoulder blocked his view. Oddly, Andrea wasn't flailing about, trying to swing back around. Instead, she seemed to be curled into a ball, hunched over the Elucidator. It made Jonah think of how kids at school would hunch over their cell phones when they got some text message they didn't want anyone else to see.

"Andrea!" Jonah yelled. "Try to, like, swim back around! Here! I'll help you!"

He kept his left hand clasped tightly over hers, both of them clutching the dog collar together. But he took his right hand off the collar just for a second, just long enough to give Andrea's arm a little yank. This was like physics, wasn't it? If they were traveling through a vacuum, his pull should bring Andrea back into place and him. . . .

Oops. It sent him swinging too far out to the left—and crashing into Andrea, as she swung back.

The dog began to bark. Katherine was screaming, "Hold on! Just—everyone hold on!" Jonah could hear that clearly, because he'd bounced back this time in a way that put his ear right in front of Katherine's mouth. He threw a quick glance over his shoulder—he thought Andrea was screaming something too, but he couldn't hear what it was.

And then he couldn't even hear Katherine or the dog, because they'd hit the part of the trip when the lights rushed up at them and Jonah felt as though his whole body was being torn apart by gravity and time. His ears roared with his own pulse, faster, faster, faster. . . . This had happened before, but what if his heart actually exploded this time?

They landed. Jonah was too blinded, too deafened, too numbed, to be able to tell where they were. They could be on a soft sandy beach, basking in the sun, or in the middle of a blizzard, constantly slammed by ice crystals. It would be all the same to Jonah. He blinked frantically, trying to recover his sight. He tried to get his hands to reach up to his head, succeeding only on his left side. . . . What was that? Had he gotten pine needles in his ear?

He did his best to brush away everything from his left ear, and that made a difference. Now he could hear someone screaming, though the voice seemed far away.

". . . lose . . ."

". . . lose . . ."

". . . you made me lose . . ."

"Who made you lose? Lose what?" This wasn't screaming. This was Katherine, sounding weak but relatively calm.

"Jonah . . . It was Jonah. . . ."

It seemed to require superhuman effort, but Jonah managed to struggle up a little and blink his eyesight slightly back into focus. Was that dog fur? Oh. The dog had landed sprawled across the right side of Jonah's body. No wonder Jonah had been able to move only his left arm. But now Dare squirmed off with an offended yelp. Once the dog moved, Jonah could see and hear much better.

"What did Jonah make you lose?" Katherine was demanding, even as she swayed in and out of focus.

Andrea had her face clutched in her hands. Her voice soared into a wail.

"He made me lose the Elucidator!"

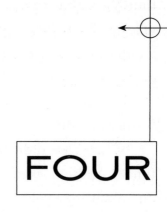

FOUR

Jonah still couldn't see very well, but he could tell that all the color had instantly drained from Katherine's face.

"Is it . . . just . . . on the ground beside . . ." Katherine began.

"No, it's gone! Completely gone!" Andrea fumed. "Jonah knocked it out of my hand when we were traveling through time!"

"I didn't . . . ," Jonah started to protest, but his lips and tongue weren't functioning yet, so the words came out more like, "Uh unhh . . ." He swallowed hard, ready to try again, and his mind flipped frantic images at him: him jerking on Andrea's arm, him crashing into Andrea's side. . . .

Maybe he had made her lose the Elucidator.

"It's okay. JB knows where we are," he said, and this

time the words came out in a recognizable way. He kept talking. "Remember, part of the time we were in the fifteenth century, we didn't have an Elucidator either, and everything turned out fine."

"Because we knew what we were supposed to do," Katherine said.

"What if we didn't even end up in the right place and time?" Andrea asked. She waved her hands like someone about to explode into hysterics. "We could be anywhere!"

"It's all in how the Elucidator's programmed," Jonah said, trying to sound more confident than he actually felt. He thought of something, and genuine confidence caught up with him. "Remember, Katherine, when JB sent Alex to the fifteenth century before he sent the rest of us? Alex didn't have an Elucidator with him. He just went where JB programmed him to go. So that's how it would have worked for us, too."

"Really?" Andrea said. "Are you sure?"

Jonah glanced at her. He must have been wrong about her being on the brink of hysterics. She looked and sounded fine now. Completely relieved. Even . . . happy.

Jonah's vision and hearing must still be messed up. She couldn't be *happy*.

"I'm sure," Jonah said, partly to convince himself. He

forged ahead to another point. "Anyhow, we know how JB does things—he tries to send kids back as close as he can to the moment when they originally disappeared. So we've got to be in—well, whatever time it was for Virginia Dare . . . er, you, Andrea . . . right when you were kidnapped."

"Hmm," Andrea said, looking around. "I guess this could be right. Close, at least." She sounded distracted, as if she'd lost interest in what Jonah was saying. Or as if she was thinking about something entirely different from Virginia Dare.

Jonah followed her gaze. All he could see were pine trees towering overhead, the branches overlapping so closely that they almost blocked out the sky. It was too hard, trying to see so far off into the distance. He looked back at their little cluster. He and Katherine were still mostly sprawled on the ground, almost exactly as they had fallen. The dog had inched over only slightly, to lie at Andrea's feet. But Andrea herself was sitting up perkily, looking completely alert. She'd even had the energy to yank her sweatshirt off and tie it around her waist, revealing a dark green T-shirt that said, *Camp Spruce Lake.*

Jonah was still at a stage where he was proud just that he could notice, *Oh, yeah. It's really hot here.* Doing anything about it was far beyond him.

"See how it is, Andrea?" Jonah said. "You're in better

shape than Katherine or me. This must be the time you belong in. Everything's fine."

"Then where's Andrea's tracer?" Katherine asked. She was struggling to sit up herself now. Pine needles showered down from her hair, and she fumbled at a cobweb that hung down into her face. "If we're in the right place and the right time, why don't we see Andrea's tracer?"

Tracers were ghostly representations of what people would have been doing if time travelers hadn't interfered. Jonah and Katherine had been completely freaked out the first time they'd seen tracers, on their last trip through time. It had also been eerie to see their friends Chip and Alex join with their tracers, blending so completely that they could think their tracers' thoughts.

The real Chip and Alex—the twenty-first-century versions—had seemed to disappear.

It would undoubtedly be the same for Andrea.

"We'll find the tracer," Jonah said, though he was thinking, *Do we have to?* The original Virginia Dare undoubtedly would have faced some life-threatening danger that Jonah and Katherine needed to save Andrea from. Once she was joined with her tracer, it would be very hard to pull her away from that danger. And now that they didn't have the Elucidator, how would they know what danger to watch out for?

Jonah stifled his fear and turned to Andrea.

"Andrea, did anybody explain tracers to you?" he asked.

"Oh, um . . . ," Andrea seemed to have make a great effort to turn her attention from the pine trees back to Jonah. "Sure. JB told me all about them." She jumped up. "So what are we waiting for? Let's go find my . . . uh . . . tracer."

She began striding off, going toward an area of the woods where the trees didn't grow as thickly. The dog, with great effort, stood up and hobbled along behind her.

"Wait for us," Jonah said feebly, struggling to get his feet. He was as tottery as an old man. Katherine was wobbly just sitting up. Andrea skipped away, past the nearest tree.

"Hurry up, then!" she said, looking back over her shoulder.

Was she *giggling*?

"No! Listen!" Jonah hissed. "You have to be careful! You can't let anyone see you! You can't let anyone hear you! You can't let anyone know we're here!"

He thought about mentioning that if they still had the Elucidator, it could have turned them invisible—invisible and *safe*. That was undoubtedly what JB had been planning, the reason he hadn't made them wear old-fashioned clothes. But if it really had been Jonah's fault the Elucidator was missing, he wasn't going to bring that up.

Andrea peeked out from behind the tree.

"We're in a wood that doesn't even have a path," she said and giggled again. "What are you so afraid of?"

Jonah tried to remember everything he knew about the Virginia Dare story. She was the first English child born in North America, in the . . . Roanoke Colony. (Wow—wouldn't his Social Studies teachers be proud of him for remembering that!) And then, hadn't the whole colony disappeared? Because of what?

Wild animals? Jonah wondered. *Hostile Indian tribes? Some enemy the English were fighting with back then—the Spanish? The French? Some other country I don't remember?*

Jonah had reached the end of his knowledge about Virginia Dare. Somehow, not knowing what he was supposed to be afraid of made things even scarier.

"Wait, Andrea!" he called again. "Come on, Katherine!"

Katherine groaned, and he took pity on her enough to reach down and give her a hand. He was still off balance, though, and for a moment it was a toss-up whether he would manage to pull her up or whether her deadweight would pull him down. Then she reached back and shoved off against a tree trunk. The whole tree shook, and a pine cone fell straight down, bonking Jonah on the head.

"Bet that pine cone was supposed to land on the other side," Katherine moaned. "We probably just changed history, right there."

"It'll change even more if Andrea gets eaten by a bear or scalped by Indians or something," Jonah said through gritted teeth.

The two of them stumbled forward, following Andrea. They wobbled terribly, bumping into each other and the tree branches. Jonah paused to take off his sweatshirt, hoping he'd do better if he wasn't so hot.

It was still hot. The air was so thick and heavy around them that Jonah almost felt like he should be swimming. His T-shirt was quickly soaked with sweat.

None of that seemed to bother Andrea.

"Don't you think . . . it's weird how . . . Andrea isn't scared anymore?" Jonah muttered to Katherine. It was hard to simultaneously walk, talk, and keep an eye on Andrea, who was practically running now.

Katherine nodded, an action that almost knocked her over. She stopped for a moment so she could speak without falling.

"Don't you think it's weird how, well . . . JB knows where we are, right?" she muttered back. "So why hasn't he dropped in a replacement Elucidator for us?" She peered over at Jonah. Her whole face was twisted with fear. "You don't think us losing the Elucidator made this Damaged Time, do you?"

"Don't say that," Jonah snapped. "Don't even think it."

But the idea had wormed its way into Jonah's head now too. No time travelers could get into or out of Damaged Time. If they'd damaged Virginia Dare's time period, no matter how well they helped Andrea, they could still be stranded here for days.

Weeks.

Months.

Years.

Forever, Jonah thought. *It could be for the rest of our lives.*

He forced himself to think only about keeping up with Andrea.

He kept losing sight of her and having to plunge desperately forward just to get the briefest glimpse of her hair or her shirt. Then he'd lose sight of her again. He finally decided it was hopeless—there was no way he and Katherine could keep up.

Just then, very suddenly, Andrea stopped.

"Can't she at least hide behind a tree until she sees what's out there?" Katherine mumbled.

Jonah realized that Andrea had stopped right on the edge of a clearing. He thought about calling out to her, ordering her to hide, but it didn't seem worth the risk. It would have been like yelling at a statue. She had frozen that completely.

Jonah crept forward, Katherine alongside him. They reached a huge tree right behind Andrea and, in silent agreement, they each peeked around opposite sides of the tree.

What's Andrea's problem? There's nothing out there!

That was Jonah's first thought. And then, because Andrea was still standing stock-still, her face a stunned mask, he looked again.

In the clearing were . . . ruins.

FIVE

What Jonah had first taken for a few downed trees out in the center of the clearing were actually the remains of a tall wooden fence. *The fence we saw in the scene when Virginia Dare was born?* Jonah wondered. A shudder ran through his whole body. That scene had seemed so happy, so hopeful, and now it was clear that everything had been destroyed. Rusting, arched metal that might have been the remains of a suit of armor lay off to one side of the clearing, beside an overturned old-fashioned trunk, half-rotting in a trench. There were no houses anymore, no people. Vines were creeping over the last part of the fence that was still even slightly upright, as if they were on a mission to pull it down too. It was no wonder that Jonah had first mistaken the scene for more wilderness: Soon it would all be wilderness again.

"I don't remember any of this," Andrea murmured sadly. Dare whined beside her, as if he was upset too.

"Andrea, you aren't supposed to remember any of it," Katherine said briskly, sounding more like herself again. Or maybe Jonah's ears were just functioning better. "You won't remember being Virginia Dare until you step into your tracer."

"No, I mean . . . ," Andrea let her voice trail off. "Maybe I just went the wrong way."

She threw an anguished glance over her shoulder, as if she expected to find some other way through the woods, away from this devastated clearing. Jonah knew she would see nothing but more trees.

"Andrea . . . , I think this *is* the Roanoke Colony," Jonah whispered. "Or what's left of it."

"Really?" Katherine whispered back. Now she was the one who seemed inexplicably excited. "Then . . ."

She gave one cautious look around before stepped out into the clearing. She peered at each tree ringing the clearing, paused for a second, then went over to the partially collapsed wooden fence. She seemed to be trying to lift the logs, to look at each one. Jonah was waiting for her to discover that that was impossible, when suddenly she let out a shriek.

"Katherine! Shh!" Jonah hissed, all his fears coming

back about wild animals, hostile natives, or some other enemy.

"This is it! This is it!" Katherine answered, her voice screeching even louder. "Come look!"

Katherine was acting like she'd discovered the Seven Cities of Gold—wasn't that one of the things the early explorers had been looking for? Jonah glanced around quickly and sneaked out to join his sister. Dare padded along beside him, and even Andrea crept forward after a few seconds.

"There!" Katherine exclaimed, pointing at the top log. "Don't you see it?"

Jonah didn't.

Impatiently, Katherine grabbed his hand and rubbed his fingers across the exposed side of the log.

"Oh, there's something carved into the tree?" Jonah asked. "Letters?"

He could feel a crescent—a *C*, maybe? And then maybe an *R* . . . He tilted his head, so he could see the log from a better angle.

"It says, *Croatoan*," Katherine said. "Croatoan!"

"So?" Jonah asked.

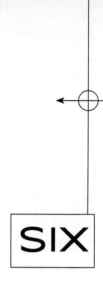

SIX

Katherine gave Jonah's chest a shove.

"Didn't you pay *any* attention in fifth-grade Social Studies?" Katherine asked. "Didn't you learn anything?"

"I know that Virginia Dare was born in the Roanoke Colony," Jonah said, feeling just as queasy as he always did when he took pop quizzes.

"And?" Katherine prompted.

"And then everyone disappeared?"

"And?"

This was getting annoying.

"Katherine, you had a better teacher than I did. I bet Mrs. Rorshas never even told us."

Katherine rolled her eyes.

"She *had* to. This is, like, the best part of the whole story!"

"So, what is it?" Jonah challenged.

Katherine dropped her voice down low, making it creepy and mysterious.

"Virginia Dare's grandfather, John White, was in charge of the colony. He went back to England to get more supplies. He meant to come right back. But for some reason—"

"The war with Spain," Andrea muttered. "The Spanish Armada."

"Oh, yeah, the Spanish Armada," Katherine said. "Because of that, it was *three years* before he made it back to Roanoke. And by then, everyone was gone. Even the houses were gone!"

"I knew that," Jonah said defensively.

"But the colonists left behind one clue." Katherine had begun using her normal voice again, but now she made it spooky once more. "It was the word *Croatoan*, carved into wood. Carved . . . right . . . here." She pointed straight down.

Jonah had to admit Katherine had a flair for story-telling. And if there was only one clue, he probably should have remembered it. He'd probably missed the word *Croatoan* on the test. Mrs. Rorshas had always given hard tests.

"Okay, okay, I should have known that," he said. "But

still—so what? We already knew this was Roanoke."

"John White thought that the word *Croatoan* meant that his colonists had gone to another island, to stay with the Croatoan Indians there," Katherine said. She put her hands on her hips, obviously ready to issue a challenge. "So if Virginia Dare went to Croatoan Island, why did JB return Andrea to history at Roanoke?"

"Maybe John White was wrong?" Jonah retorted. "Maybe you got your history mixed up?"

"No, she's right," Andrea murmured.

She had crouched down and was tracing the carved letters with her fingers, again and again.

"How long do you think this has been here?" she asked plaintively. "Could a carving stay in wood like this, out on the open, for a long time? For . . . centuries? It could, couldn't it?" Her voice shook, as if she might start crying again if Jonah and Katherine didn't give her the right answer.

"*Centuries?*" Katherine repeated. "No way! Andrea, did you hit your head or something coming through time? It wouldn't need to be here for centuries. I'm not sure how old you were when you were kidnapped from history, but you were still a kid. Under eighteen. So this carving couldn't be more than eighteen years old, at the most."

"I don't think it's even that old," Jonah said. "Out in

the open, wood would start breaking down. See how it's really faint and hard to read, already?"

He kind of wanted to add, "I'm a Boy Scout. This is something I know about," just so Andrea wouldn't think he was a complete idiot.

But Andrea was collapsing against the log, throwing her arms across it and burying her face in her arms.

"No-o-o-o," she moaned. "It can't be. . . ."

Jonah peered over at Katherine, hoping she could explain Andrea's strange behavior, going from giggling to freezing to wailing in nothing flat. But Katherine only gave an "I'm mystified too" shrug.

After a moment of Jonah and Katherine staring at each other over Andrea's wailing, Katherine dropped down beside the other girl.

"Andrea, it's okay," Katherine said soothingly. She patted Andrea's back. "Remember, we're here to help you, Jonah and me. We'll take care of you."

Jonah decided if Katherine was doing the comforting, that cast him in the role of guard. He looked around, just as Dare began barking at something off to the right. Jonah caught a quick glimpse of something pale—a white shirt? White skin? He instantly dropped down with the two girls and pulled them off the top log, out of sight.

"Ssh! Stop talking! Someone's coming!" he hissed in

Katherine's ear. He slid his hand over Andrea's mouth, but the shock had evidently already stunned her into silence.

Dare kept barking, so Jonah couldn't even listen for footsteps. What if whoever it was stepped right into the clearing? Shouldn't the three kids scramble back into the woods while they still had time?

Jonah raised his head, just enough to see past the toppled logs. He scanned the scene before him: pine tree, pine tree, pine tree . . . there! Something pale was moving through the trees, coming toward the clearing. Jonah blinked, because his eyes had chosen that moment to go out of focus again. The movement he saw was blurry and indistinct; watching was like trying to keep track of a ghost.

Or . . . *not exactly a ghost . . .*

Jonah grinned and dropped back down with Andrea and Katherine.

"It's all right," he whispered. "It's just a tracer! I bet it's Andrea's!"

SEVEN

All three kids peeked over the logs now. Even Dare stopped barking and just watched silently. Now that Jonah knew he was watching a tracer, it made sense that the figure moved without rustling any tree branches, without snapping any twigs underfoot.

"There are two of them!" Katherine whispered.

Jonah scooted over so he could see from the same angle, and she was right—there were two figures gliding silently through the trees.

"Let's make sure there aren't any real live human beings with them too," Jonah whispered back grimly.

But as the figures approached, it became clear that no one else was around. When the tracers stepped into the clearing—becoming a bit more distinct in the brighter light—Katherine began to giggle.

"Uh, Jonah, I don't think either of those tracers are Andrea's," she whispered.

"Why not?" he asked. ". . . oh."

The tracers were boys—rather scantily clad boys. At first Jonah thought they might even be naked, but then he realized that they had squares of some sort of cloth or animal skin hanging down from their waists.

Katherine kept giggling.

"Oh, grow up," Jonah muttered. "You've seen boys in swimsuits before. Those . . . outfits . . . cover just as much territory. These guys are Indians. Er—Native Americans."

From some long-ago Social Studies class, Jonah remembered the name for the clothes the two boys were wearing: loincloths. *Couldn't they have come up with a less embarrassing name?* he wondered.

"Those aren't Indians," Andrea whispered, speaking up for the first time since she'd collapsed on the *Croatoan* log. "Look at their hair. The texture. It's all wrong."

Jonah squinted. It wasn't easy to examine the texture of two guys' hair when those guys were practically see-through, even if they did glow, ever so slightly. But he could kind of see what Andrea meant. Neither of the tracers had long braids or long straight hair trailing down their backs or even a ridged Mohawk on an otherwise shaved scalp—none of the hairstyles Jonah would have expected for old-timey Native Americans. One tracer boy did have longish hair, but it was very curly long hair. The other tracer boy's hair was closely cropped and wiry.

"So maybe they come from some tribe that never got its picture into any of our Social Studies books," Jonah said, shrugging.

"That guy came from Africa," Andrea said, pointing at the tracer with the shorter hair. "Or his ancestors did."

She sounded excited about this.

"Why would an African guy pretend to be an Indian?" Jonah asked.

"Hello?" Katherine said. "To get out of being a slave?"

Jonah blushed, because he'd kind of forgotten about that. He always hated it whenever they talked about slavery at school, because the teachers got a weird tone in their voices, as if they were trying really, really hard not to offend anyone. And a lot of the black kids in his class just stared down at their desks, as if they were wishing they were somewhere else.

"No," Andrea said, her voice rising giddily. "I bet it's because they're actors or something. Not very realistic ones. And this is just a movie set, and it's still the twenty-first century, and we didn't go back very far in time at all, and . . ."

She broke off because the two tracers were suddenly

both lifting bows to their chests and pulling arrows out of packs that Jonah just now noticed hanging from their shoulders.

Tracer bows and arrows? Jonah thought. *Oh, yeah, I saw a tracer battle-ax too, on my last trip through time.*

That wasn't a happy memory. Jonah didn't want to think about what these tracer boys might be shooting at, but he couldn't keep from watching the arc of the arrows, zipping through the air.

At first it seemed that they'd fallen uselessly to the ground. Something rustled amid the pine branches, but it was only a deer aimlessly strolling away. Then Jonah saw what the deer had left behind: a tracer version of itself, pierced by the tracer arrows. The tracer deer's glow was fading, growing dimmer and dimmer.

Oh, no, Jonah thought, horrified. *JB told us before that the tracers of living things stop glowing when they die.*

The two tracer Indians—or tracer Indian wannabes—shared none of Jonah's horror. They were jumping up and down and hollering (though Jonah couldn't hear anything). Then they took off running toward the tracer deer and . . . attacked it. There was no other way to describe it. Jonah was so glad that he was seeing only the tracer, ghostly version of the action, because otherwise he would have been sick.

"This isn't a movie set," Katherine whispered. "Movies always have that disclaimer, 'No animals were harmed in the making of this film. . . .'"

"Those guys are hungry, for *real*," Jonah said, turning his head because he couldn't watch anymore. The tracer boys seemed to be eating some of the meat raw, and smearing some of the blood on their faces. "Starving. Nobody could *act* that."

"But then . . . ," Andrea began. Her face twisted with anguish. She glanced once more at the two tracers, who now were hacking at the dead tracer deer with ghostly tracer knives. "I should have known he was lying. I should have known it wasn't possible, even with time travel. . . ."

"Who was lying?" Katherine asked. "Do you mean JB? What are you talking about?"

But Andrea didn't answer. She slumped back to the ground, her shoulders shaking with silent sobs. A whimper broke through, and she stifled it, but her whole body was racked by the effort. Even though she was so quiet, Jonah knew this was the most devastated crying he'd ever seen, a million times worse than any of Katherine's drama. And, like the tracer boys with the tracer deer, this was much too real for Jonah. He couldn't watch.

But, since he also didn't want to watch the tracer boys with the tracer deer, he wasn't quite sure where to look.

His gaze fell on Dare—the dog was looking back and forth between Andrea and the tracers.

Jonah reached over and grabbed Dare's collar, to hold him in place. Jonah didn't have the slightest idea how to help Andrea himself, but maybe having the dog nearby would be comforting to her.

"What's wrong, Andrea?" Katherine demanded, sounding every bit as baffled as Jonah felt. "Are you some big-time animal lover? Let me tell you, a lot more than deer got killed, back in the past—"

"I'm not crying over a *deer*," Andrea spat back at her.

"Then what are you crying about?"

Jonah knew he should tell Katherine and Andrea to stop being so loud. It was dangerous. But the time sickness, the jolt of losing the Elucidator, the horror of seeing the deer slaughtered, the devastation of Andrea's sobbing—everything seemed to be catching up with him at once. All he could do was clutch Dare's collar, which was so nice and sturdy. Jonah's fingers grazed the little pouch where JB had stashed the Elucidator, so long ago, so far in the future. Even that pouch was sturdily constructed, sturdily fastened, and so firmly attached to the collar. . . .

Wait a minute, Jonah thought.

He fiddled with the pouch, trying as hard as he could to pull it off. But it must have been connected with some perfect futuristic superstrong glue. Even using all his strength, Jonah couldn't get it to budge.

A scene played back in Jonah's mind.

Hold on—I'm scared the Elucidator is going to fall off, Andrea had said, back when they were tumbling through time, back when they still *had* the Elucidator. She'd reached over and touched the pouch, in the dark, when Jonah and Katherine couldn't see her very well. *The strap's loose,* she'd said. *I'll just hold the Elucidator myself.*

But there *wasn't* a strap. There wasn't any reason that Andrea would have needed to take the Elucidator out of the pouch.

Unless she *wanted* to lose it.

Jonah straightened up, letting go of Dare's collar. Jonah glared at Andrea, his eyes narrowed to slits.

"You're the one who lied," he said.

EIGHT

Katherine was the one who reacted first.

"What are you talking about?" she asked, switching her baffled gaze from Andrea to Jonah.

"'Jonah made me lose the Elucidator,'" Jonah mimicked in a mincing, whiny voice that didn't actually sound anything like Andrea's. "'It's all Jonah's fault.'" Okay, she hadn't exactly said that, but Jonah was mad. "She was lying!"

"Jonah, you bumped into her," Katherine said. "It was a mistake. You were trying to help. Nobody thinks you meant to do that."

It was weird to have Katherine acting like the peacemaker—the calm, reasonable one. Somehow that made Jonah madder.

"But I *didn't* do anything wrong, even by mistake. It's all *her* fault," he accused. He pointed right at Andrea. "She took the Elucidator out and threw it away. On purpose!"

The color drained from Andrea's face. She began shaking her head from side to side, frantically.

"No," she wailed. "I didn't!"

"Who are you working for?" Jonah asked. "Gary? Hodge?"

Those were JB's enemies, the ones who had kidnapped Andrea and Jonah and all the other missing kids from history in the first place. The ones who were trying to get rich selling famous kids from history to adoptive parents in the future. With Jonah's help, JB had sent both kidnappers to time prison. But was time prison a place someone could escape from?

"I'm not working for anybody!" Andrea cried. "I just . . ." She kept talking, but Jonah couldn't understand a single word because she was sobbing too hard now.

"Jonah!" Katherine scolded, hitting him on the shoulder. "You had better have a good excuse for making all those wild accusations. For making her cry!"

For an instant, Katherine sounded just like their mother, making Jonah's heart ache a little. It was entirely possible that, because of Andrea, he and Katherine would never see their parents again. But Katherine-sounding-like-Mom also made Jonah feel ashamed. He wasn't usually the kind of kid who made people cry. And the way

Andrea looked so fragile and sad had made him want to help her so much—which made him feel even more stupid, now that he knew she'd double-crossed them. . . .

How could he feel so many different things all at once?

Jonah let out a deep sigh.

"Look," he told Katherine, pointing to the pouch on Dare's collar. "This is perfectly secure. There was no reason for Andrea to take the Elucidator out. She must have been planning to get rid of it the whole time. And that's why she's been acting weird ever since we got here." He remembered her silent crying, her hesitation to shake JB's hand, her insistence that they go back in time without getting debriefed. "Really, ever since we met her."

Katherine reached down to examine the pouch on the dog's collar for herself. She pulled it this way and that, tugging on it with every bit as much force as Jonah had used. Dare whined a little—this couldn't be comfortable for him—and Katherine let go.

"Andrea?" she said doubtfully.

Andrea took a huge breath, one that threatened to turn into just another sob. But then she grimaced, clearly struggling to hold back the tears.

"I didn't mean to lose the Elucidator," she said in a small voice. "Honest. That was a mistake. But—"

"But what?" Jonah asked. He meant his voice to come out sounding cold and hard and self-righteous, like a prosecuting attorney on a TV show. But some of his other, confused emotions slipped into his voice instead.

He mostly sounded sympathetic.

Andrea sniffled. She leaned back against the fallen fence and drew her knees up to her chest, hugging them close with her arms.

"The man came to my house last night," she said. "Er—the last night before we left. I don't know his name. I don't know who he was working for. I don't think he would have told me the truth if I'd asked. I knew he was from the future. It looked like he walked right out of the wall. And he knew . . . too much. About me."

"So, what, he blackmailed you?" Katherine asked. "What had you done—murdered somebody?"

Jonah could tell Katherine was just trying to make a joke, to lighten the mood. But this was evidently the wrong thing to say. Sorrow spread across Andrea's face, and Jonah thought she was going to fall apart again. Then, just like before, a sort of mask seemed to slide over her entire expression, hiding her emotions. But it didn't happen so instantaneously this time, or so completely. Jonah felt like he could still see cracks, broken places that didn't heal.

"Nobody blackmailed me," Andrea said. "At least, not blackmail like in the movies, where it's all about money. He didn't even ask for anything in exchange."

"In exchange for *what?*" Jonah asked. "What are you talking about?" He could feel the dread creeping over him. Hairs stood up on the back of his neck; goosebumps rose on his arms. Whatever Andrea was about to say, it was going to be awful.

Andrea didn't answer his question.

"I know I was probably being stupid, all right?" she said. "I knew I shouldn't trust the man. But don't you see? If there was any chance at all, I had to try!"

"Try what?" Jonah and Katherine asked together, the words spilling out almost completely in sync.

Andrea looked up at them and blinked back tears.

"I had to try to save my parents."

Now Jonah was even more confused.

"You mean, Mistress Dare and—what would it be?— Master Dare?" he asked.

"No, no, my *real* parents. The ones I knew." Andrea seemed annoyed that Jonah didn't understand. "Back in our time. In the twenty-first century."

Jonah saw the real problem: Andrea didn't understand time travel.

"Andrea, you don't have to worry about your parents,"

he said. He almost chuckled, but stopped himself. He didn't want to embarrass her for not understanding. "They're fine—they're just waiting for us back home in the twenty-first century. All we have to do is get you out of history—the right way, this time—and then you can go home and see them again. Honest."

Jonah spoke with the same soothing tone he'd used with homesick Cub Scouts when he'd worked as a counselor-in-training at camp. Really, if Andrea had been so confused all along, why hadn't she just asked before?

Andrea shook her head.

"No, Jonah," she corrected him. "My parents aren't waiting for me back in the twenty-first century."

"Of course they are," Jonah argued. "And the great thing is, because you'll get back just a split second after you left, they won't even know you were gone."

"Don't you get it?" Andrea said. She didn't sound annoyed anymore. The sorrow in her voice crowded out everything else. "Back in the twenty-first century, my parents are dead."

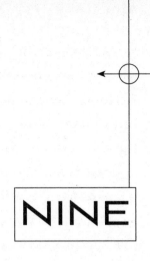

NINE

Jonah and Katherine both stared at Andrea, their jaws dropped. That wasn't a possibility Jonah would have thought of. It was too awful.

"It was a car crash," Andrea said. "Last year."

She sounded tougher now, brusque, as if she'd learned how to mask her voice as well as her facial expressions.

"I'm—," Katherine began.

"Don't say you're sorry. Don't say you can imagine just how that would feel," Andrea said. "You *can't.*"

Jonah was trying to imagine it anyway. What would it be like to lose both your mom and dad? At the same time?

"You mean, your adoptive parents?" he asked cautiously. "The ones who got you after the time crash?"

He was hoping he'd misunderstood somehow.

"Yes, my adoptive parents," Andrea said impatiently. "I said my real ones, didn't I?"

Jonah kept trying to get his head around the thought of someone losing two sets of parents by the time she'd turned thirteen. Katherine sniffed, like she might start crying on Andrea's behalf.

"I don't like telling people," Andrea said. "I usually won't. Because then they start acting like *this*." She waved her hand vaguely at Jonah and Katherine. Jonah tried to sit up a little straighter and look normal. It wasn't easy.

"But you told us because . . . because it's connected to something that man told you?" Katherine said, her voice full of bafflement. "Something . . . about the Elucidator?"

Andrea nodded.

"He promised," she whispered. "He said I could go back. He said I could stop . . ."

Andrea waited, as if she expected Jonah and Katherine to figure everything out. But Jonah couldn't think at all while he was watching the pain play over Andrea's face.

"He said you could stop . . . ," Katherine prompted. Then she gasped. "Oh, oh—I get it." Now her words came in a rush. "That man, what he told you—he said you could go back just a year in time, right? So you thought you could stop your parents from being in that crash. You thought you could save their lives!"

Andrea looked down at the ground.

"He said all I had to do was reprogram the Elucidator," she murmured.

Jonah felt the anger wash over him again.

"Couldn't you tell the man was lying?" he growled. "Time doesn't work that way. You can't go back to a time period you've already lived through. You know that! Didn't you hear anyone talking about the 'paradox of the doubles'? Or—didn't you think about what it meant that we'd been living in Damaged Time? Like Katherine was talking about before?" Jonah realized that Andrea had probably been too far ahead to hear anything when he and Katherine were talking about Damaged Time. He just leaned in closer, nearly yelling at her now. "No time travelers could get in for almost thirteen years! Practically our entire lives!"

Andrea recoiled, as if he'd slapped her.

"Nobody told me that," she whispered.

Belatedly, Jonah realized that could be true. When would she have gotten her crash course in the rules of time travel? The day they'd been trapped in the cave with all the grown-ups fighting over them? Everything was chaos that day. Nothing had been explained very clearly.

"Jonah, it was Angela who mostly told us about all that," Katherine said. Angela was the only twenty-first century adult who knew about time travel. She had taken a lot of risks to help Jonah and the other kids. "It was when we were divided up into groups—Andrea wasn't with us then."

Jonah sighed, his anger washing away. He wished he could stay mad—anger was so much easier.

"See, here's how it works," Katherine was explaining to Andrea. "When Gary and Hodge kidnapped you and the other kids from history, and JB was chasing them, you know they crash-landed into our time. Well—" she snuck a glance at her brother "—*my* time anyway. We still don't know Jonah's right time, and he's too chicken to ask."

"I am not!" Jonah argued, even as he was thinking, *How did Katherine notice?*

Katherine ignored him and kept talking.

"You were all babies, right? The ones who weren't babies to begin with were 'unaged' through the magic of time travel—and don't try to understand that, because I don't think anyone really can. Anyhow, JB or Gary and Hodge or whoever would have tried to grab you back from our time right away, if they could."

"But the time crash messed up everything, and *no* time traveler could get in or out for about the next thirteen years," Jonah added, because he wasn't going to let Katherine make it look as if she was the only one who knew what was going on. "That's how we could all be adopted and have normal lives for thirteen years. And so, when your parents . . . died . . . that would have been during Damaged Time, so no time traveler could save them. Not you, not . . . anybody."

Jonah's voice kept slowing down and getting softer as he talked. This wasn't about showing up Katherine. This wasn't like getting the right answer in school and thinking, *Hey! I knew something the other kids didn't! Go, me!* This was telling a girl she'd never see her parents again.

Andrea was biting her lip. She had her heels wedged in the dirt, her back pressed hard against the toppled fence.

"But—" she began. Then her shoulders slumped. "I know. You're right. I saw how JB and Gary and Hodge were acting. If they could have come back to get us any sooner, they would have." She was silent for a moment, then looked up at Jonah. "And, yeah, I should have known not to trust that man. I *did* know. But I still thought . . . I hoped . . ."

And then Jonah couldn't yell at her anymore about losing the Elucidator, about stranding him and Katherine in . . . well, now that he thought about it, Jonah didn't know what time period they were in. He glanced back at the tracer boys with the tracer deer once more. While Jonah and Katherine and Andrea had been screaming and crying and ranting at each other, the tracer boys had managed to truss up the remains of the dead deer. Now they had it hanging from a thick pole, which they were balancing on their shoulders as they walked away. The method they were using, with the deer slung between them, made Jonah think of a picture in a textbook. But he couldn't remember any picture in a Social Studies book that had had a caption, "If you're traveling through time and you get lost and you see people using this technique, that undoubtedly means you're in the sixteenth or seventeenth century, and . . ."

Jonah had always thought that learning Social Studies was mostly pointless. It was weird that he now wished his Social Studies teachers had taught him *more*.

"So, Andrea, when you reprogrammed the Elucidator," he began gently, "exactly what did you set it for?"

Andrea grimaced.

"I was trying to get back to June of last year, to this camp I always went to in Michigan. My parents had just dropped me off at camp when . . ." She didn't finish the sentence. She didn't need to.

June, Jonah thought. *Camp. That's why she wore shorts.*

Jonah liked being able to focus on little details like

that, so he didn't have to focus on anything else.

But Andrea was still talking.

"I thought this time around I could just keep my parents at camp an extra five minutes before they left," she said. "I thought I could make them help unroll my sleeping bag, or tell them I forgot to pack my toothbrush and they needed to get me a new one, or have them walk down to look at the lake with me . . . anything I could do to slow them down, to keep them from being on the highway beside that semi truck. . . ."

Jonah really didn't want to hear any more of this story. And Andrea seemed to be having a harder and harder time telling it.

"Okay, but the Elucidator," Jonah said. "Exactly what did you type into it? June—what? And . . . *Michigan?* The Roanoke Colony wasn't in Michigan, was it?"

Katherine rolled her eyes.

"Try North Carolina," she said.

Jonah wanted so badly to say, *Everyone hates a know-it-all, Katherine.* It would be so nice to take out all his frustration and worry and fear on her. But her face was already as white and strained and worried as Andrea's. Jonah couldn't go on the attack right now.

Andrea was shaking her head.

"It wasn't like you think," she said. "I wasn't supposed

to type in an exact date, or a GPS location, or anything. The man just gave me a code. A string of numbers."

And you fell for that? Jonah wanted to say. But how could he? Her parents were dead.

"The thing is," Andrea continued, "I worked so hard to memorize that code. I made sure I knew it forward, backward, and upside down. And I *know* I typed it in exactly the way the man told me. I checked it three times before I hit ENTER. I wanted so badly to see . . ."

This was another sentence she couldn't finish. She just sat there, frozen. She'd stopped crying now, but the tears still glistened on her cheeks. Her hair was tangled in some of the vines.

"It's okay," Katherine said gently, patting Andrea's shoulder. "We understand."

Andrea scooted away.

"But I dragged the two of you into this too," she said.

"Well, no, actually JB and his projectionist did," Jonah said, trying for a joking tone. He didn't quite succeed. He tried again. "And don't worry, it wasn't like we expected to have *fun*, rescuing you from Virginia Dare's life. Who knows? This might be a better adventure."

Both of the girls frowned at him.

"But where are we?" Andrea asked. "*When* are we? We don't know anything."

"Yeah, we do," Katherine said slowly. "We know you typed in the code exactly the way the man wanted you to. So—where we landed? That was exactly where he wanted us to land."

All three kids looked back toward the woods they'd come through. The trees were almost eerily still. Jonah looked at the ruins around him: broken down, falling apart, deserted. Desolate.

But quiet, too, he told himself. *Peaceful.*

The place they'd landed in the 1400s had seemed quiet and peaceful, too, at first. Until the murderers showed up.

Would we have met some murderer looking for Virginia Dare if we'd gone where JB had wanted us to go? Jonah wondered. *Or are we more likely to meet a murderer now? Is that what the mystery man wanted?*

"I bet Gary and Hodge are behind all this," Katherine said, pronouncing the names as if they left a bad taste in her mouth. "Somehow they got out of prison, or bribed someone from prison, or—"

"Gary and Hodge would have sent us to the future," Jonah objected. "We know this is the past."

"*Do* we know that?" Andrea asked plaintively. "For sure?"

Jonah felt bad for her: Now she was doubting everything. She looked so sad. And yet . . . even with the tears on her cheeks and the leaves in her hair and the forlorn expression on her face, she still looked better than Jonah felt. Healthier, anyway.

That was it. Another clue.

"Andrea?" he asked. "The time sickness. You didn't have it very bad when we first got here, did you? The way you could jump up and run right away . . ."

Andrea considered this.

"You're right," she said. "I wasn't paying attention when you were talking about this before, but . . . I don't think I had any time sickness at all."

"And how do you feel right now?" Jonah asked. He rushed to explain. "I don't mean whether you're happy or sad, or scared or not scared, but how do, like, your lungs feel? Your muscles?"

Andrea took a slow, experimental breath. She flexed her arms, stretched out, and touched her toes. She seemed to be concentrating hard.

"They feel . . . good," she said, sounding surprised. "Maybe better than they've ever felt before. They feel *right*. When we landed, I thought I just felt so good because I was going to see my parents again. But now . . . it's like my body still thinks everything is how it's supposed to be."

Jonah looked at Katherine.

"Chip and Alex felt 'right' in 1483, too," Jonah said.

Katherine nodded.

"You mean the friends you helped before?" Andrea asked. "This is how they felt?"

"JB said that's how people always feel in their proper time," Katherine said. "And it makes sense. I felt kind of off the whole time we were in the 1480s. And I haven't really felt right since we got here. It's not my time."

"But it is mine," Andrea whispered dazedly. She turned and traced the carved letters on the fallen fence before her. "This is the real Roanoke Colony, sometime before it all fades away into dust, sometime after I was born but before I'm supposed to . . . die."

Jonah did not like the way that word lingered in the air.

"We are not going to let you die," he said. It took a lot of effort, but he managed to stand up. He scanned the woods in every direction, as if he was Andrea's body-guard, watching out for her every minute. "We weren't going to let you die if we'd ended up where JB wanted us to go, and we won't let you die now. We're going to figure out why that man sent us back here, and we're going to fix whatever problem we have to fix, and then we're going home. All of us. Together. Safe."

Jonah couldn't have said that Andrea looked com-pletely reassured by that fervent speech—it didn't help that his voice cracked in the middle of it.

But at least she didn't say anything else about dying.

"How are we going to do all that?" she asked.

Jonah actually hadn't thought that far ahead.

"Uh . . . ," he began.

Katherine pushed herself up, so she was standing with Jonah.

"We're going to start by following those tracers," she said, pointing, even though it had been a while since the two ghostly boys had finished tying up their deer and slipped back into the trees.

"O-kay. If you say so. But . . . why?" Andrea asked.

"Because time travelers messed with them, or they wouldn't exist," Katherine said. "And some time traveler has definitely messed with us. So don't you think we've got a lot in common?"

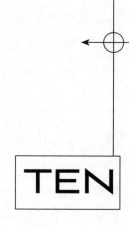

TEN

They set off into the deep woods on the other side of the clearing. Andrea and the dog didn't run ahead this time, but stayed right beside Jonah and Katherine. All of them, even the dog, kept glancing around, peering ahead before every step, as if some unknown danger could be lurking behind every tree.

"Anyone traveling through time can create a tracer, right?" Andrea asked in a hushed voice, when they'd gone just a few steps. "You just have to knock someone off his normal path?"

"Yeah," Jonah said. He was concentrating on trying to figure out which way the tracer boys had gone. Had it been *this* tree or *that* tree they'd stepped behind?

"Then couldn't it have been *us* who created those tracers?" Andrea asked. "Like, if the real versions of those boys saw us fall from the sky, got scared, and ran away? *That* could have made tracers, couldn't it?"

"Ergh. She's right," Katherine said, sagging against a tree.

"So following those tracers, maybe we're like a dog chasing its own tail," Andrea said.

Jonah wasn't fully listening. He was watching the tree behind Katherine. It shook slightly, giving off a quick glow of tracer light before returning to normal. Clumps of pine needles showered to the ground, along with a few broken twigs. But the ghostly tracer versions of the pine needles and twigs remained on the tree.

Jonah turned around. The three of them had left an entire trail of tracer destruction behind them: dropped twigs, bent branches, scattered needles. . . . It was hard to notice unless you were looking for it, but now Jonah could see the exact path he and Katherine and Andrea had followed: careening to the right a bit to avoid a downed log, swerving to the left to avoid a cloud of gnats, some of which they'd killed, leaving behind tiny tracer dots.

Wish the tracer boys had left a trail like that, Jonah thought. Then he realized: They would have. Not because the tracers were time travelers, but because there was a ripple effect to disrupted time. Because the tracer boys weren't really there, everything they weren't there to do would have resulted in a tracer. It wasn't just the deer they should have killed—it was also mosquitoes they would have swatted away, leaves they would have trampled underfoot, branches they would have bent back as they walked through the woods. And so the deer, the mosquitoes, the leaves, and the branches were all tracers now too— along with any objects the deer, the mosquitoes, and the branches should have affected.

And all of those things that were alive would glow.

Jonah squinted, peering all around. There—a line of glowing ants on the ground. There—a bird perched high overhead. There—a vine swung back out of the way. And there and there and there—dozens of glowing lights that Jonah had previously taken for glints of sunlight filtered through the trees or blurry glitches in his vision because of time sickness.

The woods were full of tracers.

"We didn't create those tracer boys," Jonah whispered. "Or, if we did, there were other tracers here first."

"Now, how could you know that?" Katherine asked mockingly.

"Because of that," Jonah said, pointing to the glowing vine. "And that." The line of ants. "And that." The bird in the tree.

Katherine gasped and put her hand over her mouth,

as if she'd just discovered the entire woods were radio-active.

"They're—they're everywhere," Andrea whispered.

"Right," Jonah said. "And how long do you think we've been here? Half an hour? An hour? No way could there be so many tracers created just in that time, just because of us."

Katherine was still looking around, her eyes huge and dismayed.

"Something's really, really wrong here," she whispered. "That's what this means."

As they stood watching, a real bird landed right on top of the glowing tracer bird, melding completely. The glow instantly vanished. Now it was just an ordinary bird on an ordinary tree branch.

"Well, there," Jonah said. "That's one bit of time that's been fixed."

He didn't want to admit how relieved he felt—or how much he wished all the other tracers glowing before him would go back to normal too.

"JB told me that people—and, I guess, animals, too—can't see tracers unless they've traveled through time," Andrea said. "How did that bird know its own tracer was there? How did it know to land in that exact spot?"

"Chip and Alex said they felt this almost magnetic pull

to their tracers," Katherine said. "The bird must have felt it too."

"They why aren't all the other tracers disappearing?" Andrea asked. "One by one, the lights blinking out, everything going back to normal . . ."

Jonah realized he was holding his breath, watching. The lights were not going out. If anything, their numbers were increasing: new pinpricks of light where insects were supposed to be flying, where seeds were supposed to be falling, where squirrels were supposed to be scampering.

"Something's holding all those tracers in place," Katherine whispered. "Something won't let time go back the way it's supposed to."

"Is it—is it my fault?" Andrea stammered. "Did I ruin everything because I didn't come back at the right time, at the exact moment that JB thought I should come back? Is this what happened when I messed up all those variables the projectionist set up so carefully?" She sniffled and waved her hand toward all the glowing remnants of tracer branches and vines and insects and ants. Her hand shook. "Does this mean I destroyed time forever?"

Jonah and Katherine exchanged glances. Jonah decided not to say, *Shouldn't you have thought of that before you changed the code on the Elucidator?* But he didn't know what to say instead.

"Well, no offense, Andrea, but how could you be that important?" Katherine asked, her voice gentler than her words. "You weren't royalty, like Chip and Alex. You were just the first English kid born in North America, and then you disappeared. That's all anybody knows about you."

"Knew," Jonah corrected automatically. "That's all anybody *knew* about Virginia Dare in our time."

Katherine glared at him.

Oh, yeah, Jonah thought. *I guess I'm not helping her argument.* But Jonah was working on a new idea, one he'd never thought of before.

And he thought it was important.

"Nobody knew what happened to Virginia Dare because nobody wrote down what happened to her the rest of her life," he said. "Well, not that we know of. But once there was time travel—time travelers could have known every single thing she did, every moment of her life."

Andrea was actually blushing now.

"And I bet you did something great," Jonah said. "I bet that's why it mattered so much that you had to be returned to time."

Katherine's glare had turned into the kind that could vaporize enemies.

"And—and—we'll make sure you get to do that thing.

Whatever it is," Jonah finished lamely. "And whenever. We'll get you to the right time. I promise."

Andrea sniffed. If anything, she looked more discouraged than ever. She crossed her arms and clutched the sleeves of her T-shirt, as if she was desperate for something to hold on to.

"Maybe we should keep walking?" Katherine suggested.

Jonah started to turn back around, facing toward the greatest number of tracer lights. But Andrea, beside him, didn't turn at the same time, the way he expected her to. He bumped against her.

"Sorry," Jonah muttered.

Still clutching her sleeves, Andrea stared at him.

I said I was sorry, Jonah thought. *What's she waiting for?*

"Oh!" she said, a baffled look traveling across her face. "Do that again. Wait a minute." She bent down and picked up a small rock, holding it out slightly from her body. "Now."

Puzzled but obedient, Jonah jostled her shoulder.

Andrea jerked back and forth, but tightened her grip on the rock. A second later, she crouched down and carefully put the rock back exactly as it had been before, eliminating its tracer. Then she straightened up.

"I was wrong," she said. "It wasn't Jonah's fault that I lost the Elucidator."

"Isn't that what I said all along?" Jonah said indignantly.

Andrea nodded.

"You were right. I'm sorry. It was just the timing of things. . . . You bumped me right after I hit ENTER on the Elucidator, so I got confused about cause and effect."

"You're losing me," Jonah said.

"There are different ways to lose things," Andrea explained. "I didn't think about how it felt different, until you bumped into me just now, when I was holding on to my sleeves. I didn't let go. And I didn't let go of the Elucidator when you ran into me the first time. It was me holding on, holding on—and then suddenly the Elucidator just wasn't there."

She collapsed her fingers against the palm of her hand, showing what it'd been like to clutch something that had vanished.

"So?" Katherine said, sounding as baffled as Jonah felt. "Why does it matter?"

"Because of the *code*," Andrea said. "The code I typed in myself—that's what made the Elucidator vanish. That man who came to visit me in secret? It wasn't just that he wanted us to go to the wrong time. He *really* didn't want us telling JB about it."

"Well, duh," Jonah said, completely frustrated now.

"Because he knew JB would put us back in the right time! All that proves is that JB wasn't your mystery man—and we already knew that!"

Andrea's face fell.

"I thought that was something important," she mumbled. "I thought I'd figured something out."

Katherine put her arm around Andrea's shoulder, somehow managing to pat Andrea's back comfortingly while she fixed Jonah with an even more scorching glare.

"You did," Katherine said. "Anything you think of is helpful."

The two girls began walking again, easily following the trail of tracer lights leading them deeper and deeper into the woods.

Jonah glanced down at the dog waiting patiently beside him.

"Looks like you're the only one who's not mad at me now," he muttered. He tugged on the dog's collar. "Come on, boy."

As they walked forward—exiled a few paces behind the girls—Jonah remembered how much he'd wanted to help Andrea from the beginning, how he'd vowed to take care of her.

How can good intentions get so messed up? he wondered.

Ahead of him, he could hear Katherine murmuring

to Andrea, "Well, you know, teenage boys. They don't always think before they speak. . . ."

Jonah tuned her out.

Hey, JB? He thought, because it would be comforting to have JB there to talk to. *Why didn't your brilliant projectionist predict that the mystery man would go visit Andrea? Why didn't he see that we'd get sent to the wrong time and lose the Elucidator? Why couldn't he forecast where we are now, so you can come and help us?*

But Jonah didn't know if that was really how the projections worked.

He did know that every minute that went by without JB showing up was a bigger and bigger sign that they were in trouble.

Around them, the tracer lights kept multiplying.

ELEVEN

They came upon their second set of ruins in an absolute burst of tracer light.

"Ooh, lots of tracers have been here," Katherine muttered, seeming to forget that she was too annoyed with Jonah to speak to him anymore. She pointed to tracer vines draped back from a clearing, tracer firewood stacked neatly beside a falling-down hut, still-standing tracer trees that evidently had been chopped down in original time.

"Or—the original two tracer boys have just been here a lot," Jonah said, because he'd been working out something like a formula for tracers in his head. The absence of one action—say, a boy not slapping a mosquito—could lead to hundreds or thousands of new tracers. Mosquitoes reproduced really fast, didn't they? So all the tracer lights Jonah had seen—that didn't *have* to mean that time was completely messed up or that they were far off from the time they were supposed to be in.

Did it?

To Jonah's surprise, Katherine didn't grumble, *Why do you always have to disagree?* She just nodded and said, "You're right. I didn't think of that."

Jonah figured that was the closest thing he was going to get to an apology for her nasty comments about teenage boys.

"Think this is an Indian village?" Andrea said, stepping out into the clearing.

"I think it *was*," Katherine said, stepping up beside her.

Jonah thought about warning them to be careful, to make sure there were no real live human beings lurking nearby before they went any farther. But what was the point? With or without the glow of tracer lights, this village had clearly been abandoned a long time ago. Granted, it was in much better shape than the Roanoke Colony. Here, about a dozen huts made from curved branches circled an open space—possibly the equivalent of a town square. But many of the branches sagged toward the ground, and a few of the huts were more down than up.

"Do you think some time travelers ruined it?" Andrea asked.

"No, because then we'd see a tracer version of the whole village in good shape," Jonah said. "And lots of happy tracer villagers . . ."

Katherine touched one of the huts with one finger, and the whole thing swayed perilously. An unmoving tracer version of the hut appeared and then vanished when the real hut stopped swaying and rejoined it. Katherine took a step back.

"Then what did happen here?" she asked. "Where did everyone go?"

"Don't know," Jonah said. He was trying not to get too creeped out by the emptiness, the desolation. Maybe there was some perfectly ordinary—even happy—explanation. Maybe the people had just abandoned this village because they'd built a newer, nicer one someplace else. What had Mrs. Rorshas said in fifth-grade Social Studies? Hadn't it been common for Indians to move around, going from village to village based on the growing seasons or animal habitats or whatever?

Jonah wasn't sure enough about that to mention it to the girls. Mrs. Rorshas really hadn't talked that much about the Indians. It'd mostly been the explorers, Jamestown and the Plymouth Colony, the American Revolution . . . all done and over with by Halloween.

Jonah didn't remember anything in that history about

Indians getting nicer, newer villages. Or happier lives.

"Look," Andrea said in a hushed voice. "You can tell they had a cornfield over there." She pointed at a rectangle of cleared land just beyond the last falling-down hut. "We're going to need food. . . ."

She didn't add, *if we're stuck here a long time.* But Jonah could tell by the others' faces that everyone was thinking that.

Jonah walked over and kicked at a downed dried-out stalk. Dare snuffled along beside him, nosing aside empty husks. This was more like the ghost of a cornfield—Jonah couldn't imagine how long ago it had last been planted. Years? Decades? Whatever food had once grown here had undoubtedly been carried away long ago, by birds and mice, if not by people.

Jonah's stomach twisted, but it was more from fear and worry than hunger. For now, anyway.

"When we catch up with the tracer boys, maybe they'll have some food we can eat," Jonah said, with more confidence than he felt. The tracer boys weren't likely to have anything but tracer food.

He began peeking into some of the huts that were in the best shape, just in case. It was dim enough in the huts that the glowing tracer boys would really show up brightly, if they were there. But the enclosed spaces made

Jonah nervous. He didn't like looking into darkness, in the midst of all this desolation.

The first hut was empty. As was the second. And the third.

In the fourth hut, something leaped out at him.

TWELVE

"AHH!" Jonah jumped back, scrambling to get out of the way. He had a quick impression of hooves and glowing eyes. *What is that—a demon?* he thought. *Where are we?*

Barking furiously, Dare streaked off into the woods after the creature.

Jonah couldn't figure out what it was until his heart stopped pounding so hard and he turned around, catching a glimpse of the tracer that remained in the hut: It was only another deer.

Or, no, it could be the very same one that the tracer boys had killed, because that one is really still alive . . . how many tracers of the same deer could there be? Jonah was picturing the one deer multiplying into dozens of tracer deer, every time it came into contact with some new disruption in time. Then Jonah realized his leftover panic was making him stupid. *There can be only one tracer of any animal. Because there is only one version of original time, only one way time is supposed to go.*

It was ridiculous, but Jonah felt much better knowing that this wasn't the same deer the tracer boys had killed. He gazed almost fondly at the single tracer version of the deer he'd startled. The tracer deer didn't even lift its head, but just kept peacefully munching on—what was that? Some sort of rotten melon?

Then Jonah noticed the commotion behind him.

"Dare, no! Come back, boy!" Andrea was calling out after the dog.

Katherine was practically falling on the ground, she was laughing so hard.

"Oh, my gosh! You should have seen your face! You're white as a ghost. You almost look like a tracer!" she screeched.

"Ha, ha," Jonah muttered. He leaned weakly against the side of the hut, which bowed dangerously inward. Jonah decided he could stand on his own two feet. He straightened up.

"Dare!" Andrea screamed, her voice echoing off the trees. "Dare!"

"Shh," Jonah said. His ears were ringing, and he didn't think he could blame leftover time sickness anymore. The screaming, the laughter, the dog and deer crashing through the woods—it was all too much noise, too much more change in this silent, deserted, tracer-haunted place. "Be quiet! Somebody will hear us! We really will ruin time!"

How much change was too much? At what point would there be too many tracers to ever fix?

Katherine's laughter softened to snorts and little bursts of giggling. Andrea called out, "Dare!" once more, but then she turned back to Jonah.

"Really, Jonah," she said soberly. "I don't think there's anyone except us and the tracers on the whole island. Can't you *feel* it?"

Someone could be hiding, Jonah wanted to say. *Like your mystery man, coming back to make us do whatever he wants us to do.* But which was worse—bringing up the possibility that dangerous, unknown people could be lurking anywhere? Or acknowledging the emptiness, the desolation, the ruin? *It feels like something bad happened here,* Jonah thought. *And, maybe . . . it's not over?*

Jonah was not going to say that.

Instead, he muttered grumpily, "How do you know we're on an island?"

"That's where the Roanoke Colony was," Andrea said. "On Roanoke Island."

Jonah threw up his hands.

"Am I the only one who didn't pay attention in fifth-grade Social Studies?" he asked.

To Jonah's surprise, Andrea laughed. But it was kind laughter. Not at all like Katherine's.

"I don't really remember hearing about the Roanoke Colony at school. I'm not sure my teacher ever mentioned it," Andrea said. "But remember that day in the cave? When they told us the names of the missing kids stolen from history, even though they wouldn't say which of us was which kid?"

Jonah nodded and shrugged.

"Yeah. So?"

"So I went home that day and decided I was going to research every single one of the girls' names I could remember," Andrea said. "I live with my aunt and uncle now and, well . . . anyhow, it's good if I can just go in my room and shut the door and have something to do."

"But—" Katherine began. Jonah could tell by the way she had her eyes all squinted together and her nose wrinkled up, that she was about to ask some really nosy question like, *Don't you like your aunt and uncle? Why not? What's wrong with them?*

"Wow," Jonah interrupted quickly. "I just went home that day and ate most of a large pepperoni pizza all by myself and then went right to sleep."

Andrea laughed again. It was a nice sound.

"That's okay—you did have that whole detour to the Middle Ages in between," she said.

"Yeah, after being in the 1480s, I was . . ." Jonah stopped himself before he got to the last word, which was supposed to be *starving*. It didn't seem smart to bring that up right now. He shifted gears. "So you really learned everything about all the missing kids from history? All the girls, anyway?"

Andrea shook her head, her eyes very solemn.

"No, and this is kind of weird," she said. "I started with Virginia Dare, and I meant to move on, but I just . . . kept . . . reading about Virginia Dare."

"Ooh . . ." Katherine let out a low, spooky-sounding moan. She'd stopped squinting—now her whole face was lit up with excitement. "So you must have known that's who you were. Did you just have this feeling about Virginia Dare? Like something subconscious, or not so subconscious, telling you, 'That's who you are. It has to be!'"

Jonah glared at his sister. Didn't Katherine remember how Andrea had reacted back in the time hollow with JB, when JB had said she was really Virginia Dare? *That's not me! That's not my mother!* she'd screamed. Was Katherine *trying* to upset Andrea again?

But Andrea didn't scream this time. She just tilted her

head thoughtfully to the side, considering Katherine's questions.

Maybe Jonah didn't understand anything about girls and their moods.

"I don't think I knew anything," Andrea said after a few seconds. "Even subconsciously. I was just really interested in the Virginia Dare story. I think it was because of the grandfather coming back—how hard he tried to get back to his family, and how many times he failed, and then when he finally made it to Roanoke . . ."

"No one was there," Katherine whispered.

Jonah should have been immune to all of Katherine's dramatics after living with her for nearly twelve years. But he couldn't help shivering at the eerie tone in her voice. Off in the distance, Dare's barking seemed to have a plaintive, desperate quality to it now.

"That's not just him barking at the deer anymore, is it?" Jonah asked.

"No—do you think he's hurt?" Andrea asked. "Fallen into some hole left by a hunter or—oh my gosh, they wouldn't have had metal leg traps at Roanoke, would they?"

She whirled around and started running toward the sound of Dare's barking. Jonah and Katherine rushed after her.

They weren't going back into the woods now, but into

an area of tall grasses that whipped against their faces and cut into their arms. Jonah began wishing he'd kept his sweatshirt on, despite the heat, just to protect his skin. But there wasn't time to stop and put it back on.

Dare's barking shifted, becoming higher pitched, more panicked.

"Something *is* wrong!" Andrea called back to Jonah and Katherine. "I can tell. We have to . . ."

She didn't finish her sentence. She just sped up.

"Wait, Andrea! You don't know what's out there!" Jonah called after her. He didn't even know what danger he should be worrying about. The mystery man, back to steal Andrea away completely? Whatever enemy had destroyed the Roanoke Colony and the Indian village to begin with? Some other danger the mystery man wanted Andrea to encounter? Pirates, brigands, murderers, thieves . . .

Listing dangers helped Jonah run faster. But the faster he went, the faster the grasses whipped against his face, against his bare arms, against his ankles. He was glad when the grasses thinned out, but then he was running through sand. It spilled into his shoes, making every step twice as hard.

And then he sped around a corner and discovered that Andrea had caught up with Dare.

The dog wasn't caught in a metal trap. He wasn't being carried away by evil time travelers or pirates. Instead, he was crouched on a narrow beach and barking furiously at something out in the water.

"What is it, boy?" Andrea asked him. "What do you see?"

Still running, Jonah put his hand to his forehead, shielding his eyes from the bright sun so he could stare out into the surf. The waves were rocking violently back and forth; it was almost impossible to tell from one moment to the next which section of the water he'd already looked at and which he still needed to scan. There was a dark shape bobbing up and down out there—or was it just a shadow?

Jonah squinted harder and ran closer to the edge of the water. The dark shape began to make sense.

"It's an upside-down boat," he said. "Smashed up, like from a shipwreck." He instantly regretted saying that word. *Shipwreck, car wreck—maybe Andrea won't think about the similarities?* "It probably happened years ago," he added soothingly. "I think sometimes it takes debris like that a long time to wash up onshore."

"Jonah, it was right side up a minute ago," Andrea said. She raced to the edge of the water. She jerked off her right shoe, then her left. She rolled up the bottom edges of her shorts.

"What are you doing?" Jonah asked.

Andrea shoved away the sweatshirt she'd knotted around her waist. It dropped onto the sand, one sleeve trailing into the water.

"There was someone in there!" she screamed. "I saw him!"

THIRTEEN

Jonah barely had a moment to think before Andrea plunged into the water.

"No!" Jonah called after her. "It's not safe!"

Jonah knew there were other objections he should be yelling at her—something about time, about how you weren't supposed to change time, about how maybe this was a trap or a trick set up by the mystery man? But she was being buffeted by the waves so completely he couldn't put two words together. She was underwater; she was back on the surface; she was underwater; she was back on the surface. . . .

Beside Jonah, Dare was now barking furiously at Andrea. The dog put one paw into the water, got hit by a huge wave, and backed out, whimpering.

"You're a lot of help," Jonah muttered. He dropped the

sweatshirt he'd been carrying, so he could cup his hands around his mouth and scream, "Andrea! Come back!"

Andrea turned slightly—maybe to yell back at Jonah—and a wave knocked her sideways, somersaulting her deeper into the water.

She didn't resurface.

"Andrea!" Jonah screamed.

He threw himself into the water and began paddling desperately toward the spot where he'd seen Andrea disappear. His shoes and clothes got waterlogged within seconds, dragging him down. But he didn't have time to tug off even his sneakers. He kept pushing forward, doggedly, even though all the water in front of him looked the same now. He couldn't remember where Andrea had vanished. He reached down, and his fingers brushed something soft—seaweed? Or Andrea's hair?

Jonah kicked hard, lifting his head high above the water, trying to gulp in a good breath before he dove down to search for Andrea.

The wind seemed to be calling his name.

"Jonah! Jonah!"

Jonah looked to the right, and it was Andrea.

"Swim—parallel—shore!" she called.

Oh, yeah. Jonah knew that. That's what you did when you got caught in an undertow.

He wasn't sure if the force tugging at him was really an undertow—or if it was just the dragging weight of his own clothes. But he did a sort of modified dog paddle toward Andrea.

"It's coming close!" she shouted.

It took Jonah a moment to realize that she meant the boat. It wasn't just coming close—it was rising up, towering over them. In a minute, depending on how the wave broke, it could be slamming down on them.

"Watch out!" Jonah yelled, just as Andrea screamed, "The man!"

Jonah glanced back at the boat, and caught a quick glimpse of a man's hand, clutching one of the splintering boards.

"This way," Jonah shouted, getting a faceful of salty water. It seemed as if an entire gallon had landed in his open mouth. He sputtered and coughed, but still managed to grab Andrea's arm and shove her toward the shore. That sent Jonah reeling backward, barely able to keep his head above water.

The waves heaved up, then hurled the boat down, down, down. . . .

It didn't hit Jonah. It hit a rock formation Jonah hadn't even known was there. The boat shattered instantly, setting off an explosion of broken boards. So now it wasn't just one boat Jonah had to watch out for, but dozens of sharp, pointed remnants of the boat, constantly being tossed by the waves near Jonah's head.

And Andrea was swimming back into the debris.

"No! Don't!" Jonah screamed.

"He's right here!" Andrea screamed back.

She'd reached the man floating in the debris. He seemed to be trying to swim, but Jonah saw that that was an illusion: His arms and legs were only moving with the current.

"Help—flip—over!" Andrea called.

Belatedly, Jonah remembered that he should actually know how to deal with this situation. He'd taken junior lifesaving lessons at the pool the past summer. But the pool had always been so calm and safe, one kid at a time jumping into the peaceful blue water to "save" an instructor flailing about in imaginary danger. There'd been no hazardous debris, no heaving waves, no actual unconscious victim.

Jonah shook his head, trying to focus.

"Uh—armpit!" he screamed at Andrea. "Grab him by his armpit!"

Either Andrea couldn't hear him, or she couldn't understand. Jonah grabbed the man himself, yanking him by the arm to pull him close, then awkwardly turning him over. Finally Jonah wrapped his own arm around the man's chest, both of them rolling in the waves together. Any of Jonah's lifesaving instructors would have frowned and pointed out everything Jonah had done wrong. Jonah knew he wasn't supposed to end up clinging to the drowning victim like this, as if he was just trying to use the victim's buoyancy to keep his own head above water. And there was something Jonah was supposed to remember about clearing obstructed airways and checking to see if the man needed mouth-to-mouth or CPR. But right now Jonah was doing well just to breathe himself—to breathe air, that is, not saltwater. Jonah was starting to forget which was which.

"Maybe—we can—go in—there," Andrea sputtered, her words coming out between waves and breaths.

Jonah looked, and the shoreline had changed. The current had flung them downwind from the sandy beach: Now they were facing rocks. And the waves were already smashing the debris from the boat against the rocks, splintering the boards into smaller boards—more dangers that Jonah and Andrea would need to avoid.

Jonah glanced down at the man in his arms. The man's chest was moving up and down, but Jonah couldn't tell if that meant he was breathing or if it was just his body bobbing in the surf, bobbing along with Jonah.

Sidestroke, Jonah reminded himself. *Just do the modified side-stroke like you're supposed to, and don't think about anything else.*

He'd only managed to take three strokes forward when something hit him in the head—something from the air, not in the water.

Now, that's not right, Jonah wanted to complain. *It's not fair for* everything *to be dangerous!*

He turned his head to look and discovered that a huge branch had fallen into the water.

"Grab on and climb out!" Katherine yelled. "Don't swim! Climb!"

Oh . . .

Katherine was at the other end of the branch. Katherine must have thrown it in.

Had Katherine been *trying* to hit him?

No, Jonah realized, she was trying to help him. The branch was a wonderful thing to hold on to while the water seemed to be trying harder and harder to dash him and the unconscious man against the rocks. Holding on to the branch, Jonah could almost stand up. He braced his feet between two rocks and yelled at Andrea, "Help me drag the man in!"

She grabbed on to the branch too. Between the two of them, they managed to jerk the man toward the shore. When they finally reached dry ground, Katherine let go of the branch and helped Jonah and Andrea yank the man out of the water. Jonah fell back on the scrubby grass, completely spent. But Andrea leaned over the man, putting her ear against his chest, her hand beneath his nose.

"He's alive!" she screamed. "He's breathing!"

Jonah didn't move. The ground seemed to be spinning beneath him. Overhead, the clouds were whipping across the sky with amazing speed. The contrasting motions— spinning earth, speeding clouds—were making Jonah feel nauseated. So he closed his eyes. But that just made him feel as if he was back in the water, being tossed back and forth by the waves. . . .

"You saved his life!" Katherine said, in awe, her voice coming from the same direction as Andrea's. "You and Jonah. That man would have drowned without you."

. . . *would have drowned* . . .

. . . *would have drowned* . . .

Jonah winced, thinking about how moments ago, standing on the shore, he'd wondered if the capsized boat in the water was a trap or a trick set up by the same man who'd convinced Andrea to sabotage her own trip through time. Jonah had been worried about Andrea drowning. But this was something else. This was him and Andrea willfully changing time. Katherine had felt guilty about knocking down a pine cone in the wrong place.

Now the three of them had saved a man's life. What if the man went on to change history even more? He might have children he wasn't supposed to have; he might turn around and kill someone who wasn't supposed to die; he might do anything.

Jonah felt sick, but he couldn't have said what was making him feel worse: Thinking that he could have stood by and let the man drown? Or thinking that maybe that was what he was supposed to do?

This setup was a trap, Jonah thought. *It was a trick.*

Back when he was in 1483, Jonah had argued with JB about taking so many chances with Chip's and Alex's lives. But even JB wouldn't have set Jonah and Katherine up with a dilemma like this one.

"Not fair," Jonah muttered. "Not fair."

He didn't know how it had worked, but he felt certain that the mystery man had planned for Jonah and Andrea to be on the beach right at that moment, right as the boat capsized. He had planned for them to have to make a choice.

Did he know what we would choose? Jonah wondered. *Does he know what will happen because the man didn't drown? Does he use projections, like JB?*

"Jonah? Are you all right?" Katherine asked.

Jonah realized he still had his eyes squeezed shut. And

he was probably moving his lips, like a little kid just learning how to read silently.

"Yeah . . . yeah . . ." Jonah didn't want to talk about tricks and traps and dilemmas with the others. Not yet. He didn't want to talk about how they might have ruined time by saving the man's life. Because that wouldn't change anything they did from here on out—it wasn't as if they were going to push the man back into the water. Jonah opened his eyes, cleared his throat, tried to remember how to act normal.

"I'm fine," he told Katherine. "Thanks to you throwing that branch in."

"Yeah," Andrea agreed. She was brushing sand from a huge scrape on her leg. "That was really smart. How'd you think of it?"

"Oh, you know me, I'm just so *brilliant*," Katherine said, grinning. She hadn't used up all her energy fighting the waves, so she had some left for clowning. She held one hand out, placed her other hand on her stomach, and dipped down in a mocking bow. "Thank you. Thank you very much." Then she shrugged. "Really, though, I just thought of it because I saw what *they* did."

"They, who?" Jonah said, baffled.

Katherine was already pointing, toward a spot directly behind Jonah.

"Them," she said.

Jonah turned around. There in the grass were the two tracer boys they'd seen earlier.

And lying between them was a tracer version of the man Jonah and Andrea had just rescued from drowning.

FOURTEEN

It took Jonah's waterlogged brain a moment to figure out what that meant.

If the two tracer boys rescued the drowning man in the original version of history, then . . .

"He was supposed to live!" Jonah burst out. "We didn't ruin history by saving him! We saved history by saving him!"

Andrea whirled around and glared at Jonah.

"Is *that* why you didn't want me jumping into the water?" she growled at him. "You think *history* is more important than a man's life?"

"No, no—" Jonah tried to explain. "I was worried about you! I—"

"If I'd gotten back to my parents the day of their crash, would you have stopped me from saving *them*?" Andrea asked.

"Of course not!" Jonah said. "I would have helped you! But . . ."

"But what?" Andrea asked, her glare intensifying.

"I don't think we would ever get that choice," Jonah said.

"Because of Damaged Time," Katherine reminded Andrea.

Jonah could have left it at that. It would have been easier. But he had too many ideas roiling around in his mind. Some of them were going to spill out whether he wanted them to or not.

"I think some things just aren't possible, even with time travel," Jonah said. He turned to Katherine. "Don't you remember JB talking about how time protects itself from paradoxes? Certain things aren't supposed to be possible." He gestured at the man who had nearly drowned, at the churning waves beyond. "*This* wasn't supposed to be possible. We weren't supposed to be here!"

Andrea patted the man's chest protectively.

"But we *are*," she said. "And we saved him."

Jonah shook his head.

"That's not what I mean," he said. "I'm not saying it right. I'm glad the man's alive. I helped save him too, remember? But don't you think there was something wrong with how it all worked? Don't you feel . . . used?"

"Used?" Andrea repeated numbly.

"Why were we here on this island, in this time period, just at the right moment to see the man drowning?" Jonah challenged.

"You mean . . . because I changed the Elucidator code?" Andrea whispered.

"And because Dare barked," Katherine reminded him. "Don't forget that."

Jonah reached over and grabbed Dare.

"How do we know he's even a real dog?" Jonah asked furiously. "How do we know he's not some . . . some animatronic thing that's supposed to spy on us and direct us wherever Andrea's mystery man wants us to go?"

Jonah rolled Dare over on his belly and felt around in his fur, looking for some on/off switch or computer chip implant. The dog yelped and squirmed away.

"Jonah, you're being paranoid," Katherine said. "It was JB who gave us Dare, not the mystery man."

"And why would he need a fake dog to spy on us?" Andrea asked. "Couldn't he watch us anyhow? Can't time experts do that, if they know where you are?"

Oh, yeah . . .

Jonah turned his face to the sky.

"We're onto you!" he yelled at the dark clouds. "We know exactly what's going on here!"

But he didn't. That was the problem. He didn't know what would have happened if the man they'd rescued had died. He didn't know if there still might be other reasons Andrea's mystery man had wanted her to go to the wrong time. He didn't know where the real versions of the tracer boys were, when they were supposed to be right here, acting like lifeguards.

He spun toward the tracer boys, as if he could catch them doing something wrong. But they were only tending to the tracer man: pulling tracer seaweed out of his hair, brushing tracer sand away from his mouth. Somehow that made Jonah angrier. He scrambled up and stood over them.

"Where are you for real?" he screamed at them. "Why aren't you here?"

He reached out toward the curly haired boy, wanting to shake his shoulders. But of course Jonah's hands went right through the tracer. And he'd been so sure that he could grab the tracer boy's shoulders that he was thrown off balance. He fell facedown in the sand.

For a moment he just lay there, not moving.

Then he felt a hand on his arm, pushing him to roll over. It was Katherine.

"Jonah?" she asked, peering down at him. "Jo-oh?"

The old baby name steadied him a little. That was

what she'd called him when they were in preschool. But that had been a long time ago. He braced himself for her to start making snarky comments about how teenage boys couldn't control their temper.

Instead, she just kept looking at him.

"I don't like this setup either," she said. "But what do you want us to do?"

"What JB sent us to do," Jonah said stubbornly. "Fix time. Save Andrea. Then go home."

And not have to think, he could have added. *Not have to worry that everything we do might ruin time. Not have to watch out for tracers.*

"But we're not where JB sent us," Katherine said. "So . . ."

Jonah could tell she was trying to choose her words very carefully, trying not to set him off again.

"What if everything's connected?" Andrea asked, looking up from beside the man they'd rescued. She was mimicking the tracer boys almost exactly, picking kelp out of the man's hair. "What if we have to fix their problems with time"—she pointed to the tracer boys—"before we can fix mine?"

Jonah felt really, really tired all of a sudden. How could they solve tracers' problems? Tracers didn't even exist, not really. They were just place holders. Signs of trouble. They were useless without their real selves.

At least we have the real version of the drowning man, Jonah thought. *Could he be a clue?*

"Hey, look," Katherine said abruptly. "Their guy's sitting up and talking."

She gestured toward the tracer man, who was looking dazedly from one tracer boy to the other. He seemed to be thanking them.

"Is our guy awake too?" Katherine reached over and tapped on the real man's shoulder. "Sir? Sir?"

The man didn't respond. His eyelids didn't even flutter. He lay deathly still.

"What's wrong with him?" Katherine asked.

She put her wrist against his forehead, feeling for a fever. She put her finger against his neck, feeling for his pulse. She put her hand on his head, ready to turn it side to side. Jonah guessed she wanted to study the bruises already showing up on his face. She stopped.

"Oh, no," she whispered.

She lifted her hand.

It was covered with blood.

FIFTEEN

Jonah was amazed that Katherine didn't start screaming, "Ew! Ew! Get it off me!" and start running away from the man. She did look a little pale. But she just wiped her hand on a clump of beach grass and said faintly, "Maybe, if there's something we could use as a bandage . . ."

"My sweatshirt!" Andrea volunteered. She took off running down the shore, to the spot where she'd left her sweatshirt and shoes right before she'd rushed into the water.

"How bad is it?" Jonah asked quietly.

"I forget how it works with head injuries," Katherine said. "Do they bleed a lot and always look worse than they really are? Or is it the other way around?"

Jonah didn't know.

He looked carefully at the man for the first time. It had

been easier to stay mad when Jonah wasn't looking, when he was thinking of the man as just part of some trick or trap—or a clue—not as a real live, flesh-and-blood person. But the man was real. Beneath his tattered white shirt, his chest rose and fell in shallow breaths, and Jonah almost felt like cheering at each sign that the man was still alive.

"He's old," Jonah said, surprised.

The man had wrinkles beneath the sand caked on his battered face. Along with his thinning white hair, he had a white beard that might have looked dapper and well trimmed if he hadn't just gone through a boat crash.

"Why would an old man go out in a boat by himself?" Jonah asked.

Before Katherine had a chance to answer, Andrea was back and handing Katherine two sweatshirts. She'd picked up Jonah's, too.

"The one sleeve dragged in the water a little," Andrea said breathlessly. She pulled her shoes back on; she hadn't taken the time to do that before.

"That's okay," Katherine said. "If we just wrap them around like this . . . and press against the wound . . ."

Andrea held her hand firmly on the sweatshirts, even when the blood began to show through. She glanced back at the tracer man behind them.

"Why doesn't *he* need a bandage?" she said.

Jonah walked over to the tracer man and studied the back of his head.

"He doesn't have any big cuts like that," Jonah said.

That was probably the reason the tracer was sitting up and talking—even weakly—while the real man lay still and unmoving.

And what does that do to time? Jonah wondered dizzily. *Is this man's head injury part of the trap or the trick? Or is it just . . . something that happened?*

"It doesn't make sense," Andrea complained. "Both men were rescued the same way. Right?"

"You and Jonah were just a little later getting the man away from all those broken boards," Katherine said apologetically. "From where I was standing, I could see the one tracer boy swim out to him while you were still floundering about, getting thrown around by the waves."

Jonah wanted to protest, *We were doing the best that we could!*

But then, to his surprise, Katherine added, "And I was a lot slower holding the branch out to you . . ."

Just then a sudden gust of wind shoved against them, practically knocking Andrea over. Both girls were forced to hold their hair back so it didn't whip into their faces. Andrea peered up at the sky, where the dark clouds were now racing even faster.

"I think there's a storm coming," she said, shivering in her wet clothes. "That's why the water's so choppy."

Katherine frowned.

"The man's not even conscious," she said. "He can't stay out here in a storm."

A bolt of lightning slashed the sky, followed by a crack of thunder. Andrea looked up appealingly at Jonah.

"Will you help us get him to safety?" she asked. "And then worry about what it all means for time?"

"What kind of a person do you think I am?" Jonah asked indignantly. "You think I'd leave a hurt old man out on a beach in the middle of a storm? Of course I'll help!"

"Thanks," Andrea said, smiling at him. Even with her hair blowing around, the smile made her look pretty again.

Am I being used again? Jonah wondered. *Did Andrea's mystery man know that I'd react to her like that? Did he know this storm was going to blow in? Did he cause it?*

Or was Jonah just being paranoid, as Katherine had said?

"Okay, great," Katherine said. "We're all willing to help. But what are we going to do? Even working together, I don't think we could get him back to that Indian village, and there's nowhere else to go. . . ."

Without thinking about it, all three kids looked toward the tracer boys.

They were casting anxious looks at the sky as well. They jumped up and grabbed another downed branch which, as soon as they moved it, turned into a tracer as well, with the original branch still lying flat on the ground. This branch had slick, shiny leaves and several rather large offshoot branches, but the tracer boys dragged it effortlessly across the ground. When they reached the tracer man, they gently eased him into a crook between the main branch and one of the offshoots. Then they tugged on the other end of the branch, pulling the man along behind them.

"The very latest in ambulance transportation, circa— what? One thousand B.C.?" Katherine muttered.

"Who cares! We'll try it!" Jonah said.

He ran over and grabbed the end of the branch, but it wasn't quite as light as the tracer boys had made it seem. Jonah had to do a lot of tugging and jerking to maneuver the branch into place beside the unconscious man. Then, no matter how the three kids tried, the best they could do was roll him facedown onto the branch.

"One of us will have to walk beside him, holding him on," Katherine directed.

Ahead of them, the tracer boys were marching steadily along, the man perched on the branch sliding smoothly behind them.

For Jonah, Katherine, and Andrea, it was more a matter of tugging, jerking, and snarling at one other, "Can't you push any harder?" and "I'm doing my best—can't *you* push harder?" Jonah began to have a lot more respect for the tracers. They may have looked scrawny and malnourished—and they were wearing ridiculous clothes and evidently belonged to a culture that hadn't figured out how to invent the wheel. But they were incredibly strong. In Jonah's time, they probably would have won several Olympic gold medals for *something*.

Jonah couldn't have said how close they'd gotten to the deserted Indian village—halfway back? Two-thirds of the way?—when the blinding rain began.

This is impossible, he wanted to say. *I give up.* But how could he say that when Andrea and Katherine were still pushing and pulling and tugging and yanking, even as water streamed into their eyes, twigs stabbed into their arms, and mud slipped against their shoes? So he kept trying too.

The tracers were just a dim glow ahead of him. And then, suddenly, they were out of sight.

"No! I can't—" Jonah screamed. Rain pounded against his face, drowning out anything he tried to say.

"Let's go into the same hut," Katherine said, speaking directly into his ear.

The same hut? *Oh . . . The Indians went into one of the huts in the village,* Jonah realized. *That's why I can't see them.*

He got a final burst of energy, pulling the branch even harder. Then he dropped the branch and tugged the man into the dim but dry hut. All three kids collapsed in a heap, not even caring that they had fallen right on top of the tracer boys.

SIXTEEN

For a while, Jonah just lay of the floor of the hut. At least the rain wasn't pounding down on him anymore. But his shoulders ached from fighting the waves and struggling with the branch. His legs felt as if they'd been rubbed raw, walking all that way in wet jeans. His clammy T-shirt clung to his skin, the saltwater that had soaked into it stinging against the dozens of scrapes and cuts he'd gotten scrambling over the rocks.

"Ohh," Katherine moaned. "I need a hot shower."

"Dry clothes," Jonah mumbled.

"Make it a nice warm robe for me," Katherine said. "And my fluffy bunny slippers."

"Hot soup," Jonah said. "Mom's chili maybe?"

"Stop it!" Andrea said fiercely. "That just makes it worse, wishing for things you can't have. You know?"

Jonah could tell she wasn't just talking about clean, dry clothes and hot food.

"Sorry," he muttered.

Andrea ignored him. She sprang up and began fussing over the unconscious man.

"We put him down on the dirt floor and he's got cuts all over him, and they're going to get infected if we're not careful. But the water's coming off his clothes and hair, and that's turning the dirt into mud . . . how did people do it, hundreds of years ago?" she ranted. "How did they stay clean and healthy?"

A lot of them didn't, Jonah thought. *A lot of them died.*

He wasn't going to say that to Andrea.

She was adjusting the way the sweatshirts were tied around the man's head and muttering, "At least we can keep the cut on his head up and out of the mud . . . we should rinse it off, but where are we going to get clean water?"

Jonah noticed that one of the tracer boys had stepped out of the hut—it was a little hard to keep track of someone who was *under* you and who could move right through you. But the boy was just now coming back in, carrying a tracer version of a hollowed-out gourd in his hand. The boy bent down beside the tracer man and gently lifted the man's head, so the man could drink out of the gourd.

"I'll go see where he got that," Jonah said.

He stepped out of the hut into a stiff wind. Oddly, the rain had stopped—it had lasted just long enough to make the final part of their trip back to the village really, really challenging. But the sky was still dark and ominous, and the dim light made it hard to see where Jonah was going. He practically tripped over the hollowed-out water barrel before he saw it.

The twin of the tracer boy's gourd was floating about halfway down in the barrel.

Oh . . . they just used this to catch rainwater, Jonah thought. *That's why there's not much water in there—there wasn't much rain.*

He filled up the gourd as best he could and stumbled back toward the hut.

The tracer boys had started trying to build a fire while Jonah was away. Jonah handed the gourd over to Andrea and then stood watching the tracers. They piled together sticks and twigs and dried-out leaves; one of the boys was twisting a pointed stick against the groove of a stick below it.

"If those guys can start a fire that way, they're superheroes," Jonah said. "We tried that in Boy Scouts, and even the scoutmaster couldn't get a flame going. It's impossi . . ."

The ghost of a flame flared out from the tracer boys'

fire. Moments later, the flames were crackling across the dried-up leaves, spreading to the small twigs.

Katherine snorted.

"Shows how much you learned in Boy Scouts," she said.

"But . . . but . . . I could start a fire with a magnifying glass," Jonah protested. "Or, I saw this thing online, where you use a Coke can and a chocolate bar—"

"Do you see any of those things lying around here?" Katherine asked.

"Maybe I could try doing it just like the tracers," Jonah muttered.

He saw that the sticks and twigs and dry leaves that the tracer boys had used were still in the hut. In original time, the way time was supposed to go, they'd been stacked up neatly. But right now they were scattered about, probably by squirrels or badgers or some other animals looking for food.

Jonah began picking up the sticks and laying them in the exact pattern the tracer boys had used. It was eerie reaching into the blazing tracer fire. Jonah kept flinching and bracing for pain. But the tracer flames felt like nothing. Like air. Dust. Empty space. He breathed in tracer smoke—so wispy, like the ghost of a ghost. It didn't even have an odor.

MARGARET PETERSON HADDIX

When all the sticks and chunks of wood were arranged, he tucked in the twigs and leaves as kindling. Then he found the same pointed stick the tracer boy had turned to create enough friction to spark the first flame. Jonah twisted it back and forth in the palms of his hands, the friction warming his hands, at least. He kept the image in his head of the way it had worked for the tracer boy—like magic. One moment the boy had just been rubbing two sticks together, and the next, he had a roaring fire. Jonah tried not to think about how things had worked in his Boy Scout troop: He and his friends had tried and tried and tried, and then the scoutmaster had brought out the matches.

Jonah didn't have any matches now. There wasn't a backup plan.

He kept trying, long past the point where he and his Scout friends had given up.

"There!" Katherine shrieked, leaning down close to watch. "You did it!"

Jonah sat back and looked. If there had been a flame, Katherine had just blown it out.

"Stay back!" he ordered.

The two tracer boys were sitting around their fire staring into the flames, cryptic expressions on their faces. *They* probably didn't feel cold and wet, even though they were practically naked. *They* probably weren't worrying that the man that they'd pulled from the waves might die from infected mud. They definitely weren't worrying that time had been irreparably harmed or that they'd been set up in some elaborate trap.

Even though Jonah knew that they were staring into their own fire and had no way of knowing that Jonah was there—because he hadn't been, in their time—Jonah felt like they were watching him. Their cryptic expressions seemed to be hiding scorn at Jonah's constant failure, trying to start a fire.

"I can so do it!" Jonah muttered, rubbing the sticks together faster than ever.

A leaf crackled and began to smoke—real smoke, not ghostly tracer smoke. A tiny spark leaped from one leaf to another.

"Whoo-hoo!" Jonah cheered. "Take that, Scoutmaster Briggs! *That* should be the test for Eagle Scout!"

"Oh, good," Andrea said, flashing a rare smile at Jonah. "Now the man can dry off next to the fire."

"We can *all* dry off next to the fire," Katherine corrected.

The fire was tiny, and there was no more dry wood around for making it bigger. Jonah had never had to solve any math problems where X was the size of a fire; Y was the rate at which water evaporated, and Z was the likelihood that someone would survive after nearly drowning, bashing his head, and lying in germ-infested mud or that three kids would manage to outsmart someone who had sabotaged their trip through time. Jonah knew the fire couldn't make *that* big a difference. Still, it felt like the fire was a big deal. It felt like they all had a chance now.

"Here," Jonah told Andrea. "I'll help you move the man closer, so he warms up faster."

Jonah shoved at the man's waist. Katherine shoved at his shoulders. Andrea gingerly moved his head. Jonah's main goal was to keep from pushing the man all the way into the fire, so he wasn't paying attention to much else. He'd forgotten that the tracer boys had placed the tracer man right next to their tracer fire, which was in the same spot as Jonah's fire. He'd forgotten what happened when a person joined with his own tracer.

Jonah gave the man's body one final shove, and suddenly the glow of his tracer went out. The man had slipped exactly into the outline of his tracer.

The man's color instantly improved. His lips moved, even though his eyes remained closed.

"Greedy privateers," he muttered. "Thinking of naught but money . . . Coming to Roanoke too late in the season . . . Dangerous winds, dangerous seas . . .

Help! The rocks! The rocks! Beware the rocks!" He took in a ragged gasp. "No! No! Our ship! We're doomed! All will perish. . . . It's happening! Oh, dear God! All have perished but me!"

Jonah jerked the man back away from his tracer.

SEVENTEEN

"What'd you do that for?" Andrea demanded.

It had been only an instinct, unthinking fear. The man and his tracer were both still moving their lips, but soundlessly, now that they were apart. Jonah could tell what each of them was saying only because it was almost exactly what he'd just heard: *All perished but me; all perished but me; all perished but me. . . .*

Jonah shivered.

"What's wrong?" Andrea asked harshly. "Can't you take hearing another sad story?"

Jonah rubbed his hands hard against his face.

"No, I just—what if it's too confusing for the man, being joined with his tracer, thinking with his tracer brain?" Jonah asked, trying to come up with an explanation that sounded reasonable. "The tracer knows he was saved by two boys dressed like Indians, not three kids in T-shirts and jeans or shorts. And then if he sees us but not the tracer boys—because people can't see tracers in their own time—that will really mess him up."

"But this guy never saw us save him," Katherine argued. "He'll just think the tracer boys saved him and left, and then we arrived. . . . We saw people rejoin their tracers after seeing different things before, back in the 1400s. I don't think anything bad happened then, because of that."

Jonah was still figuring out other problems.

"You think, when the man wakes up, it's going to be okay for him to see us in our twenty-first-century clothes?" Jonah demanded. "Here, now, where we really don't belong? When it's all a setup by some mysterious time traveler who lied to Andrea?"

"No," Katherine admitted. She winced, probably thinking about how she'd poked at the man back on the beach, trying to wake him up: *Sir? Sir?* That had been a mistake. They were lucky the man hadn't awakened.

Very deliberately, Katherine pulled her hand back from the man's shoulder.

"Hold on. Are you saying you just want to . . . sneak away?" Andrea asked incredulously. "Leave the man alone when he's hurt?"

The man was still mouthing his silent lament: *All perished but me; all perished but me; all perished but me. . . .*

Moving just as deliberately as Katherine, Andrea grabbed the man's hand and held on tight.

"Shh, it's over now," she whispered to him. "You're safe." She looked back up at Jonah and Katherine. "Didn't you hear him? He's the only survivor of some awful shipwreck. So nobody would know to look for him. He's just as stranded as we are. We can't abandon him!"

Jonah shook his head.

"Nobody's saying we should abandon him," he said. "We're just trying to figure out how to take care of him without ruining time."

But was that possible? Or was this another trap, one where they'd be forced to endanger time, no matter what?

"I wish we still had the Elucidator to make us invisible," Katherine said.

Andrea sighed.

"Sorry about that," she said. She stared into the fire for a moment, her face almost as inscrutable as the tracer boys'. "No. You know what? I'm *not* sorry. If I hadn't changed the code on the Elucidator, this man would be dead right now." She squeezed his hand. "Do you know how much time I've spent the past year wishing it was possible to go back and save someone from dying?"

"Andrea," Katherine said. "This doesn't change any-thing about your parents. You still can't save them."

"I know, I know, but . . . this is one little victory over death, all right?" Andrea said fiercely. "One way to stick it to death and say, 'Ha, ha, this is one person you can't have yet. Yeah, you're going to win in the end, but not right now. Not this time.'"

The man still could die, Jonah thought. *And is it really a victory over death if he was supposed to be rescued in original time anyhow? Or is it more of a victory over . . . time?*

Andrea's face was flushed, as if she'd said more than she'd meant to. Jonah had to look away, because he couldn't think straight, watching her.

"Should we hide, except when we *have* to be in here taking care of the man?" Katherine asked. "Should we put the man back with his tracer, and leave him like that, because that'd be putting time back the way it's supposed to be? Or should we keep him away from his tracer until we can find the real versions of the tracer boys? How *are* we going to find the real boys . . . and Andrea's tracer . . . and whatever else we need to fix time and get out of here?"

She sounded completely perplexed.

This must be what Andrea's mystery man wanted, when he told her to change the Elucidator code, Jonah thought, staring into the fire. *He wanted us confused. So he could make us do . . . what?*

Jonah's thoughts twisted like the smoke flowing up toward the chimneylike hole in the roof. While he watched, the smoke completely combined with the tracer smoke, so it was indistinguishable. And, he realized, the fire now flamed out and drew in at exactly the same rate as the tracer fire.

Not scientifically possible, Jonah thought. *Two fires, started at different times, by different people, should not be identical.*

But that was how it worked when time was trying to fix itself. Given a chance, the tracers always took over.

Unless some time traveler intervened.

"The man who lied to Andrea," Jonah said slowly. "He's not standing here telling us what to do. But he's put us in all these situations where we have to make choices. And I think he's manipulating things so we always make the choice he wants."

"Like the way he got me to change the Elucidator in the first place," Andrea said, scowling.

"Exactly," Jonah said. "So I think we should stop doing what the man expects, what we would normally do. We have to do the opposite instead."

Katherine squinted at him.

"You're saying we *should* abandon—" she began.

"No, no," Jonah said, before Andrea got upset again.

"Nothing that extreme. I really don't think we should let this man see us, but he's unconscious and it's pretty dark in here anyway, so I'm not going to worry about it tonight."

"You're talking about whether or not we put the man back with his tracer," Katherine said, catching on quickly.

"Right," Jonah said. "I was feeling guilty for pulling him away before, for interfering with time like that."

"And I was going to say that if we put him back with his tracer, maybe we'd hear more," Andrea said. "About him, anyway, even if that doesn't help with *my* problem with time."

"I agree," Katherine said. "So, normally, we'd be deciding to push the man back together with his tracer."

"So we won't. We'll keep them apart," Jonah said. He tugged the man a little farther away. He looked up at the dark sky, through the hole in the roof. "How do you like that, Mr. Elucidator Code-Changer? We're forcing your hand!"

"But what if we really do ruin time, doing that?" Andrea asked.

"We won't," Jonah said, hoping he sounded confident. "Because that's what your mystery man is trying to do. We're showing him he can't trick us into playing along. It's like chess or Stratego, games like that, where sometimes you have to use reverse psychology."

"Jonah, you're terrible at chess and Stratego!" Katherine objected.

"I am not," Jonah said. "Not anymore. Remember a few years ago, when I used to go over to Billy Rivoli's house and play board games? I got a lot better."

Katherine frowned, but then she shrugged.

"It's not like I have any better ideas," she admitted.

Across the fire, the tracer boys were lying down, settling in for the night. Dare curled up at Andrea's feet. Andrea let out a jaw-splitting yawn.

"I guess it's worth a try," she said.

Jonah lay down, feeling surprised that Katherine and Andrea hadn't argued more.

We're all too tired to think straight, he thought. *But my idea will work. I hope.*

The truth was, Jonah really didn't like Stratego or chess or games like that. There was too much planning, too much strategy, too much trying to figure out your opponent's plans ten moves ahead.

What was that really complicated game Billy was always trying to get me to play? Jonah tried to remember. *The one where you weren't just competing against one other person, but there could be five or six people, all trying to win?*

Jonah remembered the name of the game just as he was slipping off to sleep: Risk.

He woke hours later, to darkness and the sound of screaming.

"Stop! Stop! Halt the battle!"

EIGHTEEN

Jonah sprang to his feet, his heart pounding. He gazed frantically from side to side. The fire was barely even embers now, but the dim glow of the tracers cast a little light into the darkness, onto the arched walls of the hut.

Hut . . . we're still in the hut . . . I don't see any battle anywhere. . . .

The man they'd saved from drowning was thrashing about on the floor. He seemed caught in the grip of some unceasing agony.

"These are the wrong savages!" he screamed. "They aren't the ones who killed George Howe! They're Manteo's people! Oh, Lord, forgive us—forgive us this blood on our hands!"

Dare whimpered at the loud shouting. Jonah saw that Andrea and Katherine were awake now too. Andrea sat up and reached over to pat the man's shoulder.

"Shh," she said soothingly. "You're okay. It's just a dream."

"Andrea, stop talking to him!" Jonah hissed. He tried to stay back in the shadows, out of sight. "He'll see you!"

"Don't worry—he's talking in his sleep again," Andrea whispered back. "He doesn't have his eyes open."

Jonah thought about rushing forward and pulling Andrea away, just in case. But it seemed as if that would be even more disruptive.

And just then, the man began to sob.

"Oh, Eleanor, we were star-crossed from the start," he wailed. "What Fernandez did . . . the enmity Lane left behind . . . killing over a communion cup . . . Oh, how can I leave you now? With the wee babe . . . in this wilderness, under constant threat from mine enemies . . ."

Even in the dim light, Jonah could see Andrea stiffen. For a moment she sat completely frozen, a shadowed silhouette. Then she moved her hand. She wrapped her fingers around the man's hand and held on tight.

"Oh, Father," she whispered. Her voice broke. Jonah saw her lower her head, gulping for control. After a moment, she raised her head and went on. "You are the only one who can go. You must talk to Sir Raleigh. He'll listen to you. Only you can save us."

Sir Raleigh? Jonah thought. *What's Andrea talking about?*

The man seemed to know.

"What if Sir Raleigh thinks I abandoned my duty?" the man moaned. "Oh, 'tis a dreadful choice. To stay, to go . . . I see evil encroaching, either way. If evil befalls you—"

"It won't be your fault," Andrea said firmly.

"But 'twas I who brought you here! My child! And I will not be here to protect you!"

The man seemed to be getting more and more upset. Across the hut, the tracer boys were stirring now. One propped himself up on his elbow, to stare over at the man. He spoke.

Of course Jonah could hear nothing, but he thought he could almost get the gist of the boy's words from his expression, from the clipped way he opened and shut his mouth. His words would be something like, *You. Sleep now. No more noise.*

"Oh, no," Katherine moaned.

"What's wrong with you?" Jonah muttered.

"The tracer boy's talking to our guy. Which means . . ."

"The man we saved joined with his tracer again," Andrea finished for her, quite calmly.

Jonah looked back at the tracers again. He'd never been good at waking quickly and instantly thinking clearly. He squinted, counting and recounting the tracers. One. Two.

Clear enough. But there should have been three tracers in the hut—even without counting any random tracer bugs or other tiny tracer detritus. Maybe he'd miscounted. One. Two. Two tracer boys.

No tracer man.

"Our guy could have just rolled over in his sleep, and, boom, that was it, he was with his tracer again," Katherine was speculating.

Like the smoke, like the flames, Jonah thought. *I knew tracers worked like that.*

"We need to pull him away from his tracer again," Jonah said, sighing. "Then one of us should sleep between him and his tracer."

Wearily, Jonah moved toward the man and reached for his arm. But Andrea blocked Jonah's way.

"Leave him alone!" she commanded.

Jonah blinked, even more confused. He'd just had trouble counting to two—and now he was supposed to figure out Andrea?

"Andrea, remember the experiment we're doing?" Katherine said softly. "Jonah's plan?"

Jonah himself was having a hard time remembering.

Oh, yeah—we're not going to be used. Not going to fall for any tricks or traps. Not going to put the man with his tracer . . . going to do the opposite of what anyone would expect . . .

Andrea laughed, a little wildly.

"Isn't this weird?" she asked. "You don't want to be manipulated, so you're going to manipulate this man? Use him as a pawn, to keep from being pawns yourself?"

Jonah winced at the bitterness in her words.

"That's not how I meant it," he muttered. He guessed he should explain everything all over again, but he was so tired. It was the middle of the night. Jonah just wanted to pull the man away from his tracer and go back to sleep.

He started to reach for the man once more, but this time Andrea actually shoved him away.

"I won't let you," she said. "I'll stop you, no matter what."

"Andrea, this isn't a game," Jonah said, bewildered. "Just—"

"You're right," Andrea interrupted. "It isn't a game. But you're the one treating it like one. Chess! Stratego!" Her voice arced wildly again. "This is this man's *life*. This is his dearest dream, what he's been working toward for years. . . ."

"What are you talking about?" Katherine asked.

"We have to keep this man with his tracer," Andrea said. "He has to see me. I have to talk to him."

"What?" Jonah said. "But that could really ruin time!"

"Oh, time," Andrea said scornfully. "What has it ever

done for me? Besides taking away my parents . . ."

"Andrea," Katherine began. "You can't blame—"

"I *can*," Andrea said. "And I do. And I don't care." She bent over the unconscious man as if she was going to try to shake him awake.

Now it was Jonah's turn to reach out and try to pull her back.

"Did your mystery man come back and tell you more lies?" he asked. "Is that why you're acting like this?"

"No!" Andrea said, struggling against Jonah's grasp.

"Then what changed?" Jonah asked, holding on. "You agreed with Katherine and me before. Why do you care so much about keeping this man with his tracer?"

Andrea lifted her head, so her chin jutted out. Even in the near-total darkness, Jonah could see how determined she was. Her eyes glistened.

"Because," she whispered. "Now I know who he is."

NINETEEN

Jonah let go of Andrea's arms. He was too stunned to say or do anything else. For once, he was glad that Katherine was so rarely at a loss for words.

"Andrea, I really don't think you do understand," Katherine said, almost snippily. "How could you know? Who could this man possibly be, that would—"

"He's my grandfather," Andrea said. "John White."

Katherine gasped.

Jonah was struggling to catch up. Andrea's grandfather . . . had they somehow missed the chance to save her parents' lives, but zoomed back instead to rescue her grandfather? No, her real grandfather—her twenty-first-century, adoptive grandfather—wouldn't be from Virginia Dare's lifetime. This would have to be Virginia Dare's grandfather, the one Andrea had read so much about. The one who had captured her interest in the Virginia Dare story in the first place.

I think it was because of the grandfather coming back, Andrea had said. *How hard he tried to get back to his family, and how many times he failed, and then when he finally made it to Roanoke . . .*

Jonah gasped now too, only a little after Katherine.

"How can you tell it's him?" he asked.

"He keeps talking about Eleanor, which was his daughter's name—my . . . mother's name. My birth mother's, I mean." Andrea sounded defensive.

"I bet a lot of women were named Eleanor back then," Katherine said.

"The other names he said were people at Roanoke too—Fernandez, Lane, George Howe . . . And what he was saying about a battle with Manteo's people? That was this really stupid sneak attack the Roanoke colonists made on an Indian village. They figured out in the middle of it that they'd attacked their own friends," Andrea said.

"John White wouldn't have been the only colonist in that battle," Jonah pointed out, proud that he could come up with something logical.

"But John White *was* the only colonist who left Roanoke to sail back to England to talk to Sir Walter Raleigh to get supplies," Andrea said. "He didn't want to. The other colonists had to beg him. They told him he was their only chance."

"And he was talking about a baby," Katherine said thoughtfully. "That would be . . ."

"Virginia Dare," Andrea said. She dropped her voice to a whisper. "Me."

She gently patted the man's shoulder again, and it was almost as if she was claiming him, agreeing to be his granddaughter. Jonah blinked, trying to see better in the nearly nonexistent light. He knew something important had just happened. Did Andrea *want* to be Virginia Dare now? Was this something else that Andrea's mystery man had manipulated her toward?

When we got back to 1483, Chip and Alex wanted to be Edward V and Prince Richard, too, Jonah remembered. *But that was after we found their tracers.*

Andrea might have found her grandfather, but they still didn't have a clue where her tracer was. Jonah glanced across the hut to the glowing tracer boys, sprawled out flat again, looking soundly asleep. Those tracers were even more proof that time and history were out of whack.

"I thought you said the grandfather didn't find anybody when he came back to Roanoke," Jonah said accusingly. "Just the word *Croatoan* carved into wood. Not two

Indian boys." He gestured toward the tracers. "Er—two boys dressed like Indians."

"Something must have changed," Andrea said. "Even without us interfering. Or maybe the historical accounts are wrong?"

She looked down at the man—John White?—who had settled back into a peaceful sleep again. He was even smiling slightly, and it seemed as though he was responding to Andrea's voice. As if he knew her. But how could that be? Sure, he'd seen her as a baby, but not after that—not in any version of history—until she and Jonah had fished the man out of the waves.

Jonah shook his head. Really, history was complicated enough without there being multiple versions.

"What was supposed to happen when John White came back to Roanoke?" Jonah asked. "In the accounts you read?"

"It was three years before he made it back," Andrea said. "That wasn't just because of the Spanish Armada—he had all sorts of bad luck. It was like nobody cared about Roanoke but him. He was on one ship that was attacked by pirates, and he got cut up in a sword fight. And then, when he finally found a ship that would take him to Roanoke, he wanted to bring a bunch of new colonists with him, but the captain wouldn't let him."

"Why not?" Jonah asked.

"The captain didn't want all those extra people taking up space on his ship. He was hoping to make a fortune privateering, and he wanted the room for all his treasures." Andrea's voice was bitter, as if the ship's captain had personally offended her.

"What's *privateering?*" Katherine asked.

Jonah was glad that she'd asked the question, that she was the one who looked dumb.

"The man—Mr. White?—didn't he say something about privateering?" Jonah asked.

"*Governor* White," Andrea corrected. "He was governor of the Roanoke Colony. Though"—she grinned, seeming almost cheerful now,—"the colony was just a hundred and sixteen people, so it's not that big a deal."

"But, privateering . . . ," Katherine reminded her.

"Oh, yeah." Andrea shrugged. "It was like being a pirate, only legal. English ships would go out and attack Spanish ships and steal all their treasure. And then they'd just pay a certain percentage to the English government, like taxes, and everyone thought it was okay. It was *patriotic.*"

"That's crazy!" Jonah said.

"Yeah, I bet there weren't any Boy Scouts involved in that," Katherine said.

"Well, there wouldn't be, because Boy Scouts weren't

founded until . . ." Jonah realized that Katherine was teasing him. And he'd fallen for it. He cleared his throat. Maybe if he pretended he hadn't said anything, nobody else would notice. "Why didn't Mr.—er—*Governor* White get on a ship that wasn't doing that privateering stuff?"

Andrea tilted her head to the side, considering this.

"I think, back then, pretty much all the English ships going to America were privateering," Andrea said. "One of the reasons the English wanted the Roanoke Colony in the first place was so they could stash stolen treasures there, and hide from the Spanish, and get food and water."

"They never told us that in school!" Katherine protested.

"Yeah, well, it doesn't sound very noble," Andrea said. "Who wants to hear that your ancestors were a bunch of thieves?"

Jonah kind of did. He might have remembered the Roanoke Colony better if Mrs. Rorshas had talked about pirates and stolen treasure.

Katherine looked down at the sleeping man.

"But this guy wasn't bringing a bunch of treasure with him to Roanoke," she said. "He was alone in a rowboat."

"He wasn't supposed to be," Andrea said grimly, her voice low. "It was supposed to be several men who rowed from their ship to Roanoke Island. And then after they saw the word *Croatoan*, Governor White wanted to go on to Croatoan Island and look for the colonists there. But this horrible storm blew up—a hurricane, I think—and caused lots of problems. So they had to leave. And that was it. Nobody ever looked for the colonists on Croatoan Island."

Andrea was practically whispering by the end of her story. She was probably just trying to keep from disturbing her grandfather, but the effect was creepy. Jonah shivered, almost as if he was one of the colonists abandoned on the opposite side of an ocean from everyone he knew.

What if it's like that for me and Katherine and Andrea? he wondered. *What if we're abandoned in the past, the way the colonists were abandoned in America?*

Jonah had an image in his head of JB hunched over some sort of computer monitor, desperately searching for the three of them. JB *would* search. Jonah was certain of it. But time was—well—endless, wasn't it? What if JB never found them?

What if that's part of the plan? Jonah wondered. *What if Andrea's mystery man wants us to stay lost forever?*

"Are you sure you remember the story right?" Jonah asked Andrea. His voice came out too harsh and accusing, almost as if he was mad at her again. "If this is John White, he didn't even make it to *Roanoke* Island before the storm hit. I think that could have been a hurricane we rescued him from!"

Andrea twisted her hands together, an agonizing gesture.

"There are a lot of things that don't fit," she admitted.

"The shipwreck, too," Katherine said. "There wasn't a shipwreck in the original story, where everyone died but John White, and he escaped in a rowboat." Her face turned white. "Do you think Andrea's mystery man caused the shipwreck?"

"No, because John White's tracer was talking about the shipwreck too," Jonah said. "That was part of original time."

"Some of the details must be a little off in the historical accounts," Andrea said. "Maybe the historians lied?" She brushed a lock of hair from her grandfather's forehead. "We can get the real story tomorrow. I'm sure he'll wake up then, and I can talk to him. . . ."

And they were back to that, to Andrea's determination to talk to the man-joined-with-his-tracer, no matter what.

"Andrea," Katherine began, "you can't do that. Especially now that we know who this is, that he's connected to you . . . We know we aren't in the right time. We know your tracer isn't here. We know these tracers *are* here"—she gestured toward the boys on the other side of the fire,—"and so we know two kids are missing. There's too much that's already messed up! We can't risk—"

"I. Don't. Care," Andrea said.

Jonah started to say, "But—" and Katherine started to say, "Listen—"

Andrea shook her head at both of them and kept talking.

"*You* listen," she said. "I know what you're going to say. I know you think your plans and your strategies are important, and it really, really matters to outsmart the man who lied to me, and to protect time, like it's some perfect, priceless jewel. But it isn't. It doesn't matter. None of that matters. Life *isn't* like a game. You'll see. When you lose the people you love most in all the world—when you lose everything . . ." She was getting choked up. Jonah could hear the tears in her voice. She gingerly touched John White's sleeve. "This man came all the way across the ocean to find his family. He risked his life for that. So if I'm one of the people he's looking for—and I *am*—I'm not going to hide from him. I'm going to tell him who I am!"

There had been a moment on Jonah and Katherine's last trip through time when they had come so close to violating a sacred rule of time travel that JB had yanked them out of the fifteenth century in nothing flat. Jonah found himself hoping that that would happen to Andrea right now. Wasn't she threatening to upset everything about time? Didn't she need to be yanked out of the past?

Nothing happened. Andrea sniffed once, defiantly. Her grandfather let out a soft moan. One of the tracer boys turned over in his sleep, his arm disappearing in Dare's fur. And the fire that Jonah had worked so hard to build flickered out.

There's proof then, Jonah thought grimly. He realized, in spite of everything, he'd been holding on to just a bit of hope that JB knew exactly where they were and that, somehow, everything was going according to plan. If JB's projectionist really was the best ever, couldn't he have predicted that Andrea would change the Elucidator code, that the Elucidator would vanish, and that Jonah and the others would save the drowning man? Wasn't it possible that the three kids might do something on their own that was better than what they could do with JB bossing them around? It had kind of worked that way in the fifteenth century.

But what Andrea wanted to do—that was just reckless. JB would never allow it. So there was no way that JB knew where they were. Nobody knew where they were.

Except Andrea's mystery man, Jonah thought.

It wasn't a comforting thought.

"Andrea—" Jonah began.

"My mind's made up," Andrea said. "I'm not going to change it."

She leaned down to whisper in John White's ear, but Jonah could hear every word she said.

"Tomorrow. We'll talk tomorrow. . . ."

TWENTY

Jonah expected to lie awake the rest of the night, worrying and trying to figure out the right argument to make to Andrea, to stop her.

This is like Risk, he thought. *There are too many sides, too many complications. There's what Andrea wants and there's whatever her mystery man is trying to do and there's original time and there's the historical account. . . .*

It was hard to stay awake in such complete darkness, in such complete despair and confusion. Jonah drifted off, and the next thing he knew, there was sunlight streaming in through the doorway of the hut.

The sunlight was odd, though: It didn't seem to filter all the way down to the floor of the hut. Jonah couldn't make out the lumps that would be Andrea's sleeping form, and Katherine's, and John White's. He couldn't even see any tracers.

Jonah sat up quickly. The problem wasn't with the sunlight. Or his eyes. The problem was that he was the only person left in the hut.

Jonah was about to give himself over to panic when he heard a snoring sound coming from right outside the hut: It was a deep, masculine sound and had to belong to John White. Jonah couldn't fathom why the girls had moved the sleeping man out of the hut—was Katherine trying to get him away from his tracer? Or was Andrea trying to keep him with it? But it was so good to hear the man snoring, to know that he was still soundly asleep, to know that nothing irreversible had happened yet. Jonah let himself relax a little, and he went back to thinking of arguments to use on Andrea.

She doesn't care about time, but she cares about her grandfather. . . . What if we tell her she can't talk to him because that might worry him, she might scare him. . . .

Something tickled at Jonah's brain—an idea, something he might have thought of the night before, right before he fell asleep, or even in the middle of sleeping. Something important about Andrea. But he wasn't awake enough; the idea slipped away, just a tease.

Along with the snoring, Jonah could hear a girl's muffled voice outside—it was too muted for him to tell if it was Andrea's or Katherine's.

Katherine's more likely to be talking, but Andrea's more likely to talk softly, he thought, grinning slightly to himself.

Then he heard the rumble of a man's voice in response.

Jonah froze, straining his ears. It had to be just the man talking in his sleep, right? Talking deliriously again? It *couldn't* be John White answering Andrea, who was so disdainful of time that she might have said something like, *Hi, Gramps. Long time no see.*

Suddenly Jonah knew the perfect argument to use on Andrea, the idea he'd almost thought of earlier. The idea he should have thought of hours ago, when there was still time to stop Andrea.

Was there still time now?

In one motion, Jonah jerked to his feet and crashed out the door of the hut. He almost tripped over Dare, who was stretched out, sound asleep, just outside the doorway—oh, great, it had been the *dog* snoring. Jonah whipped his head from side to side, looking for Andrea, looking for her grandfather.

Andrea was sitting right in front of him in the clearing, her back mostly turned to Jonah, her mouth open. What if she was about to say the words that would ruin everything, right now?

Jonah dived toward Andrea. He thought he would just

get close by and whisper in her ear, but he miscalculated. He ended up tackling her, knocking her to the side. He scrambled to right himself, to get his mouth next to her ear, to tell her what he'd just figured out.

"Andrea, it was only three years!" he hissed. "You said so yourself—Governor White came back to Roanoke after three years! That means . . . he's looking for a granddaughter who's only three years old!"

TWENTY-ONE

Andrea didn't react right.

In Jonah's wildest dreams, she might have thrown her arms around him and given him a big kiss and burst out, "Oh, thank you! Thank you! You saved me from ruining my life! And my grandfather's!"

Jonah didn't really expect *that*.

But he was kind of hoping for an "Oh, you're right—I should have thought of that!" Or at least a "Thanks—you stopped me just in time!"

Andrea just lay in the dust and mumbled, "Whatever."

Jonah slid back.

"You didn't say anything to him yet, did you?" he whispered.

Andrea shrugged.

"Doesn't matter."

"Doesn't matter?" Jonah repeated incredulously. "Of course it . . ."

Jonah stopped talking, because Katherine came up just then and shoved him back into the dust.

"Jonah, you are a total idiot! What if John White had seen you?"

Jonah looked around and replayed everything in his mind. He'd come running out of the hut—and John White was sitting right on the other side of the clearing, in between the two tracer boys.

Jonah crouched down.

"He's looking right at us!" Jonah hissed to Katherine. "What should we do?"

He'd been so concerned about Andrea ruining time by talking to John White, and now what had he done himself?

Suddenly he had an idea.

He jumped up and waved at John White.

"Aye, matey," he said, trying to sound like an old-timey sailor. All he could think of was Johnny Depp in *Pirates of the Caribbean*. "Sailing out on the sea for a long time, you can get to wearing some mighty strange clothes. And acting strangely too. But it be time to sail again, so I promise you, you will never see us again."

He slipped into the woods, gesturing for Andrea and Katherine to follow him.

Katherine burst out laughing.

"At least sometimes he's a funny idiot," she said to Andrea.

Andrea gave a halfhearted smile.

"Shh!" Jonah hissed. "Careful!" He kept motioning for Andrea and Katherine to come into the woods with him, out of John White's view. "He can see you!"

"He can't see us," Andrea said. "Or hear us."

"Of course he can! His eyes are open!" Jonah whispered. "He's awake."

"Come and look for yourself," Katherine said.

Jonah hesitated, then inched back into the clearing.

He could tell John White was joined with his tracer because the tracer boys, on either side of him, were taking turns placing some sort of food in his mouth. They were treating him like an invalid, tearing the food into such tiny morsels he didn't even have to chew.

And, just as Jonah had said, John White's eyes were wide open.

Er, no, they're not, Jonah corrected himself.

Or were they?

Jonah's brain seemed to be having a war with itself, trying to decipher what he was seeing. It was almost like the first time he'd seen his friend Chip join with his tracer, when it seemed as if Chip had vanished but he really hadn't.

Ohhh, Jonah thought.

John White had his eyes shut.

His tracer's eyes were open.

Jonah turned to Katherine.

"How's that possible?" Jonah asked. "Is he joined with his tracer or not?"

"You tell me," Katherine said. She swallowed hard. All the laughter was gone from her voice.

"It's not right," Jonah said. "This isn't how tracers work."

It was unnerving, the old man's steady gaze and peaceful slumber, simultaneously. It was like double vision, or a double exposure.

Or a huge time error.

"It was weird enough watching Chip and Alex join with their tracers, when we could still kind of see their different clothes and their different hair," Katherine said. "And the fact that, sometimes, they were different ages from their tracers. But this is the same man, in the same clothes, in the same place. . . . Why can't he meld with his tracer completely?"

"It must be because the real man hurt his head," Andrea said glumly.

"Or . . . maybe it protects him from having to figure out why he can't see the tracers?" Jonah asked.

"There were real people around tracers back in the 1500s, and none of them were half awake and half asleep," Katherine complained.

John White said something to one of the tracer boys, but even though the real man moved his mouth, he made no sound.

"We can't hear him either?" Jonah asked. "But I thought—"

"We can—sometimes," Andrea said. "Katherine and I think it's only when he says something he would be thinking with both his tracer brain *and* his real brain. A minute ago, he was talking about how hot it is."

Jonah shook his head. John White's eerie gaze bothered him more than he wanted to admit.

"Andrea, when that mystery man came to your room back in the twenty-first century, and told you to change the Elucidator code, are you sure he didn't say anything about it making tracers act weird?" Jonah asked.

"All he talked about was how I could save my parents," Andrea said in an icy voice. "I told you."

Jonah racked his brain for some other explanation.

"Well . . . maybe this is normal, after all, and we just don't have enough experience with tracers to know," Jonah said. He thought hard. "Remember that time in 1483, right when the assassins grabbed Chip and Alex?

Alex was kicking and fighting, but his tracer was asleep. That's sort of the same thing. Just reversed, who's sleeping and who's awake."

"That was just for a few seconds," Katherine said. "John White and his tracer have been like this all morning, ever since Andrea and the tracer boys dragged them out here. This feels . . . permanent. Like he's stuck."

Is this something Andrea's mystery man planned too? Jonah wondered. His plan from the night before for outsmarting the mystery man seemed hopelessly naive. Jonah couldn't understand anything about their opponent's strategy.

Jonah's stomach growled, reminding him he'd had nothing to eat in, well, centuries.

"Maybe if we eat some of their food, we'll be able to think better and figure this all out," he said.

"Great idea," Katherine said. "Except I think that's the deer they killed yesterday. For us, it's still alive and running around the woods. Want to go hunting with a bow and arrow?"

"We don't have a bow and arrow," Andrea pointed out. "Just the tracers do." She slumped down beside John White, sounding completely discouraged. "We don't have anything."

"Oh, hey—there was some melon in that hut where I saw the other deer," Jonah said, because he had to offer something. The melon had looked slimy and unappealing the day before, but it was the only possible food Jonah could think of.

Jonah stood and walked into the hut where he'd frightened the deer. The melon vines stretched across the dirt floor, their leaves pale and limp from growing indoors, with the only light coming from broken places in the roof. Jonah bent down to search under the leaves. Every time he lifted a leaf and then let go, it quickly settled back together with its tracer. *At least the leaves are obeying all the tracer rules*, Jonah thought. He found the remains of the melon the deer had been eating, but it was just a glob of mush that left slime on Jonah's hand when he brushed it by mistake.

"Find anything?" Katherine said behind him.

Jonah wiped his hand on a leaf and discovered a hard green, baseball-size melon underneath.

"Just this," he said, holding it up.

"Better than nothing, I guess," Katherine said. "We can split it on a rock, divide it three ways."

"Four," Andrea corrected from outside the hut. "My grandfather needs some real food too."

Jonah wasn't sure what the nutrition rules were for someone sort of joined with his tracer, but sort of not. He looked at the melon in his hand. Regardless of whether they each got one-third or one-fourth of it, it wasn't going to be enough.

"Are you sure that's the only one?" Katherine asked.

Jonah ruffled the pale, anemic-looking leaves before him, setting off a ripple of even paler tracer leaves.

"See anything I missed?" he asked sarcastically. "Geez, there's not even a whole tracer melon left anym—" He broke off. He looked back down at the leaves. He lifted the slimy leaf where he'd found the melon.

The leaf itself instantly developed a tracer, but there was no tracer melon underneath.

Jonah shoved aside the nearby leaves. He found the remains of the rotten melon the deer had eaten part of. It had just an edge of tracer light along its top, where Jonah had brushed against it and carried some of it away. But there was no tracer of the small green, hard melon in Jonah's hand.

"It's not supposed to be here," Jonah mumbled, more to himself than Katherine. "Maybe it's not even from this time. I moved it, and it didn't leave a tracer."

He turned the melon over and over again in his hand. Its surface was rough and ridged, except for one section where the pattern of webbing seemed almost carved into the rind.

No, Jonah thought. *That's not webbing. Those are letters. Words.*

He flipped the melon over, and this put the letters right side up. Now Jonah could read the words in the crude lettering:

EAT. ENJOY. YOU'RE DOING GREAT.

CAN'T SAY MORE.

-SECOND

TWENTY-TWO

Jonah dropped the melon.

"I am not eating this," he said.

Katherine was leaning so far over Jonah's shoulder she was able to catch the melon before it hit the ground.

"Ooh—words," she breathed. "Is it an Elucidator?" She brought the melon up toward her mouth and began yelling: "JB? Anyone? Hello? Are you there?"

Nothing happened.

"An Elucidator wouldn't come with instructions to *eat* it," Jonah said. "And it's not from JB."

Katherine bent lower over the melon and touched the words with her finger.

"Second?" she said. "Is that a name?"

"It has to be," Jonah said. "Think it's the same person who told Andrea to change the code on the Elucidator?"

Katherine looked back over her shoulder.

"Andrea?" she called. "Look at this."

Andrea patted her grandfather's arm, whispered, "I'll be right back" in his ear, and came over to look at the melon.

"Is this . . . typical?" she asked, squinting down at it with a baffled expression on her face. "Did you see anything like this in the fifteenth century? Messages on food?"

"Oh, no," Katherine said.

"I think JB would think it was wrong," Jonah said. "Interfering too much with time. And dangerous, because someone native to this time period might see it. But this Second guy—who knows what he thinks?"

Katherine rolled the melon side to side, so Andrea could read the whole message.

"Does this sound like it might have been written by that guy who came and visited you and told you to change the code on the Elucidator?" Katherine asked her. "Can you analyze the—what do they call it in Language Arts class? The diction?"

"'Analyze the diction'?" Jonah said incredulously. "It's not even ten words! That's like telling her to analyze a text message!"

"I don't know about any of that," Andrea said. "But the way this is carved? It *does* look like his handwriting."

Jonah and Katherine stared at her.

"When he gave me the code, he wrote it out, so I could memorize it," Andrea explained.

Katherine nodded excitedly.

"So the guy who sabotaged us calls himself Second," she said, acting like she was Sherlock Holmes making a brilliant deduction. "And he's the same guy communicating with us now."

Jonah didn't see any reason for excitement.

"Communicating?" he said bitterly. "That's not communicating." He pointed at the melon. "'You're doing great'?" He yelled up at the sky, "We are *not* doing great!"

He suddenly realized that the melon might be a response to their experiment from the night before—or to Andrea's deciding to keep John White with his tracer, no matter what. Either way, the message was annoying. Insulting. Patronizing. Jonah threw his head back farther and yelled even louder: "We don't want to do 'great' for you!"

"Calm down," Katherine said. "Second. Let's see. Second place? Second rate? Second-in-command? Second, as in, not a minute or an hour, but a really, really short period of time?"

"Who cares?" Jonah asked disgustedly.

"If someone calls himself Second, there's got to be a reason," Katherine said.

"Yeah, maybe his parents didn't have any imagination

with names, and he's just their second kid," Jonah said. He shoved at the melon in Katherine's hands. "I don't like this guy, and I'm not going to pretend this makes any sense. And I am *not* doing anything he tells me to do. Eat this? I'd rather starve!"

Andrea turned to Katherine.

"What about you?" she asked. "Are you going to eat it?"

Katherine stared down at the melon, her face scrunched up in concentration.

"No," she finally said. "It's too much like *Alice in Wonderland*. 'Eat me,' and then it's something that makes you grow or shrink. Or . . . it's like having a stranger offer you candy. Everybody knows you shouldn't take that."

"This isn't candy," Andrea said. "It's a melon. And we're hungry."

"Do *you* think we should eat it?" Katherine challenged.

Andrea bit her lip.

"You two can do whatever you want," she said. "But . . . I'm going to."

"What?" Jonah said.

"Look, my grandfather needs to eat, or he's never going to get better," she said. "But if there's a chance this is dangerous, I'm going to try it myself, first."

She took the melon out of Katherine's hand and hit it

against a rock sticking up in the dust. The melon broke into even halves, revealing five brown pellets where there should have been the fruit and seeds.

"Five?" Katherine muttered.

Andrea flipped over one of the pellets, which was a slightly lighter shade of brown. It had the words, "For Dare," carved into its surface.

The others weren't labeled.

"Okay, then, at least test the food on the dog first," Jonah suggested.

"No, I'll be the test case," Andrea said.

She hesitated for a second.

"Don't do it," Jonah said. "Please."

Andrea popped a pellet into her mouth.

TWENTY-THREE

Jonah had a sudden image in his mind of the girl in *Willy Wonka and the Chocolate Factory* puffing up and turning blue after chewing defective gum.

"Spit it out!" he yelled at Andrea.

Andrea swallowed instead.

"Okay, you guys can watch me for the next couple hours, and then we'll know if it's safe to give this to my grandfather," she said calmly.

Jonah shook his head.

"You're crazy," he said.

Andrea shrugged.

"Time will tell, won't it?" she said, grinning slightly.

"That's not funny," Jonah objected.

Andrea scooped the other four pellets out of the melon half and put them in her pocket. Katherine and Jonah watched her warily.

"Look, I feel fine so far," Andrea said. "Not so hungry anymore, but maybe that's just my imagination. It couldn't work *that* fast. Let's just . . . go on, okay?"

Go on, Jonah thought dazedly. *What would that mean? Fixing time? Rescuing Andrea?*

Those had been his original goals, but everything was so mixed-up now. How could they fix time when it just kept getting more and more messed up? How could they rescue Andrea when she was determined to do crazy things like talk to her grandfather and eat suspicious food?

Right then, out of the corner of his eye, Jonah saw one of the tracer boys pat John White's shoulder and stand up. The tracer boy was nodding, nodding. . . . Had John White's tracer just asked him to do something? The old man's tracer was still speaking, but he kept blinking, as if he was fighting off sleep. He seemed to be struggling to get the words out before he slipped toward unconsciousness, toward joining the real man completely.

The tracer's eyes closed, and now Jonah could hear what he was saying because the real man was speaking, too.

"Find it," John White murmured. Clearly the tracer and the real man were thinking the same thing. "Please find it, I beg of you."

The tracer boy nodded once more and began walking out of the village.

"Did you hear that?" Jonah asked Katherine and Andrea. "This is a clue! We should follow him, see what he's looking for!"

Andrea shook her head, firmly.

"I'm staying with my grandfather," she said.

"But this is something for him!" Jonah said. "Maybe it's connected to you! Or your tracer!" He turned to his sister. "Katherine?"

Katherine was grimacing.

"You go," she said. "I'll stay here with Andrea."

Her gaze flickered from Jonah to Andrea to John White. She cocked her head and made a face. Jonah could tell what she was thinking: *Andrea's not going to leave her grandfather, and there's no way we can trust her alone with him. Who knows how many different ways she might try to ruin time?*

"So I should go . . . alone?" Jonah asked. He wasn't scared—of course he wasn't scared. But it was a little weird to think that he would be going off on his own without a cell phone, without an Elucidator, without any way to communicate with anyone. "If you two go somewhere before I get back, uh, carve a map on a tree or something, okay?" he said, trying to make a joke of it.

"That didn't work out so great for the Roanoke colonists," Andrea muttered.

She walked over to Dare, who was still snoring, and gently shook him awake. She held out his pellet of food in her hand and he eagerly gobbled it down.

"Now you'll have energy to go with Jonah and keep him company," Andrea told the dog. She pushed him forward. "Hurry! Before you lose the tracer!"

"Um, okay then," Jonah said. He took off after the tracer, the dog at his heels. He had to stop himself from turning around and saying to Andrea and Katherine, *Are you sure you two don't want to come too?* Or, *You'll come after me if I get lost, won't you?*

When he was pretty sure he and Dare were out of earshot of the girls, Jonah turned to the dog.

"Don't think this means I trust you," he told Dare. "I am still watching you, to make sure you're not animatronic or a decoy or a spy or something."

The dog licked Jonah's hand.

"I mean it," Jonah said sternly. He addressed the sky, "And, Second, you can't fool me either. I am not eating your food, and we are not blindly going along with any of your plans. Got it?"

Jonah hoped that Second had not planned for Jonah and Dare to go off with the one tracer boy while Katherine and Andrea were left behind for . . . what? The danger Jonah had been fearing all along?

You're being paranoid, Jonah told himself. *Just like Katherine said.*

To distract himself, he concentrated on looking around, watching everything carefully. The tracer boy seemed to be following the same trail he and the other boy had taken the night before, when they'd dragged John White back to the village on the tree branch. Jonah would have expected the whole trail to be lined with tracers—bent-back grasses, footprints, other dents and gouges in the sandy soil. But the trail ahead was almost completely clear of tracer changes.

Because of the violent storm? Jonah wondered. *Or . . . because of the branch that Andrea and Katherine and I were dragging behind the tracer boys?*

Jonah watched the tracer boy in front of him trample a clump of grasses. A crumpled tracer version of the grasses instantly appeared. Jonah purposely dodged it.

Dare stepped on the grasses instead, tamping them down in the exact same pattern as their tracers.

Jonah found that unless he concentrated very hard, he automatically walked in the exact same footsteps as the tracer boy in front of him, erasing almost all of his tracer prints. Or the dog did it for him. And even though the tracer boy was barefoot and Jonah was wearing sneakers—and the dog had paws—they all seemed to leave very similar markings on the trail. It happened again and again, the boy creating a tracer, Jonah or the dog erasing it.

Weird, weird, weird, Jonah thought. *Is it time making me do that, healing itself? Or is this part of Second's plot too?*

It was so frustrating not to know. He wished he'd paid more attention to the habits of tracer objects the last time, in the fifteenth century. But they really were hard to see. And there hadn't been so many of them then. They hadn't seemed so . . . threatening.

Time is so much more messed-up here, Jonah thought, shivering despite the bright sunlight.

Jonah forced himself to catch up with the tracer boy.

"You know, it'd be nice if it turned out that you were going off to talk to your girlfriend, who's babysitting a little three-year-old girl named Virginia," Jonah muttered. But John White had said, *Please find it, I beg of you—it,* not *her.* Jonah didn't have any hope that things could end so easily.

The tracer boy turned and stared directly at Jonah. He couldn't have heard Jonah, but it was unnerving how the tracer was looking toward Jonah so coldly, so calculatingly. In a split second the boy had an arrow out of his pouch and lodged against his bow. A split second later, the arrow was zinging toward Jonah.

Jonah threw himself at the ground. He lay there for

only an instant—his heart pounding, his shoulder throb-
bing from the impact—before he rolled to the right, just
in case the boy was already loading again, aiming again.

Why is he shooting at me? He's not supposed to be able to see me!

Dare raced toward Jonah, barking furiously. Jonah
smashed into thick grasses and dared to look up. Off in the
distance, some sort of bird—a duck? a goose?—was rising
into the sky, squawking its protest against Dare's barking.
And, slightly behind it, the bird's tracer rose like a shadow,
its wings flapping just as frantically, its beak opening and
closing just as angrily. Only, the tracer couldn't have been
bothered by the barking. It was protesting . . .

Being shot at, Jonah realized. *The boy was shooting at the
bird, not at me.*

Jonah's heartbeat slowed slightly; his tensed muscles
slipped out of panic mode. He rolled his head to the side
so he could see the tracer boy, who might right that minute be putting another arrow against his bow and aiming for some tracer groundhog or beaver waddling near
Jonah.

But not at me, Jonah thought, hoping to calm down his
reflexes. *The tracer can't shoot me. Even if he did, the tracer arrows
can't hurt me. Got it?*

But when Jonah looked up at the tracer boy, he wasn't
slipping another arrow into his bow. He was letting his

bow slip to the ground, his shoulders slumped.

The tracers are worried about food too, Jonah thought.

Jonah sat up, studying the tracer more carefully. This was the one with the longer, curly hair. It was hard to tell skin color with a see-through tracer, but Jonah didn't think this boy's skin would be much darker than Jonah's with a tan. The boy's nose and lips were narrow; his eyes would have been round if he hadn't squeezed them into such dejected-looking slits.

"I guess you could be English," Jonah muttered. "Are *you* one of the lost colonists?"

But then, why was he dressed like an Indian? What had happened to all the other English colonists if he was the only one left? And why was this boy hanging out with the other tracer, the one Andrea was so sure had come from Africa?

Jonah shook his head, trying to shake away the questions. At the same time, the tracer boy shook his head and slung his bow over his shoulder again. Dare whimpered.

"Come on, boy," Jonah told the dog, almost forgetting that he suspected him of being a decoy or a spy. "We're going on."

The dog stayed a few steps behind Jonah and the tracer the rest of the way. Maybe the bow and arrow had spooked him, too; maybe he was afraid that Jonah would suddenly throw himself to the ground once more. But Jonah found himself trying to stay as close as possible to the tracer boy. It was a shame Jonah couldn't hear the tracer's thoughts just by stepping into his space. Several times the boy stopped and Jonah walked right into him, his knees raised at the same height as the boy's knees, his arms swinging at the same angle.

To understand another man, you must walk a mile in his moccasins, Jonah thought, remembering a phrase an old scoutmaster had been fond of—a phrase that Jonah and his friends had laughed at so hard that one of his friends had even peed in his pants during a campout years ago. Even now (well, now in Jonah's regular time), all someone had to do was whisper, "moccasins" during a flag-raising or some other supposedly solemn ceremony, and the whole troop would instantly be fighting giggles.

But walking where the tracer boy walked, and following his gaze whenever he turned his head, Jonah could tell: The boy was hunting. Hunting without much hope that he'd find something.

"So there's not enough food on this island, not even for just two boys," Jonah whispered. "So why are the two of you here?"

It was just another layer of mystery: Why were the tracer boys on Roanoke Island? Where were their real versions? Why didn't John White's return to Roanoke match up with history? What was wrong with him and his tracer? Where was Andrea's tracer? Why had Second wanted to send Andrea someplace apart from her tracer? Who was Second anyway?

Before Jonah ran out of questions—or came up with a single answer—they reached the shoreline and the tracer boy went to stand on a small spit of land jutting out into the water. Jonah thought maybe it was the same spot where Katherine had stood yesterday to throw the branch out into the water. But he wasn't sure. He hadn't exactly had time for sightseeing before.

The tracer boy stood gazing out at the choppy waves. He put his hand against his brow to shield his eyes against the sun and turned slowly, methodically scanning the water before him. Jonah did the same. But Jonah was done in about three seconds—*yep, there's a lot of water out there. And maybe a bit of land out there to the right—too far away to really see without binoculars.* Meanwhile, the boy was still staring, as if each square inch of water was more fascinating than the last. Once he finished studying the water, he shifted to peering out along the coastline just as thoroughly.

Suddenly the boy's mouth opened and closed—if Jonah had had to guess, he would have speculated that the boy had said something like, "There it is!" The boy jumped down from the outcropping of land and began to run along the shore. Dare barked at the unexpected movement.

"Okay, okay—ssh!" Jonah hissed at the dog. Jonah took off after the tracer boy.

Debris from the storm had washed up onto the shore, so Jonah had to dodge dead jellyfish, spiky shells, and, here and there, splintered scraps of wood.

From John White's boat? Jonah wondered. It was frightening how small the wood fragments were, how thoroughly the wind and water had smashed them to bits.

The tracer boy was several steps ahead of Jonah; now he stopped and bent down among some rocks. He seemed to be searching frantically along the water's edge, all but ignoring the waves that slapped against his bare legs.

If he's going to this much effort just to find a single crab or a single clam, I give up, Jonah thought.

Suddenly the tracer boy rose up, hoisting a tracer version of a rectangular box onto his shoulders.

No, not a box, Jonah corrected himself. *A chest. A treasure chest?*

TWENTY-FOUR

Jonah scrambled over the rocks, hoping he could get to the real chest before the tracer boy moved away. As far as Jonah was concerned, one rock looked pretty much like any other. Without the tracer boy standing there, Jonah might have to search for a long, long time.

The tracer boy stepped to the next rock, the tracer chest balanced on his shoulder. *It was that other rock where he bent down and found the chest,* Jonah thought, *the rock shaped like a witch's nose. . . .* The tracer boy was walking faster now. He was three rocks away. Jonah crouched low and dived forward, straight through the tracer boy.

The witch-nose rock was hard, with razor-sharp edges.

"Note to self," Jonah mumbled. "Don't tackle rocks."

He'd scraped both the palm of his right hand and his right knee—ripping right through his blue jeans. And, for the first time, Jonah realized that his dive might have been for nothing: *What if some time change affected the chest, too, and the real one isn't here?* he wondered.

But it was right there at the base of the witch-nose rock. Waves still slapped against the lower half of the chest, but it was wedged in so tightly that it wasn't being battered like the boards from the boat.

Jonah reached down and tugged on the handles. Once again, Jonah was in awe of the tracer boy's strength: Jonah had to tug so *hard*, and the tracer boy had picked up the chest as if it was nothing.

Maybe it wasn't wedged in as tightly, in original time, Jonah rationalized.

Grunting, he managed to free the chest from between the rocks and drag it up to more level, dry ground. The chest was fairly small—not much bigger than Jonah's backpack for school. Jonah turned it on its side and started trying to figure out its latch.

Dare began barking.

"Don't worry, boy, if it's a million dollars' worth of gold coins, I'll share," Jonah muttered. "Or if it's the clue to solving all our mysteries, you'll get to go home too."

Dare kept barking.

"Okay, okay—what?" Jonah looked up.

Dare was twisting back and forth between Jonah and

the tracer boy. But the tracer boy was barely visible now. He hadn't stopped to look at what was in the chest. He was just carrying it away, back toward the Indian village. Only his head and the tracer chest on his shoulder showed above the tall grasses.

"Never mind," Jonah told the dog. "We can find our way back on our own."

Dare whined and tilted his head to the side, as if he didn't trust Jonah's sense of direction. Or, as if he wanted Jonah to picture how worried Katherine and Andrea would be if the tracer boy showed up back in the village and Jonah was nowhere in sight.

Jonah fiddled for a moment longer with the latch, which was made of some sort of ornate metal. But he couldn't really focus anymore. His hands shook.

"All right," Jonah told Dare. "Since you miss the girls so much . . ."

Jonah lifted the chest and stepped to the next rock. At first he tried to hold the chest in front of him, by both handles. But that made it hard to walk. His legs kept hitting the chest.

Jonah glanced ahead at the tracer boy, at how effortlessly he carried his tracer chest.

When in Rome . . . , Jonah thought, one of his mother's expressions. Only, here would it be, *When on Roanoke Island, do what the fake Indians do?*

With difficulty, Jonah managed to raise the chest to the level of his shoulder and slide it into position. He staggered forward.

"Really, I am in good shape," Jonah told the dog. "I play soccer. And basketball."

His arms were going numb from holding the chest up so high.

In the end, Jonah found he had to drag the chest most of the way, just to keep up with the tracer boy. He didn't even look at the ridges he made in the sandy soil. He kept himself going by imagining exactly what sort of treasure might be inside. Gold coins actually wouldn't be very useful right now—maybe the chest contained food that John White had brought from England.

Surely the trunk was watertight enough that the food wouldn't have been ruined? Surely, if there was food in both the tracer and real versions of the trunk, that would mean it was safe to eat?

Jonah was afraid he might begin drooling, thinking of this possibility.

Maybe the chest contained weapons meant for hunting food: knives, compact bows and arrows.

Maybe Jonah was adapting to this time period a little too well: He was actually hoping for weapons instead of gold.

The tracer boy entered the Indian village with the

bearing of a warrior coming home from a great victory. A few steps behind, Jonah decided the least he could do was put the chest back on his shoulder before he walked into the village. He stumbled into the clearing on the tracer boy's heels.

"Oh, no, Jonah, what happened to you?" Andrea gasped.

Jonah looked down. Beneath the torn place in his jeans, his knee was caked with dried blood. He had scrapes from the rocks on his arms, as well as his hands. He put on a grin, hoping he just looked like some battered action hero at the end of a movie. Indiana Jones, maybe. Or Jason Bourne.

"I found a treasure chest," Jonah offered. "It was a little rough, getting to it."

He hoped Andrea and Katherine didn't notice that the tracer boy wasn't so battered.

"You think John White really was doing some of that privateering himself?" Jonah asked, to distract them. "Stealing Spanish gold?"

"No, no, not him," Andrea said, wincing. "It couldn't be. . . ."

The tracer boy was placing the tracer chest down on the ground, in front of John White. Jonah was surprised to see that the real man was completely joined with his tracer—both men were sleeping. But the second tracer boy was shaking the tracer man awake.

"Quick—put the real chest where the tracer chest is," Andrea said. "So my grandfather won't be confused if . . ."

"Quick"? Jonah thought. *Do you know how heavy this is?*

But he managed to drop the chest onto the ground in roughly the proper location. The chest didn't join completely with its tracer; it didn't shift into position the way a person would have.

Or, like a person should, Jonah thought.

Katherine nudged the real chest into place, exactly lined up with the tracer.

"Just in case," she muttered. "At least we can do that much to fix time."

Andrea crouched down in the same spot as the tracer boy. She began jostling her grandfather's shoulder the same way, too.

"Wake up," she whispered in his ear. "Oh, please, wake up!"

Jonah looked at Katherine. She shook her head.

"He's been asleep the whole time," she said. "That's better for us, but . . . it's breaking Andrea's heart."

Andrea was shaking her grandfather's shoulder harder and harder.

"Andrea, you're going to hurt him!" Jonah said sharply.

Andrea let go and slumped down to the ground. She put her head in her hands.

"Why doesn't anything work?" she moaned. "The food pellet didn't hurt me, so I gave him the food. I gave him water. I cleaned his wound again—he should be healing! He should be awake!"

Katherine moved over and gently put her arm around Andrea's shoulder.

Hey! I could have done that! Jonah thought. He remembered how he'd vowed, way back at the beginning, to take care of Andrea. He hadn't realized how complicated that would be. He was glad that Katherine seemed to know what to do.

"Let's just watch," Katherine said softly. "See what happens."

The tracer version of John White was awake now. Jonah found that it really bothered him to look at the old man's face, with the eerie staring eyes superimposed over the closed eyelids.

"Open it," John White whispered, the tracer and the real man together. And then the tracer sat up, his upper half separating from the real man. Jonah winced—that didn't look right either. But then he got distracted, watching the tracer.

The tracer John White was still talking, though Jonah couldn't hear him anymore. He gestured, clearly giving directions for exactly *how* to open the chest. The boy who'd found it was crouched by the chest, his hands on the latch.

"We might as well see what's inside too," Jonah said, trying to sound casual, as if he was used to half tracers giving ghostly instructions.

He put his hands in the exact same position as the tracer boy's and mimicked every movement. When the boy finally raised the lid, Jonah had to push a little harder. He hoped neither of the girls noticed how much it strained his muscles.

"So what's in there?" Katherine asked. "Andrea's family fortune?"

The tracer boy was already lifting the first item out of the chest. Jonah looked at it, did a double take, and then glanced down into the open chest.

"Paintbrushes?" Jonah said in disbelief. "Who bothers carrying art supplies halfway around the world?"

TWENTY-FIVE

"John White did," Andrea said quietly, pride in her voice. "He was an artist. Is. That was his job on all his trips to Roanoke Island. He was supposed to record views of the local people, the local plants and animals. To get more people to come here. And just to show what everything was like."

"Let me guess," Katherine said. "Nobody had invented cameras yet?"

Andrea shook her head.

"John White has been widely praised in modern times for his sympathetic depiction of Native Americans," she said, as if quoting. "It's a tragedy that so little of his work survived."

Jonah shook his head. Art supplies! Whatever happened to going back to England for everything the colonists needed? Like . . . food? And whoever heard of an artist also being a governor? Were the English *trying* to make their colony fail?

The tracer boys were pulling other things out of the chest, so Jonah did the same. Quill pens. Little jars that must have contained inks and paints. Tablets of blank paper. Tablets full of pictures.

The papers and jars were wrapped in cloth—no, it was clothing: another shirt just like the one John White was already wearing and two dresses that seemed to amaze the tracer boys.

"I bet he was bringing those for Eleanor," Andrea murmured.

The tracer boys held the dresses up against their own chests and laughed, just like the football players at school who had dressed up like cheerleaders for Halloween.

"Oh, grow up!" Katherine muttered.

John White's tracer must have said something similar, because the tracer boys quickly put the dresses back into the chest. At the old man's direction, they picked up a tablet instead and began looking through the pictures. John White waved his arm, apparently telling the boys, *Turn the page, turn the page, that's not, the picture I want to show you.* . . . Jonah pulled the real version of the same tablet out of the chest, so he could turn pages along with the tracer boys.

On the first page was a drawing of an Indian village with huts made of curved branches. Jonah looked at the picture, then glanced the disheveled huts around him.

"Do you think . . . It's a drawing of this village we're sitting in right now, isn't it?" he asked, holding up the page so Andrea and Katherine could see.

"Yes," Andrea whispered. "Except . . . everything's in good shape. And there are people."

The drawing was actually full of people. Indians—dancing, cooking, laughing, harvesting healthy-looking corn . . . They practically jumped off the page, they looked so alive. Jonah could see on their faces how happy they were, how proud they were of their thriving village.

Where had they gone? What had happened to them?

The tracer boys were holding the tracer tablet out to John White, pointing to a particular picture. Jonah could practically hear them asking, "Do you mean this one?"

John White's tracer nodded vigorously, tears glistening in his eyes.

Jonah glanced at the picture the tracer boys held up and quickly flipped through his tablet until he located the same drawing.

It was a woman holding a tiny baby tightly wrapped in a blanket. The woman's hair was pulled back from her face rather severely, but her eyes shone with love.

John White's tracer swallowed hard, struggling to regain his composure. He weakly lifted his arm and swiped it through the air, telling the boys to turn the page again.

The next picture—which Jonah turned to in the real version of the tablet as well—was of an Indian. He stood proudly, posing with his chin held high. He was wearing nothing but a loincloth, unless you counted the tattoos on his chests and the feathers in his hair. The word at the bottom of this page was *Manteo*.

"Manteo was the Indian who got along with the English the best," Andrea said. "Do you think these boys know him? *That* might be a clue!"

But the tracer boys were already shaking their heads. John White's tracer grimaced and lowered his head into his hands.

"No, no—don't give up!" Andrea exploded. "*I'm* here! Look at me!" She waved her hands in front of the tracer's face, but of course he looked right through her. She dived through the tracer and grabbed the real man by the shoulders.

"Why can't *you* see me?" she shouted. "Why can't you hear me? Why don't you know I'm here?"

"Andrea," Katherine said softly. "I don't think—"

But Andrea had stopped yelling. A horrified expression was spreading over her face.

At the bottom of the page were the words *Eleanor and Virginia*.

Katherine gently touched the woman's face in the picture.

"She looks a lot like you, Andrea," Katherine murmured. "I didn't notice when JB was showing us that DVD . . . or whatever that was." She laughed a little, an embarrassed-sounding snort. "But she'd just given birth then. Maybe women don't look like themselves when they've just given birth."

Jonah wasn't going to comment about *that*. He peered down at the picture: It was definitely the woman from the scene JB had shown them. And she did look like Andrea or like what Andrea could look like in ten or fifteen years.

He looked over at Andrea, wanting to compare. Bu Andrea had turned her face to the side.

Meanwhile, the tracers were still conferring over th picture. Both tracer boys were shaking their heads, shru ging apologetically. Disappointment clouded the face John White's tracer.

It was so clear what each of the tracers had been s ing. John White had been asking if the tracer boys ever seen his daughter and granddaughter, if they k where his family was.

The tracer boys had said no.

"Look at him," she mumbles. "Without his tracer he looks . . . he looks . . ."

Awful was the word that jumped into Jonah's mind. Without his tracer, John White was ghostly pale, but with beads of sweat trickling down into his hair. His cheeks were sunken, the hollows almost an ashy gray.

"He looks like he's going to die," Andrea whispered. "Quick! Help me put him back with his tracer!"

But just as she started to tug on his shoulder—before Jonah had a chance to even think whether that was the right thing to do—John White's tracer lay back down, rejoining the real man completely, even down to the closed eyes. *Was* the tracer giving up?

No. He was still struggling to speak, even as he seemed to be slipping toward unconsciousness.

"Please," John White said, the tracer and the man talking as one now that they were back together, thinking alike. "Please take me to Croatoan then. Canst thou take me to Croatoan Island?"

Jonah glanced up just in time to see the tracer boys nodding their heads yes.

TWENTY-SIX

"That's it!" Andrea exclaimed. A smile spread across her face, instantly hiding the anguish. "That's how everything is supposed to work! I understand now! We'll all go to Croatoan, and that's where we'll find my tracer! It makes sense, if that's where the Roanoke colonists went. And when I'm with my tracer, my grandfather will be able to see me. . . . He'll be whole again; there won't be anything throwing him off. . . ."

She bent down and hugged her grandfather's shoulders. The real version of the man flinched and she sat back.

"Andrea, remember, your tracer will be a three-year-old," Jonah cautioned. "When you join with your tracer, you'll have to go back to being a preschooler again—not that they probably had preschool in this time period."

Andrea's smile trembled slightly, but she replied

evenly, "I don't care. It'd be worth it, being a little kid again, if that's how things are supposed to work for my grandfather to see me."

How things are supposed to work, Jonah thought, a little dizzily. It wasn't just the lack of food that was making his head spin. Was this what JB would want for them? Was this the way to fix time and rescue Andrea? Or was this another setup?

"What if this is just part of Second's plot for us?" he asked. "You said in original time, John White never made it to Croatoan Island. He never saw you or anyone else from his family again!"

"But they're taking him!" Andrea said, pointing. Already, one of the tracer boys was bending down, as if preparing to carry John White away. "The historical accounts that I read were wrong about other things—they must be wrong about this, too!"

"Or Second is tampering with time again," Jonah said darkly. "Tricking us . . ."

"How could he?" Katherine said. "Andrea's right—if the tracers are taking John White to Croatoan, that's how original time went. Tracers are always right—er—accurate, I mean. They have to show how time really went."

Jonah squinted at the girls.

"How did John White know to ask to go to Croatoan?"

Jonah asked. "He hasn't even been to his old colony yet, to see the word carved in wood."

"Maybe he was actually *leaving* Roanoke Island when his rowboat broke up, and we rescued him?" Katherine suggested. "Maybe he was here two days ago, went back to his ship, and then came to Roanoke again only because the ship was wrecked?"

"None of that's what history says," Jonah said stubbornly.

"But this is what *time* says is supposed to happen," Katherine said, gesturing toward the tracers.

"You want to make time go right, don't you?" Andrea asked softly. "Don't you think we should go to Croatoan with the tracers?" She was looking at Jonah, not Katherine. And, for that matter, Katherine was looking at Jonah. Both of them were waiting to see what he had to say. He thought about making a dumb joke: *Hey, America isn't a democracy yet. You don't have to wait for my vote!* But they were all in this together. Andrea and Katherine did need to hear Jonah's vote.

Jonah frowned, trying to think through everything.

"I guess you're right," he finally said. "Nobody was at the Roanoke village, and we saw the word *Croatoan* with our own eyes, so we know that part of the story's true. And if all the tracers are going to Croatoan Island and that's where Andrea's tracer probably is . . . what good would it do to stay here?"

"Exactly!" Andrea said, grinning.

Jonah tried to keep himself from noticing once again how pretty Andrea looked when she was happy. He wanted to be able to think clearly. He wanted to be able to analyze this new development for ulterior motives or secret behind-the-scenes plans by Second. Could things really fall into place this way? Or . . . was there more reason than ever to be suspicious?

"If we're going to keep up with the tracers, we'd better get moving," Katherine said.

While one tracer boy crouched beside John White, the other was pouring water on the site of their fire from the night before. Then he went toward a hut at the far end of the village, at a distance from all the others.

"I'll go see what he's up to," Jonah volunteered.

He reached the hut just as the tracer boy began putting strips of dried meat into a deerskin bag.

Venison jerky from that deer they killed? Jonah wondered. *But where did they dry it?*

The tracer boy poured water on the floor of this hut too. For the first time, Jonah noticed that there had been a tracer fire going here as well.

Oh, this is a smokehouse. . . . They must have come straight here and started the fire right after they shot the deer, before they went to the beach and rescued John White, Jonah realized. *They could have been getting up every few hours through the night, to turn the meat.*

It bothered him that he hadn't noticed any of that—he hadn't even thought to wonder about where they'd cooked their meat.

What else am I missing? Jonah wondered. *What else am I just not paying attention to?*

He realized he hadn't looked into all the huts in the village the day before—or since, even after he discovered the melon with the message from Second.

"I really don't want any more messages from that guy," he muttered.

But as he walked back toward Katherine and Andrea and John White, he poked his head into every hut along the way. All of them were empty and dark, their dirt floors bare except for the occasional unhealthy-looking plant. The melon plant in the broken-roofed hut looked like it was thriving, by comparison. Jonah glanced into that hut quickly . . . and then stopped.

There on the floor, nestled among the melon leaves, were two jars. Jonah bent over and picked them up.

They left no tracers.

And they each had the same words engraved on their stoppers:

WITH MY COMPLIMENTS.

-SECOND

TWENTY-SEVEN

"What's this? Ketchup and mustard for the little food pellets?" Jonah muttered.

He pulled the cork out of one of the jars and got a whiff of the thick purplish liquid—it was paint.

In fact, the jars were identical to the ones in John White's trunk.

"You have a really sick sense of humor, Mr. Second," Jonah murmured. "Given everything we don't have—all the *answers* we don't have—and you just send us more paint?"

"Jonah! What are you doing? Come on!" Katherine called from outside the hut. "The tracer boys are leaving!"

Jonah came out of the hut waving the jars of paint.

"Look what else Second left for us," he said. "'With my compliments,' he says. *I* say we take a stand: Second, we don't want your stupid presents!"

He tossed the jars back into the melon plant. They broke off several of the leaves, creating a line of tracer leaves.

Katherine frowned at him.

"No, wait," she said. "We should take those along. Not leave behind any more time mess-ups than we have to, you know?"

"All right, all right," Jonah mumbled. He fished the jars back out of the melon leaves. He went over to the trunk and dropped them in with John White's other art supplies.

"I'm glad we're getting away from this creepy island and that creepy hut and that creepy guy Second's gifts," Jonah said. Somehow, he was sure Croatoan Island would be different.

"Some help?" Katherine muttered.

Jonah realized that Katherine and Andrea were attempting to pull John White across the clearing, following the tracer boy carrying the old man's tracer.

"Oh, right. Sorry," Jonah said.

He rushed over to the girls. They had been trying to tug the old man by his armpits, but with all three of them working together, they were able to lift him up, almost into a standing position. John White's head sagged forward; his legs dragged uselessly.

"We've—got to—get him back with his tracer!" Andrea grunted.

Ahead of them, the tracer boy placed John White's tracer in the crook of the branch they'd carried him on the night before. Much less gracefully, Jonah, Katherine, and Andrea settled the real man into the same spot.

"Now he looks so much better," Andrea said.

It was true. John White's color instantly improved. The sweat beads disappeared from his face. And even though his eyes remained closed, his whole countenance looked more peaceful now.

Does it really help John White that much to be with his tracer, like Andrea thinks? Jonah wondered. *Or is it just that the tracer's healthier, and that's what we see?*

Dare began barking. The second tracer boy was carrying the tracer chest over to put on the branch beside John White.

"Right. Don't worry—I'm getting it, boy," Jonah muttered.

He was glad that Andrea and Katherine were looking down at John White and didn't notice that Jonah just dragged the chest. No, now the girls were peering through the trees ahead of the branch. As Jonah heaved the chest onto the branch—almost splintering it—he realized that they were looking at a small sliver of water visible through the woods.

"Do the tracers think this branch is going to float?" Andrea asked. "If we're going to a whole different island . . ."

Jonah hadn't thought of that. There was too much to keep track of.

"John White would fall off," Katherine said. "He wouldn't even make it across a puddle, if this was all he had holding him up."

"Surely . . . ," Andrea began.

She broke off because the one tracer boy was pushing the branch forward—all by himself.

"Show-off," Jonah muttered.

The other boy was walking down toward the water.

"We have to push too!" Andrea said. "We can't let my grandfather get separated from his tracer!"

It took all three of them heaving and shoving to get the branch lined up again with the tracer boy's branch. Fortunately, from that point, there was a slight downhill tilt, so the main problem was controlling the branch's slide.

The next time Jonah looked up, they were at the water's edge, and the second tracer boy was a few yards down the shore. He disappeared behind a tree. Then he reappeared *on* the water—in a tracer canoe.

"Oh, there's a canoe," Jonah said. "That's how it's going to work."

He was a little annoyed with Andrea and Katherine for scaring him. Of course the tracer boys wouldn't try to sail an old man and a treasure chest from one island to another on a splintery, unstable branch.

Jonah dashed over to the tree where the tracer boy had stood just a few moments before. This was like searching for John White's treasure chest. Jonah just had to look in the same spot where there'd been a tracer. Granted, the tracer boy had disappeared behind the tree, but he'd reappeared so quickly in the canoe that the real version of it would have to be right there.

Jonah looked down.

No canoe.

He looked to the right.

Nothing.

To the left.

Nothing.

Jonah peered far down the shoreline, in both directions, then out into the water, as far as he could see. Nothing, nothing, nothing. There wasn't a real canoe anywhere in sight.

"Oh, no," Jonah groaned, dread creeping over him. "Oh, no."

It made so much sense that the tracer boys would have a canoe. They'd been alone on an island, after all—they had to have gotten there somehow.

But they weren't here for real, Jonah thought dizzily. *In our version of time, they weren't here. So . . . neither was their canoe?*

Jonah didn't want to trust that conclusion. He leaned weakly against the tree, trying to think through everything again, trying to come up with a different answer.

The tracer boy was angling the canoe up against the shore. He held the canoe steady while the other boy helped the tracer version of John White climb into the canoe. Then the second boy loaded the chest and the pouch of venison jerky. He shoved the canoe out into deeper water before jumping in and grabbing a paddle.

Then, without a backward glance, both boys paddled away with John White's tracer.

TWENTY-EIGHT

"Hey!" Andrea screamed, waving her arms uselessly. "Wait for us!"

The tracer boys kept paddling.

"Jonah! Hurry up with that canoe!" Katherine yelled.

"There isn't a canoe!" Jonah yelled back. "Not a real one!"

"What?" Katherine hollered back.

Both girls scrambled out toward the water's edge, to look up and down the shoreline for themselves.

"Maybe the branch would work better than we think?" Jonah said.

The branch was already sagging down into the water. A wave hit it, and Andrea reached back just in time to keep her grandfather from toppling over. He would have fallen in if they'd been out on the open water.

"Or we could swim?" Jonah revised his suggestion. "I carried John White yesterday. . . ."

Katherine fixed him with a withering glare. She didn't have to say, *Are you crazy? Do you want us all to drown? Can't you see how far away the nearest land is?*

The nearest land was just a sliver on the horizon. Everything was so flat, Jonah wasn't even sure it *was* land. The thin layer of green and brown might have just been a trick of the eye.

And who knew how far it might be to Croatoan Island?

"Second!" Andrea screamed at the sky. "If you really want to help us, give us a canoe! A canoe! That's all we need!"

Nothing happened. No canoe floated down from the sky.

Andrea slumped against her grandfather's side.

"It figures," she muttered. "Second's just been toying with us all along. And now look at my grandfather!"

John White's skin looked clammier than ever. A pained expression covered his face, as if he was being poked in the back by various twigs and other sharp, pointy off-shoots of the branch.

"Maybe the stuff I thought was paint is actually medicine?" Jonah suggested.

"Wouldn't Second tell us that if he really wanted to help?" Katherine asked. "So we wouldn't poison Andrea's grandfather by mistake?"

"If Second really wanted to help, he'd tell us something besides, 'With my compliments' and 'You're doing great,'" Andrea muttered. "And—oh, yeah, 'Here's how you can save your parents'—and it's all a *lie*."

Jonah gazed at Andrea. He could see the tears welling in her eyes.

"Forget Second," he told her. "We *are* going to get off this island. We're going to get away from Second's plans, and we're going to catch up with the tracer boys, and we're going to find your tracer—even if we have to make our own canoe out of this . . ."

Log, he was going to say. There was a downed log floating in the water right at the shoreline. It had been there from the first moment that Jonah had begun looking for a canoe. But a breeze blew some dead leaves away just then, and Jonah saw that the log was actually tied to a tree with some sort of primitive braided rope.

Why would someone tie up a log? Was the log maybe not just a log?

Jonah glanced up at the tracer boys in their tracer canoe, paddling off into the distance. He squinted, trying to think what the underside of the canoe might look like, the part submerged in the water. He remembered something from Boy Scout camp, the year the water sports instructor had gone on and on during orientation about "respecting the history." The instructor had seemed like a crazy old man, but hadn't he said something about how Native Americans used to make canoes by burning out the insides of logs? Wouldn't that mean that the outside of a canoe would still look like a log?

Jonah nudged the side of the log with his foot, rolling it back a bit. Jonah hadn't pushed hard enough to completely flip the log over, so when it settled back into place, it displaced a huge wave of water. Jonah jumped back too late to avoid getting soaked.

But he'd seen enough. He'd seen that the other side of the log was hollowed out.

"I found the canoe!" he screamed. "I found the canoe!"

"Well, get it over here!" Katherine said. "Before we lose sight of the tracers!"

"You have to help!" Jonah yelled back. "I can't do everything!"

Which was unfair, because Katherine and Andrea had worked just as hard as Jonah had, pushing John White on the tree branch. But Jonah was wet and tired and hungry and sore, and he knew he was going to have to jump into the water to turn the canoe over.

They were all wet and tired and sore—and irritable—

by the time they got the canoe untied, turned over, emptied of water, and loaded with John White and his chest. It took all three of them trying five times before they managed to flip the canoe. They might have succeeded on the fourth try, except that just as they were heaving the canoe up, Katherine said, "Wait a minute! What are we going to use for paddles?"

Jonah lost his grip on the side of the canoe, and it smashed down on his shoulder, knocking him under the water. He surfaced in the air pocket under the canoe.

Oh, yeah, he thought, remembering something else from the crazy water sports instructor at Boy Scout camp. *This is how you're supposed to turn over a canoe. From underneath.*

Something was banging against his head, so he grabbed hold of it as he dipped down, kicked to the right, and resurfaced outside the canoe.

"I figured out how we should do this!" he told the girls, lifting his arms high in the air, triumphantly. He decided not to mention that he should have known all along.

"And you found a paddle!" Andrea exclaimed.

Jonah looked at the thing in his hand. It was a carved piece of wood, vaguely paddle-shaped. Huh. Maybe the crazy water sports instructor at Boy Scout camp had said that was the best place to store paddles, under an overturned canoe.

In the end, once all three of them had dived under the canoe and heaved it into the air, they also found another paddle and a wooden object that looked like a rake. They didn't have time to figure out what that was for—the tracer boys were paddling farther and farther away—so they just tossed the rake into the canoe. Even after they added John White and his chest, there was plenty of room left for all three kids and Dare.

Didn't the guy at Boy Scout camp say that sometimes these canoes could hold as many as twenty men? Jonah thought. *Or was that something that Mrs. Rorshas told us about the Indians?* He wasn't sure. He felt too dizzy and disoriented and exhausted to think clearly. And now he and one of the girls were going to have a paddle a canoe that was supposed to be powered by twenty men?

He decided not to mention that to the girls.

"I'll take the front," Jonah offered, stepping into the canoe. "Can one of you push off?"

"I'll do it," Andrea volunteered. "Hurry!"

The tracer boys and their canoe were getting smaller and smaller off in the distance.

Once Jonah and Katherine had settled into position, Andrea was surprisingly quick pushing off from the shore.

"Go!" she yelled.

"You paddle—opposite side from me!" Jonah yelled

back over his shoulder. He wished there'd been time to review canoeing strategy. "Katherine, tell Andrea—"

"She knows!" Katherine yelled forward, from where she was crouched beside John White and his chest. "She's already doing it. Just go faster."

Jonah paddled desperately. The shoulder the canoe had slammed down on ached with every stroke, but it helped when he switched sides.

"Switch!" he yelled back to Andrea.

"She already did!" Katherine yelled forward.

Jonah kept paddling.

At first, it seemed that they were going only fast enough to keep the tracers from lengthening the distance between them. But then, slowly, almost imperceptibly, Jonah realized that they were gaining on the tracers.

Am I paddling that much faster? Jonah wondered, feeling rather proud that he could outpace the muscular tracers. Then he took a quick glance over his shoulder and realized: He wasn't the one doing such an awesome job paddling. It was Andrea.

She was paddling frantically, her paddle re-entering the water only a split second after she'd pulled it out. And she pulled the paddle through the water at exactly the right angle to create the most force, to propel the canoe forward as quickly as possible.

Oh, yeah, Jonah remembered. *Andrea went to camp too. And she ate that food pellet, so she should have more energy than me. Maybe it had steroids in it? Maybe the pellet made Dare peppier, too?*

Jonah didn't have time to follow that thought.

"Good job!" he yelled back to Andrea.

"Just keep paddling!" Katherine screamed at him.

The paddling was starting to feel grim to Jonah, like punishment. As long as they kept the tracers in sight, did it really matter if John White was joined with his tracer every single second?

He dared to glance back at John White again. How could it be? How could the man look even paler than before? And—was he shivering? Shivering in all this heat, when Jonah himself had just gotten out of the water and was already sweating again?

Jonah went back to focusing on nothing but digging his paddle into the water, shoving it back, pulling it out. Digging, shoving, pulling; digging, shoving, pulling . . .

With great effort, they drew close to the tracer canoe. The tip of the kids' canoe touched the end of the tracer version.

"All right!" Katherine cheered. "Almost there!"

Jonah's arms felt like they were almost ready to fall off. He'd been holding on to the paddle so tightly, for so long, that he couldn't even feel his hands—which was a good thing, because they had blisters now. He thought he could put on a final burst of speed and draw even with the tracers. But how was he supposed to keep paddling after that?

The canoe lurched forward—Andrea was paddling harder than ever. This shamed Jonah into paddling harder too.

Jonah slipped through the body of the first tracer boy. He drew even with the tracer John White's feet, with his stomach, with his head. The canoe wavered—losing ground, gaining, losing, gaining—and then with one last yank of his paddle, Jonah ensured that the real canoe and the tracer canoe occupied the exact same space.

Jonah glanced at the second tracer boy, who paddled alongside Jonah.

"Hey," Jonah mumbled. "Isn't it time for your coffee break? Er—venison break?"

This seemed hilarious to Jonah in his thirsty, hungry, exhausted state. He couldn't really see the tracer boy except as an echo of himself: an arm separating every now and then from Jonah's own, an extra nose leaning forward occasionally from Jonah's face. It was like talking to his own shadow, like slipping through fog.

And then, quite suddenly, the tracer stopped seeming like a shadow or fog. It stopped seeming like a tracer, too—it seemed like an actual boy, with actual arms and legs and a torso and head, trying to take up the same space as Jonah himself. It was like having someone fall on him from out of the sky and leap up at him from underneath and dive into him from every other side, all at once. And like time and space had hiccupped and the other person somehow had a stronger claim to the place where Jonah was sitting than Jonah did.

Jonah immediately fell out of the canoe.

TWENTY-NINE

Jonah hit hard, the chilly water a huge shock against his sweaty skin. He slipped beneath the surface but gave a fierce kick and came up sputtering. His legs were already cramping; it seemed to take a huge amount of effort just to keep his head above water.

This is why they always made us wear life jackets at camp, Jonah thought. *Be prepared, and all that.*

Jonah would have to settle for a backup plan.

Let's see. Find something to grab on to, something that floats, to hold yourself up?

Jonah had fallen out of the canoe in the middle of acres and acres of water. He was so far from shore that finding a random branch or log floating nearby would require divine intervention. Or *Second's* intervention, and Jonah wasn't going to count on that. But he had been holding on to a paddle when he'd fallen into the water . . .

Jonah actually lifted his hands up in front of his face, looking at them carefully. Maybe he was still holding on to a paddle?

Nope. His hands were empty.

"Jonah!" Katherine screamed, the sound distorting because of all the water in Jonah's ears. "Swim back to the canoe!"

Oh. Well, that would do. That would be something to hang on to.

Jonah had surfaced with his back to the canoe, but it was a little odd that he'd practically forgotten it was there. Maybe his mind didn't want to deal with the weird thing that had just happened to him in the canoe?

Jonah took a deep breath and whirled around.

The canoe was several yards away now, getting farther and farther ahead of him. But it had turned back into two separate canoes again—or maybe one and a half? One and three-fourths?

Jonah decided this wasn't one of those times when precise numbers mattered.

The tracer version of the canoe was starting to break away again—not in a straight line, but off at an odd angle, swinging wildly back and forth. No, it was the real canoe that was swinging so wildly, as if paddled by maniacs.

In the front of the real canoe, in the spot where Jonah had sat only moments earlier, was a boy with short dark hair and pierced ears and a T-shirt that said, *Sarcasm—just one of my specialties.* The boy was staring down at the paddle in his hand with a baffled expression on his face.

From the back of the canoe, Andrea was yelling at the Sarcasm boy, "Keep paddling! We'll explain everything later. But for now—keep paddling!"

Jonah hoped Andrea would be able to explain everything to him later too.

When she wasn't yelling at the boy at the front of the boat, Andrea was arguing with a boy—or was it two different boys?—sitting practically on top of her. Jonah blinked and squinted, trying to correct the double vision. The boy he could see now, like the one he thought he'd seen only a moment before, had dark skin. His hair was cut quite close to his head, almost shaved, and he wore a Beatles T-shirt. Jonah blinked again, and suddenly that boy was gone, replaced by the other boy. This boy was naked from the waist up—the only part Jonah could see— and his hair was cut in a strangely familiar style.

Oh, yeah. He looks like one of those tracers we've been following around. . . .

While Jonah watched, the back end of the canoe lurched to the side, and Beatles T-shirt boy was back, with only the tracer version of naked-chest boy beside him.

"No, no, you've got to paddle exactly the same way as your tracer!" Andrea screamed. "You've got to sit in the same place! You've got to keep it together so I can go help that guy in the front!"

She shoved the boy to the right—an amazing feat, since he was taller and bigger than she was. And then she wrapped her hands around the boy's hands on the paddle and plunged it into the water, trying to pull the canoe back into place, lined up with its tracer. And . . . to pull the boys into their places, lined up with their tracers?

That's who those boys are, who appeared out of nowhere, Jonah thought, his brain finally starting to catch up. *Sarcasm T-shirt boy and Beatles T-shirt boy—they're the real versions of our tracer buddies, the fake Indians.*

Jonah did nothing but tread water for a few seconds, basking in the glow of actually having figured something out. He refused to let any more questions into his mind— certainly not any of the disturbing, unanswerable questions that threatened to creep in.

"Jonah, would you stop goofing off out there?" Katherine screamed. "We need your help!"

Oh, so she wasn't interested just in saving his life? She wanted him to solve all the problems with the canoe?

"Katherine, you go to the front and paddle!" Andrea yelled. "We're losing the tracers!"

"Not until we rescue Jonah!" Katherine screamed back.

Okay, so maybe she did care about saving Jonah's life.

Did Andrea care so little that she was willing to leave him behind?

Jonah slipped slightly lower in the water, his cramped legs shooting with pain, his exhausted arm muscles barely compensating. The water was over his chin and mouth now; he had to tilt his head slightly to keep his nose above the waterline. For the first time in his life, he could understand how someone who knew how to swim might drown anyway.

"Jonah, swim!" Katherine commanded. "Stop treading water and swim!"

Treading water was easier—and he was so tired—but Jonah obediently launched his body toward the canoe. His flutter kick did nothing—how about a frog kick? Scissors kick? Butterfly kick?

It turned out that Jonah was worthless at everything right now except a modified dog paddle. Still, he struggled forward. Katherine leaned dangerously over the side of the canoe, holding out her hand.

"Don't tip us over!" Andrea hollered, real panic in her voice.

"Lean . . . other . . . way . . . ," Jonah panted.

Andrea and Katherine both leaned away from Jonah. Even Dare scrambled back as Jonah grabbed the side of the canoe and, with his last burst of energy, lunged up and over the edge.

For a moment, everything seemed like it could go in any direction. Jonah could pull too hard, tipping the canoe toward him. The girls could lean too far the other way and overturn the canoe in the opposite direction. For all Jonah knew, a hundred more boys could suddenly land in the canoe out of nowhere, completely sinking it with their weight.

But what happened was that Jonah landed inside the canoe, sprawled slightly on top of John White. The canoe rocked, Dare barked . . . and Jonah closed his eyes, completely spent.

The canoe's rocking settled into stillness.

"Katherine," Jonah heard Andrea say, softly.

"I'll paddle now," Katherine said.

Jonah was barely aware of anything for a while after that. The canoe sped forward, but it was like gliding now, smooth and seemingly effortless. Effortless for Jonah, anyway—he had no effort left in him.

Once he thought he heard Katherine say, "Oh, so that's what the rake is for," and then he thought something wet

"More like a fish net," Katherine said. "But close enough."

Jonah would have preferred, say, a cheeseburger and fries, but the fish really did smell good. And it wasn't some suspicious pellet that had come from Second.

"Come on," Katherine said, tugging on Jonah's arm.

Jonah let her lead him toward the fire. He was surprised at how weak he still felt. Surely that wasn't just from canoeing and treading water and swimming.

I was tired before I fell out of the boat, he thought. *But I didn't feel this bad until that guy dropped on me . . . jumped up at me . . . tackled me. . . .*

Jonah's brain still kept dodging away from thinking about that moment. He stumbled past the two boys, who were taking fish from a sort of improvised wooden rack by the fire. One by one, they placed the cooked fish on huge leaves—stand-ins for plates, Jonah guessed.

"Uh, hey," Jonah mumbled, because it seemed kind of rude not to say anything.

Jonah thought he saw one of the boys separate from his tracer long enough to nod stiffly at him, but he couldn't be sure.

"That's Brendan," Katherine said. "He's really nice. But he and Antonio are trying to stay with their tracers as much as they can, until they're sure the tracers are just going to sit still for a while."

---

and slimy hit his ankle. But he might have been dreaming. He was dreaming a lot. He dreamed that he was at Boy Scout camp, and there were four new water sports instructors, some guys named John, Paul, Ringo, and George. Jonah thought they looked kind of familiar.

He dreamed that he was in art class in school, and the teacher, Mr. Takanawa, was announcing that they would draw nothing but Native Americans for the rest of the year.

He dreamed that he was at a fish fry, and the air was full of the smell of smoke and cooked fish. And even though Jonah was starving, he couldn't make himself wake up to eat. But Katherine was shaking his shoulders, and she wouldn't give up. She just kept shaking and shaking and shaking, and her "Jonah, wake up! Jonah, wake up!" kept getting louder and louder and louder. . . .

Wait. That dream wasn't a dream. It was real.

Jonah managed to open his eyelids a crack.

"Finally!" Katherine exploded. "You were starting to scare us!"

"Huh?" Jonah mumbled. He'd been asleep—how was that scary?

He forced his eyes open a little wider. He was still in the canoe, but he had it completely to himself now. And, unless Katherine had magically developed the ability to sit on water, the canoe wasn't floating anymore, but resting on land.

Weakly, Jonah propped himself up on his arms, and saw that they were on a sandy beach, the canoe pulled carefully above the high tide mark.

"Croatoan?" Jonah mumbled. "Is this Croatoan Island?"

"We're not there yet," Katherine said. "We . . ." She stopped and bit her lip. Then she tried again, in an overly cheerful voice. "We're just making a stop along the way."

Jonah nodded, too dazed to analyze the reason she'd bitten her lip, the reason she'd stopped herself from telling him something. He squinted, trying to bring his vision into focus, to look past Katherine. A few yards away, Andrea and Dare sat near a crackling fire with John White and the tracer boys.

No, Jonah corrected himself. *They're not tracers now. They're real—the tracers and the real versions of the boys joined once more.*

If Jonah squinted really hard, he could make out the slightest hint of a Sarcasm T-shirt and shorter hair on one boy, a Beatles T-shirt and cropped hair on the other.

"Brendan and Antonio," Katherine said. "That's their names. Well, their twenty-first-century names. They have Indian names too."

"I thought they weren't Indians," Jonah muttered. He

peered over at the two boys again. If they were going to fi[t] into Jonah's notion of Indians, one's skin seemed too dark[,] the other's, too light. And in both cases, Jonah though[t] their hair was wrong for Native Americans.

On the other hand, they both acted as if they fel[t] completely comfortable walking around in nothing bu[t] loincloths.

"Neither of them was born an Indian," Katherine sai[d.] "But an Indian tribe adopted them both." She grinne[d.] "Kind of ironic, huh?"

Jonah let his eyelids slip shut again. Maybe h[e] wasn't really ready to wake up. Not if it involved thin[k]ing about Indians who weren't really Indians, and ado[p]tions and . . . how had those boys just appeared out [of] nowhere, anyhow?

Katherine jostled his shoulder.

"Stop that!" she said. "You need to stay awake so y[ou] can eat."

"Eat?" Jonah mumbled, opening his eyes again. "E[at] what?"

"We were fishing in the canoe—well, mostly it w[as] Brendan and Antonio," Katherine said. "They were rea[lly] good at it when they were with their tracers, you kn[ow,] because their tracers knew what to do. Remember t[he] paddle that looks like a rake?"

"It's a fishing rod?" Jonah asked.

Something about the way she put that bothered Jonah, but his brain wasn't working well enough yet for him to figure out why.

The second boy—Antonio?—said something to Brendan just then, but Jonah didn't really catch it. He couldn't even tell if it was English or another language.

"They're speaking an Algonquian dialect," Katherine said.

"How'd you know that?" Jonah asked. Was this something else he should have learned in fifth-grade Social Studies?

"They told me," Katherine said. "We had a long time together out in that canoe."

Jonah noticed for the first time that Katherine's face was sunburned and—he brought his hand to his face—his was too. He looked back over his shoulder and saw how low the sun was in the sky.

"So we were in that canoe all day?" he asked. "I was asleep all day?"

"Pretty much," Katherine said. "Now do you see why we were worried?'

Jonah shrugged this off. He didn't want to seem too wimpy in front of two boys he didn't even know. But how could he have slept all day?

Antonio picked that moment to stand up and stretch, revealing perfect six-pack abs. This made Jonah feel even wimpier, since every muscle in *his* body felt rubbery and sore and pathetic. But Jonah wasn't going to let the other boy see how intimidated he was. He gave the boy a hard look.

Then he did a double take.

"Wait a minute!" Jonah said. "I know you! Weren't you wearing a sweatshirt with a skull on it? Back in the cave?"

In the time cave, the day Jonah had learned that he was one of the missing children from history, there'd been a small subgroup of kids wearing skull sweatshirts. They'd gone out of their way to be rude to Jonah and Katherine; if he hadn't had so much else to worry about, Jonah would have been afraid of them.

Now the boy standing before Jonah seemed to quiver, his twenty-first-century self separating slightly from his fake-Indian self. Jonah could see just the hint of the Sarcasm T-shirt at the boy's neckline, just the edge of a tracer at the back of the boy's head.

"Yeah—so?" Antonio growled. "What's it to you?"

Jonah recoiled. In his experience back home, that was the kind of thing bullies said right before they started looking around for someone to punch. Jonah had almost always taken comments like that as a cue to slip away, out of range of anyone's fists.

But that was before he'd survived the Middle Ages,

before he'd defied time experts to rescue his friends, before he'd rescued a drowning man, before he'd stood on messed-up Roanoke Island yelling at Second.

Jonah stepped closer to Antonio.

"Then you're a famous missing kid from history, like me and Andrea," Jonah said. "Who are you, really? Why did JB send you back that way, like . . . right on top of us?" Jonah was proud he could force those words out, describing what had happened. "Didn't JB know we were there? Does he know now? What are you guys supposed to be doing here?" Jonah's brain still wasn't exactly functioning normally, but he found he could come up with plenty of questions. A brilliant one occurred to him, one that made him almost stammer with excitement. "D-do you have an Elucidator with you? Can you let us talk to JB?"

Katherine put a warning hand on Jonah's arm.

"Jonah, it wasn't JB who sent Brendan and Antonio back in time," she said.

"Then—who—?"

"Some guy named Second," Antonio muttered. He narrowed his eyes and added tauntingly, "Know him?"

THIRTY

"You're working for Second?" Jonah said.

He took one step closer to Antonio and would have punched him squarely in the jaw if Katherine hadn't had her hand on Jonah's arm. Katherine jerked his arm back and then quickly grabbed his other arm, before he could even think about getting a left-handed jab in instead.

And Jonah was so embarrassingly weak that he couldn't pull away from her.

"Katherine, stop it!" he yelled.

"No—you stop it!" Katherine yelled back. "You're being an idiot! Antonio isn't working for Second any more than we are! And neither is Brendan!"

"How can you be so sure?" Jonah asked, struggling against her grasp.

"Because I've been talking to them all day, while you

were asleep," Katherine said. "And then you wake up and Antonio says two or three words to you, and you think you know enough to start beating people up?"

"It only took one word," Jonah muttered. *"Second."*

"You are just like all the white men who come here, to our land," Antonio said. "You start fighting and stealing and killing before you know anything."

Antonio had to separate even farther from his tracer to say this. Right as he was speaking, his tracer stepped completely away from him, carrying fish toward Andrea's grandfather. Antonio stopped and clutched his head.

"That was so weird!" he said. "It was like I was thinking with my own brain, but I was thinking the way my tracer would have. . . ."

Jonah thought about saying, *Yeah, buddy. You're a white guy too. Did you ever think of that? Hasn't your tracer ever looked in a mirror? And what did I steal or kill?* But Katherine was glaring so intensely that Jonah decided he shouldn't push things.

"Let's all just sit down and eat," Andrea said anxiously. "Then we can figure everything out."

"Here," Katherine said, thrusting a fish on a leaf into Jonah's hands. "You're just grumpy because you're hungry."

That was exactly the kind of thing Jonah's mother would have said. Jonah didn't want to think about what his mom would have said if she'd seen him trying to punch someone. To distract himself, he looked down at his fish.

The fish looked right back at him—or seemed to. Its little beady eye was still attached. So were all its scales and fins.

"Don't go asking for fish sticks instead," Antonio said sneeringly.

Jonah swallowed hard.

"I wouldn't do that," he said.

"I'm sure it's delicious," Katherine said faintly. She poked at her own fish and seemed relieved that it didn't move. She looked as if she'd almost expected it to jump off the leaf, flop over to the water, and swim away.

"But it's not what you're used to, right?" Brendan said. "Sorry. We were trying to stay with our tracers—we didn't know how to cook the fish any other way but how they would cook it." He expertly pulled away some bones and put a chunk of fish into his own mouth. "It really is good."

Again, there was something about the way Brendan talked about staying with his tracer that bothered Jonah. Jonah looked at Katherine, who shook her head warningly. Now, what did that mean?

"At least they got a fire started," Andrea said, taking a fish-on-a-leaf for herself and Dare, before going back to sit near her grandfather. "At least we don't have to eat it raw."

I managed to get a fire started back on Roanoke Island, Jonah wanted to protest. *These guys aren't so great!*

But he wouldn't have known to use the rakelike paddle to catch fish. He wouldn't have known how to build the wooden rack that held the fish over the flames. He wouldn't have known the way to Croatoan Island . . . assuming Brendan and Antonio did.

Jonah took a bite of fish—it really was okay, as long as he didn't think about it having a face. And as long as he spit out the bones. He chewed carefully and tried to think about how to ask all the questions churning in his mind without once again ending up on the brink of a fight with Antonio.

"Are we close to Croatoan Island?" he finally said, trying to sound casual, even unconcerned. He looked around. They seemed to be in some sort of cove, sheltered from the water and wind. A thick woods started several feet behind them. "It feels like we're a million miles away from anything. Like maybe nobody's ever been here before."

Antonio snorted and separated from his tracer enough to say, "Shows what you know. People camp here all the time. You can tell, just by looking." He pointed behind him, toward some vague indentations in the sand. "There was a war party over there, back in the spring." He pointed to the right, to a darker patch of sand. "A smaller group camped there, but they'd had a good day of hunting, so they took up a lot of space."

Jonah couldn't tell if Antonio was making this up or not.

"Okay, but Croatoan—" he persisted.

Katherine caught his eye and shook her head, ever so slightly.

"Would you stop bugging us about Croatoan?" Antonio snapped. "Our tracers aren't thinking about that right now!"

Katherine was shaking her head furiously now.

"Great fish!" she said, in a too-bright, completely fake voice. "Andrea's grandfather seems to like it a lot too."

Perplexed, Jonah followed her gaze. Brendan and Antonio, both completely joined with their tracers again, were taking turns placing small chunks of fish in John White's mouth. John White once again had the eerie closed real eyes/open tracer eyes, but he was eating with gusto. Between bites, the old man's tracer would murmur. Jonah guessed he was just saying thank you, but it was infuriating not to be able to hear.

"Do your tracers know what John White is saying?" Jonah asked, changing his approach.

"Why do you care?" Antonio asked, before Brendan could answer.

All right, then, Jonah thought. *That was supposed to be a safe question.*

Antonio opened his mouth again. This time he didn't separate from his tracer, but spoke as his tracer would have.

"It is to my great and unutterable joy that this old man shall live to see many more dawns and dusks," he said.

Jonah couldn't help snickering.

"Did you just say something about 'unutterable joy'?" he asked.

Antonio separated from his tracer enough to blush.

"Hey! I'm speaking Algonquian here," he said. "You're not supposed to understand!"

Andrea blinked at Jonah in amazement.

"You even understand Algonquian?" she asked.

"Uh, no—I mean—I didn't think I did," Jonah protested. He looked over at Katherine, who had an oddly guilty look on her face. "Wait! Do you think it was because of the translator thingies JB put in our ears before we went to the fifteenth century that last time?"

Antonio whirled on Katherine.

"You girls understand too?" he asked. "You mean, all afternoon when we were talking in Algonquian—"

"*I* didn't understand," Andrea said. "I didn't get any translator thingies in *my* ears."

Katherine sheepishly wrinkled up her nose.

"I didn't want to say anything, because I thought you might be embarrassed," she admitted. "But what you were saying, it was so poetic . . . so lovely . . . I didn't want you to stop." She all but fluttered her eyelashes at Antonio.

Oh, please, Jonah thought. *You think you're going to get out of this one by acting cute? This guy's nasty!*

"Well, then, uh," Antonio stammered.

He hovered, almost completely relaxing back into his tracer's face. But suddenly he jumped up, totally leaving his tracer behind.

"Oh, no!" he hollered. "I am *not* saying that!"

His tracer stood up, too, almost as if he intended to chase Antonio down.

"Stay away from me!" Antonio yelled, darting around the fire to dodge his tracer. "Just stay away from me!" He turned and raced into the woods.

"Wait!" Andrea called after him. She sprang up.

Brendan separated from his tracer to put his hand on Andrea's arm.

"Leave him alone," he said. "He'll be back. There's not really anywhere for him to go."

Antonio's tracer did nothing but take another fish from the fire and settle back into his seat beside John White.

"I can take over feeding my grandfather," Andrea said.

But her grandfather's tracer had fallen asleep, just like the real man. Andrea felt his forehead.

"You think John White is going to be all right, don't you?" Andrea asked Brendan. "I mean, your tracer thinks so?"

"Yes," Brendan said. "He does."

Jonah noticed that Brendan had carefully separated his head from his tracer just as his tracer was starting to speak too. Of course, since it was only the tracer speaking, Jonah couldn't hear what he said. And the translator thingies in his ears *hadn't* given him the ability to read lips.

"Just what was Antonio's tracer going to say, that Antonio didn't want to say?" Jonah asked Brendan. "What did your tracer say back to him?"

"Oh, just lots of lovely poetic stuff," Brendan said, grinning. He slipped back toward rejoining his tracer completely, stopped, groaned, and then stepped entirely away from it. He stood awkwardly beside his tracer for a moment, then flopped down in the sand a few feet away.

"I think I'll be sitting this one out for a while, too," he said.

"What are they talking about?" Andrea asked. "More about my grandfather? Something about what they expect to see at Croatoan?"

"No," Brendan said, grimacing. He looked over at the two tracer boys, who both wore solemn expressions even as they gestured toward the darkening sky, the water, the woods. "Now they're discussing . . . um . . . becoming men."

Katherine giggled.

"You mean, they're talking about puberty?" she asked.

Jonah wouldn't want to talk about that in front of Katherine and Andrea either.

Brendan shrugged.

"Sort of, but not . . . well, not how we think of it," he said. "For them, it's this whole—rite of passage? Is that the right term? They have to prove their bravery and their honor and their loyalty to the tribe. They have to show they're willing to die if they have to, and kill if they have to, and . . ." He stared into the flames for a moment.

"And?" Katherine prompted.

Brendan shook his head.

"And I can't really explain. They think about *everything* differently."

"But they aren't thinking about Croatoan Island?" Jonah asked. "Even though we're going there?"

Brendan's face looked troubled as he shook his head again.

"No, and . . . I don't understand why," he said. He winced. "Not that I understand much of anything right now."

"You're a famous missing kid from history," Katherine said in a soothing voice, as if this was supposed to help. "JB told you in the time cave that you were going to have to go back to the past."

So Brendan had been in the time cave too. Of course he had. He just hadn't been obnoxious like Antonio, so Jonah hadn't remembered him.

"Yeah, but why didn't JB come and get me himself, like he did Andrea?" Brendan asked. "Who's this Second guy? Why didn't he tell me anything? He just shows up in my bedroom one night when I'm listening to my iPod, and the next thing I know, I'm in that canoe, my iPod's nowhere in sight, and Andrea's yelling at me to paddle the same way as my tracer. I didn't even know what a tracer was!"

"Sorry," Andrea said, "I was just worried about keeping my grandfather with *his* tracer."

"Yeah, yeah, I get it," Brendan said, shrugging. "It's not your fault." He looked down at the fish bones in his hand and tossed them into the fire. "You know, I was really hoping to be some great African king who just got lost because he ran off with his girlfriend or something. And it turns out, I'm a not-so-native Native American?" He turned to Jonah and asked plaintively, "Have you ever heard of some famous African American/adopted Indian named One Who Survives Much?" His voice cracked, and he stopped.

"One Who Survives Much is Brendan's Indian name," Katherine explained to Jonah. "Antonio's other name is Walks with Pride."

"Yeah, and we never studied either of those dudes at my school," Brendan said. Jonah could tell how hard he was trying to sound like he didn't really care. "Did you at yours?"

Jonah shook his head.

"No, but—" He looked over at Katherine and Andrea. "Remember what I was saying about Andrea being Virginia Dare? That maybe she's famous for things in the future that we don't know about in the twenty-first century? Time travel could make lots of new people famous in history. People who did really brave things that nobody wrote about, but time travelers witnessed with their own eyes. . . ." Jonah was liking this idea more and more. "Especially when it's someone like you, because, um . . ."

"Because I'm black?" Brendan asked. "Because people in America weren't writing down much of anything that black people did in . . . what year did you say this is?"

"It's 1590," Andrea said. "We know, because that was the year that John White came back to Roanoke."

"Okay. So I'm supposed to be doing something brave that makes me famous in 1590?" Brendan asked. "Or I already did it, and I'm already famous, and this is the year I'm supposed to disappear?"

"Or is this just some random year that Second sent you to, because he's sabotaging you and Antonio the same way he sabotaged Andrea?" Jonah asked bitterly. "You tell us—have you or your tracer already done something that would make you famous hundreds of years in the future?"

Brendan furrowed his brow.

"I—don't know," he admitted.

"How can you not know?" Jonah asked. "If your tracer—" Jonah broke off because Katherine kicked him in the leg just then. "Oof!"

Jonah turned to glare at Katherine, but she was cutting her gaze from Jonah to Brendan to Andrea and back to Jonah. Jonah had seen her do that little trick before: This was just like her, "Let's not talk about this in front of Mom and Dad" code.

Great, Jonah thought. *Another mystery. Why doesn't Katherine want me to talk about this in front of Andrea and Brendan? How is this different from what we were talking about a few minutes ago, when she wasn't kicking me?*

"What song were you listening to on your iPod when Second showed up?" Katherine asked quickly, as if this were urgently important.

"Cold War Kids—'Something Is Not Right with Me.'"

Fits, huh?" Brendan said. "It'd be funny except"—Brendan gestured at the empty water before them, the dark woods behind them,—"look where we are now."

Just then, some sort of animal howled in the woods. Dare stiffened and let out a low growl, deep in his throat. Then he whimpered and backed away.

"Chicken," Jonah muttered. But he had chills traveling down his spine as well. The howl was answered by another howl—was it wolves? Coyotes? Bobcats?

The underbrush rustled at the edge of the woods, a ripple of movement through the shadowy giant leaves.

Something was running toward them.

THIRTY-ONE

Jonah sprang up and darted to the side, holding his arms out protectively in front of Katherine and Andrea. He didn't know what was coming toward them, but it seemed like a good idea to stay on the opposite side of the fire.

The last clump of giant leaves parted, revealing . . .

Antonio.

He was sprinting toward them at top speed, hightailing it across the sand.

"Is something chasing you?" Jonah yelled at him.

Antonio didn't answer. He bent his head down, focused only on running. His feet barely touched ground. When he was still several feet away from the other kids, he suddenly leaped, launching himself upward in an amazing arc.

That's going to hurt when he lands, Jonah thought. From

Jonah's perspective, it looked like Antonio was trying to dive into the sand.

No, Jonah realized. *Into his tracer.*

Antonio collided with his tracer in mid-air. The tracer had just stood up to carry fish bones toward the fire, so for an odd moment Antonio and his tracer looked like a monster with two heads and four arms and four legs sticking out at strange angles—and with skeletal fish attached to two of his hands. Then Antonio's body straightened out, twisted around, and completely melded with his tracer.

"Is something chasing you?" Jonah screamed again at Antonio.

Almost imperceptibly, Antonio separated from his tracer just enough to shake his head. No. Nothing was chasing him.

Still, Jonah gazed off into the woods for a few moments, watching for rustling in the undergrowth. Nothing but wind moved the giant leaves.

"What was that all about?" Katherine demanded.

Another howl rose up from the woods.

"Brother Wolf speaks most eloquent—" Antonio-joined-with-his-tracer began. But then Antonio jerked his mouth away from his tracer's mouth. "Crazy tracer!" he muttered.

Brendan dipped his head into his tracer's head, then pulled back again.

"Our tracers know the wolves won't come near the fire," he explained. "The tracers aren't afraid. But when we're apart from our tracers, we never know . . ."

Apart from his tracer, Antonio was terrified of the wolves, Jonah realized. Even now, separated only slightly from his tracer's head, Antonio had sweat pouring down his face and was panting heavily, gulping in mouthfuls of air. This was a particularly bizarre sight since his chest, still joined with his tracer's, rose and fell with a calm, even pace.

"My tracer's not afraid of anything," Antonio said. He separated from his tracer a little more, to turn toward Brendan. "Is yours?"

Brendan shook his head.

"Not really," he said slowly. "I mean, he knows terrible things could happen—we could starve, we could be attacked, we could die a million different, horrible ways—but if that happened, he knows it would just be the will of—"

"Don't say it!" Antonio ordered. "Don't say 'Great Spirit,' or anything like that, because that's not how it translates—it doesn't translate, and they'll just laugh. . . ." He separated his arm from his tracer's to gesture angrily at Jonah, Katherine, and Andrea.

"Us?" Katherine said, with fake innocence. "Say it in Algonquian, and Jonah and I will understand. We'll help you translate."

"Never mind," Antonio muttered. He turned angrily away. Surreptitiously, he slid his head closer to his tracer's, so that barely anything except his mouth remained separate. "The tracers are cleaning up and getting ready to camp overnight," he said gruffly. "Brendan, you'd better get back together with your guy so we can do this the right way."

"Okay," Brendan said, shrugging.

"Jonah, while they're doing that, could you help me with something over by the canoe?" Katherine asked.

"What?" Jonah said.

"I, uh, think I might have lost a ponytail rubber band," Katherine said. Jonah glanced at his sister.

"It's in your hair," he said.

She shook her head, her ponytail flipping side to side.

"Not *that* rubber band," Katherine said. "A different one. It could mess up time forever if we don't find it."

Even though he'd slept all day, Jonah was still really tired. Just the thought of standing up seemed beyond him, not to mention having to walk over to the canoe and search for some stupid little rubber band that was probably buried under three inches of sand by now. How much could one rubber band matter anyway? Second had tossed whole jars of paint into the wrong time period.

And five kids and a dog.

"Wouldn't Andrea do a better job looking?" Jonah said. "She's a girl. She knows about stuff like ponytail rubber bands."

Katherine shot a glance toward the other kids. Antonio and Brendan, completely joined with their tracers now, were bent over the fire. Andrea, with Dare beside her, was gazing down at her sleeping grandfather. None of them was looking toward Jonah and Katherine.

Katherine jabbed her elbow into Jonah's side.

"Ow!" Jonah cried. "What—"

But Katherine already had a finger poised over her lips. She jerked her head to the right, toward the direction of the canoe. Then she quickly pointed to herself and Jonah, and started thumping the fingers of her right hand against the thumb, like someone operating a puppet.

"Oh, you mean—" Jonah began.

Katherine shook her head firmly and pressed her finger against her lips once more. She grabbed Jonah's arm and began tugging.

"Okay, okay, I'm coming!" Jonah muttered.

They walked several steps, and as soon as they were out of earshot of the others, Katherine burst out, "You are so dense! You would be the world's worst spy! Any of my friends would have caught on about ten *years* ago that I wanted to talk to them alone!"

"Well, duh," Jonah mumbled. "They actually care about ponytail rubber bands."

Katherine rolled her eyes. Then, near the canoe, she dropped to her knees and began sifting sand through her fingers.

Jonah groaned.

"*Please* tell me you didn't really lose a rubber band," he said.

Katherine paused long enough to glare up at him.

"No, but you need to *look* like you're looking for a rubber band," she reminded him. "In case they're watching." She tilted her head, indicating the other three kids.

Reluctantly, Jonah knelt down beside his sister and began scooping up random handfuls of sand. His knees ached. His shoulders ached. His head was still woozy— the day of sleeping in the sun, having nightmares, hadn't come even close to curing him. Worst of all, he was getting chills again, the little prickles of fear all along his spine that warned of some approaching danger.

"What's wrong with you?" he asked Katherine, his

voice coming out rough and accusing. "Don't you trust Antonio and Brendan after all?"

Katherine brushed aside sand, revealing more sand.

"It's not that," she whispered. "It's—I don't trust their tracers."

THIRTY-TWO

Jonah dropped a whole handful of sand, sending up a puff of dust.

"Are you crazy?" he asked. "Did you get sunstroke this afternoon? What do you mean, you don't trust the tracers? They're tracers! They're not really there! They don't know we're here! They don't care if we're looking for a rubber band or not. To them, we don't even exist!"

The dust floated up to his mouth and nose, making him cough. While he was coughing, he thought of a new argument.

"The way I see it, the tracers might be the only ones we *can* trust!" he said. "We know they're doing what they're supposed to be doing because, duh, they're tracers! They have to be accurate! I like Andrea—"

"You like her too much," Katherine said.

Jonah ignored this.

"—but she doesn't care what happens to time," he continued. "Brendan *seems* okay, but how can we know for sure that he and Antonio aren't working for Second?"

"You didn't see them the first hour or so," Katherine said. "They were completely clueless and scared out of their wits. They didn't know anything."

"Yeah, but as soon as they joined with their tracers, they should have known . . ." The next word Jonah had intended to say was *everything*. But he stopped. He remembered Brendan saying he didn't know if his tracer had done anything great; he didn't know what the tracer thought about Croatoan Island. He didn't even know what year it was. And Antonio—maybe he wasn't just being a jerk when he'd refused to talk about the distance to Croatoan because, "Our tracers aren't thinking about that right now!"

"You think . . . ," Jonah began. He had to try again to get the words out. "You think the tracers are keeping secrets?"

Katherine nodded, her eyes huge and frightened. Now that they were away from the other kids, Jonah could see how scared she really was—and how fake her brave face and cheerful chatter had been before.

"Didn't Chip and Alex know everything their tracers knew, back in the fifteenth century?" Jonah interrupted. "Didn't they know everything right away, from the first moment they joined with their tracers?"

"I *think* so," Katherine said. "That's how they always acted. Whatever we asked them, they had answers. Unless it was something their tracers didn't know either."

"But maybe we only asked them questions about things they'd been thinking about anyway," Jonah said.

"Yeah," Katherine agreed. "We never tested them with anything like, 'What color shirt was your tracer wearing a week ago Monday?'"

"*I* couldn't answer that," Jonah said. "With or without a tracer."

"Oh, right," Katherine said. But she didn't launch into any mocking rant about how he was just a stupid boy, and she could remember every outfit she'd worn since starting sixth grade.

"Do you think the *tracers* are working for Second?" Jonah asked.

Katherine frowned, considering this.

"I don't think they could," she said. "It's like you said, they're tracers. They can't change." She hesitated. "Maybe I shouldn't have said I don't trust them. Maybe that's not the right way to put it. How could any of this be the tracers' fault? They're just what we see, and the problem's deeper than that. The whole setup is messed up."

"Because of Second," Jonah growled. "He's behind this."

Katherine nodded.

"He must have done something to keep Brendan and Antonio from melding with their tracers right," Katherine said.

Jonah struggled to get his aching brain to follow this thought. It seemed every bit as impossible as finding a rubber band buried on a vast beach. *Brendan said Second pulled him straight out of time from his room back home— Second didn't take him to a time cave or time hollow first,* Jonah remembered. *Could that be the problem?* Jonah didn't know why this would matter. The time hollows had always seemed like conveniences, not essentials. Why couldn't Brendan and Antonio go straight from the twenty-first century to . . .

Jonah's head throbbed, and he saw what he had been missing.

"I bet the problem was the way Brendan and Antonio came back," Jonah said slowly. "Antonio landing . . . on top of me."

This was still hard to talk about. It was like the moment back home when Jonah had first seen a time traveler seem to vanish into thin air, changing dimensions. Jonah's brain had tried so hard to recast the memory, to turn it into something else—something believable.

Now it felt like Jonah's brain was trying very hard to get him to forget completely. The memory already seemed distant and hazy, like something from a dream.

Oh, no, Jonah thought. *I am not letting go.*

"You know, when Antonio . . . arrived . . . that felt wrong," Jonah said. "I bet Second did it that way on purpose."

Katherine nodded, still deadly serious.

"I was looking right at you," she said. "And, for a moment, it was like there were three people in the exact same spot—you, Antonio, and the tracer."

Jonah felt chills again.

"That's how it felt to me, too," he admitted. He could bear thinking about that moment only in a roundabout way, as if he had to sneak up on the memory to catch it.

Katherine evidently wasn't so limited.

"And then for a split second after that, you and the tracer both disappeared," Katherine said, her voice low and troubled. "Maybe I blinked. Maybe I just missed seeing you fall out of the canoe. But where did the tracer go? Before, anytime we saw someone joined with his tracer— back in the fifteenth century, with Chip or Alex—it was always the tracer we could see, more than Chip or Alex. But with Antonio and his tracer, it was like the tracer blended into Antonio, not the other way around. I could see Antonio's T-shirt better than his tracer's back."

Jonah shook his head, trying to make sense of Katherine's words.

"Not just then," Katherine said. "Ever since he got here, anytime he's not thinking with his tracer's brain, he's terrified. It was like he couldn't even hear half the things Andrea and I told him in the canoe. That's why he keeps saying all those mean things, trying to make it so we don't see how scared he is."

"Oh, come on, Katherine," Jonah scoffed. "Have you been listening to too many of those bullying assemblies at school? That's the kind of thing a guidance counselor would say!"

"That doesn't mean I'm wrong, does it?" Katherine challenged.

Jonah was about to make a snappy comeback or—to his surprise—maybe to grudgingly agree. But suddenly, across the beach, he heard Andrea scream.

"For real? Are you serious?" she yelled at the top of her lungs.

Jonah was already running toward her when he realized: No matter how loudly she was screaming, she didn't sound upset.

She sounded delighted.

"But that didn't last," he said. "The tracers look normal now." He glanced back toward the others clustered around the fire. Antonio and Brendan, still joined with their tracers, were very clearly wearing nothing but loincloths. "Well, normal for 1590s Native Americans." He cleared his throat, trying to get rid of the last of the dust. "When did Antonio and his tracer start looking right again? And do you think Brendan and his tracer were messed up at first too?"

"I don't know," Katherine said. "I started looking around for you, and when I glanced back at Antonio and his tracer, everything was like . . ." she gestured toward the two boys, moving completely in concert with their tracers.

"You mean Antonio and his tracer were following all the rules of tracerdom, as we know them," Jonah said, back to joking a little bit, because he couldn't stand being so deadly serious all the time. "Except for Antonio—and Brendan—not knowing everything their tracers know, and *maybe* that's not that different from the last time. Maybe we just didn't notice it before. Nobody broke any other tracer rules after that, did they?"

Katherine bit her lip.

"I know you were asleep all afternoon, but . . . haven't you been paying attention since then?" she asked. "Haven't you noticed how easy it is for Antonio and Brendan to move in and out of their tracers?"

Jonah gaped at his sister, his brain finally catching up.

"*That's* why kept you shaking your head at me!" he said. "You didn't want me to notice. . . ."

"No, I didn't want you to say anything in front of the others," Katherine said. "Andrea's already sick with worry about her grandfather, and Brendan and Antonio are plenty freaked out as it is."

"So you want to protect them, but it's okay to worry me?" Jonah said jokingly.

"Yeah. Because . . . ," Katherine took a deep breath, and for a moment Jonah was afraid that she was going to say something sappy like, *Because you're my big brother,* or *Because we're in this together.* Or even, *Because I trust you most of all.* Jonah wasn't sure he'd be able to take it if she did that. Instead, she just frowned and said, "You know how people are supposed to behave with their tracers. You've seen it before. You already know something's wrong with John White and his tracer, even though that might just be because of his head injury."

"Antonio and Brendan don't have head injuries," Jonah said.

"Right," Katherine said. "So isn't it weird that they have to *try* to stay with their tracers? With Chip and Alex

it practically took nuclear warfare to keep them *away.*"

"Yeah," Jonah agreed. He almost added, *Or true love.* But this was not the right time to tease Katherine about that.

Katherine hit the palm of her hand against the sand. They'd both given up on pretending to look for a rubber band.

"I hate this," she said. "We know Second did something wrong again, and we know everything's messed up, but it's like we're boxed in—we don't know what we can do about it."

Another trap, Jonah thought. *Or is it just another trick?*

He looked back at the other kids: Andrea hovering near her grandfather, Brendan banking the fire, and Antonio . . . well, it looked like Antonio was posing, showing off his six-packs abs in front of Andrea. He was talking to her, too, probably saying, *Look at me. Aren't I hot?* Jonah clenched his fists.

"Are you *sure* it wouldn't help to punch Antonio?" he asked.

"Would you stop that?" Katherine said. She shoved at Jonah's fists, knocking them uselessly against the sand. "None of this is Antonio's fault. Can't you tell he's scared out of his mind?"

"Well, yeah, when he heard the wolves." Jonah snickered. "Did you see how fast he was running?"

THIRTY-THREE

Jonah skidded to a stop in the sand right by Andrea and Brendan and Antonio. Katherine sprinted up behind him. By then, Andrea was grabbing Antonio in a tight hug.

"Thank you!" she cried. "Thank you!"

She hugged him again before letting go.

Antonio took a step back, just enough to blur away at the edges of his tracer. He barely missed stepping on Dare.

"What did I do?" Antonio asked, stunned.

"You told me the right *year*," Andrea said, her face glowing. "The year!" She looked over at Jonah and Katherine, and her grin grew bigger. "We were wrong, what we thought, and what I told Brendan, and he didn't know any different. But Antonio, my new best friend Antonio did. . . ." She threw her arms around him once more, before jumping back, too excited to stand still. "It's not 1590, after all!"

"Uh, really?" Jonah said blankly. "And that's a good thing because . . . ?"

Andrea laughed gleefully.

"You don't get it, do you?" she said. "Come on, Jonah, you were the one who figured this out before! When you were wrong!"

Jonah could feel his expression getting blanker. Still, Andrea only laughed more giddily.

"Virginia Dare was born in 1587," she said. "She—I—wasn't even a month old when my grandfather went back to England for supplies. He came back and found his colony deserted three years later, in 1590. So, you guys thought, John White, deserted island—it must be 1590. Doomed trip for him, no chance for us."

Jonah was sure he hadn't made everything sound so simple-minded.

"But," Andrea said. She held up one finger for dramatic effect. "But! We don't know about anything John White did after 1593. He wrote a letter describing his ill-fated 1590 voyage, and it was published in a book by a guy whose name I can't remember. And for all anybody knows, John White might as well have died the day after he mailed that letter. But he didn't! He didn't!"

"You know that?" Katherine asked cautiously. "How can you be so sure?"

"Because!" Andrea crowed. "Antonio here remembers when he—er, his tracer—"

"It was both of us, really," Antonio said. "Together. Before Gary and Hodge kidnapped me and made it so there was a separate tracer. When I was just a Spanish kid about to be adopted by Indians."

"Okay, okay," Andrea said impatiently. "What matters is that Antonio remembers what *year* he sailed from Spain, and how long he's been in North America. Antonio?"

Antonio flashed her a puzzled look.

"I still don't get why this is such a big deal. But . . . it was 1597," he said. "Three years ago."

"So don't you see? That means it's 1600 now!" Andrea exclaimed. "A new century! A completely different trip! And I'm thirteen years old!"

Andrea might as well have said, *Ta-da!* She seemed that thrilled with her revelation.

Everyone else just looked at her. Even Dare tilted his head quizzically.

"So?" Jonah finally said. "What's the big deal about being thirteen?"

"Are you Jewish?" Katherine asked. "That whole bar mitzvah—er, bat mitzvah thing—"

"No! That's not it!" Now Andrea sounded exasperated that the others didn't understand. "I mean, I'm the right age for the year! I'm the age my grandfather would expect for his granddaughter! So—it wouldn't be weird for him to see me and know who I am!"

She beamed at them, expecting everyone else to catch on. Jonah's brain was slowly cranking out, *Oh. Then that means* . . . Katherine had her mouth open, but didn't seem to have decided yet what she wanted to say. Antonio and Brendan were watching Katherine as if they expected her to tell them what to think.

Only Dare responded quickly. He began barking happily and jumping up against Andrea's legs, practically dancing around her.

"Don't you see?" Andrea said, reaching down to hug Dare, before letting him go to dance some more. "Don't you think this means that . . . that everything was meant to be? My grandfather is supposed to find me, I don't have to go back to being a toddler—everything's going to work out!"

The other kids were still squinting and stunned and trying to understand.

"Then . . . you think history's completely wrong?" Brendan said slowly. "What you and Katherine were telling us in the canoe—you said John White never found his family or anyone else from Roanoke."

"The last time. In 1590," Andrea said. "He never found anyone in 1590. But it's 1600 now, and John White came back. And this time—he doesn't *have* to fail." She snorted. "The history we told you wasn't *wrong*. Just . . . incomplete."

"You mean, nobody in history kept track of what happened to John White in 1600," Jonah said numbly. "Nobody wrote anything down so nobody knows. . . ."

Something about this—history having secrets, history hiding its holes—really bothered him. But he didn't have time to think about it because Andrea was already flitting on to another point.

"Don't you think it's because he found his family and was happy and didn't bother to write home?" Andrea asked. She giggled. "It's not like there was postal service back to England!"

She pointed out toward the water glowing with the last rays of the sinking sun. The water seemed boundless; it was hard to imagine other lands off in the distance.

"This would explain why things didn't match up on Roanoke Island," Katherine said thoughtfully. "Why John White was alone instead of with other sailors, and why he didn't see the word *Croatoan* and get driven away in a storm."

"So maybe Second didn't sabotage time that badly,"

Andrea said. "Really, the only important thing that got messed up with my grandfather on Roanoke Island was that the wrong kids saved him from drowning."

"And he got a head injury," Antonio said. Jonah was glad it was Antonio who pointed that out, because Andrea glared at him.

"Yeah, but . . . ," Andrea seemed to be trying very hard to hold on to her excitement. She glanced down, and her whole expression changed. "I bet his head injury really isn't that bad! Now that Antonio and Brendan are here for real—and he can see them, just like his tracer can—I bet the reason he's unconscious is just because of us! Because his mind can't deal with us wandering around in twenty-first-century clothes!"

She jumped up and began rummaging through her grandfather's treasure chest. Jonah knew exactly what she was looking for: the dresses. She yanked out one that was pale yellow with a pattern of tiny roses.

"Andrea, no," Katherine said sharply. "That can't be the answer. People saw Jonah and me in modern clothing back in the fifteenth century, and that didn't make anyone half-unconscious!"

"Just let me try!" Andrea said stubbornly.

She jerked the dress down over her shoulders, completely covering her T-shirt and shorts. The hem dragged down in the sand as she rushed to her grandfather's side. He was lying practically flat on his back, his tracer eyes staring toward the darkening sky. His real eyes were still closed.

Andrea knelt beside him. Something about the dress made her move differently, or she was making a conscious effort to act like a girl from 1600.

"Grandfather?" she murmured. "I have just learned of your arrival and your rescue by these fine, uh, natives. They sent word to me to come right away, and they gave me the dress you brought. So, please, please wake up. . . ."

In her own way, Andrea sounded as ridiculous as Jonah had when he was doing his *Pirates of the Caribbean* imitation back on Roanoke Island. But she was looking so hopefully at her grandfather.

He stirred, swaying side to side. Andrea clutched his hand.

"Grandfather?" she said.

John White opened his mouth.

"Treachery!" he cried out. "Betrayal! Deceit!"

Andrea collapsed in despair at his side, hiding her face in the skirt.

"Andrea!" Jonah called out. "He's not talking about you! His eyes are still closed! It's just him and his tracer thinking the same thing—it was *random*."

"The savages betrayed us, and we betrayed them," John White continued. "And I've never met a sea captain I could trust. . . ."

Jonah patted Andrea on the back.

"See—this isn't about you!" Jonah said. "It's just—you need to be with your tracer! We'll find it! I promise!"

"Go away," Andrea mumbled. "Leave me alone."

Brendan crouched beside her, leaving his tracer behind.

"Andrea?" he said. "I don't know anything about your tracer, and I don't know why my tracer hasn't been thinking about Croatoan Island. But I can tell you—Antonio and me, our tracers—we're honorable tribesmen . . . er, people. If our tracers told John White we'll take him to Croatoan Island, then that's where we're going. And that's probably where your tracer is, right?"

"That's what . . . we think," Andrea said, sniffing a little.

"Jonah?" Katherine said, in a too-loud voice. "Don't you think we should get back to looking for that rubber band?"

"Uh, right," Jonah said.

They walked together back toward the canoe.

"Are you thinking what I'm thinking?" Katherine asked.

"I don't know," Jonah said. "What are you thinking?"

This could have been part of a comedy routine, but Katherine didn't have the slightest trace of humor in her voice. And Jonah didn't feel anything like laughing.

"Maybe the people who wrote history didn't know anything about John White's trip in 1600," Katherine said. "But time travelers would."

"JB knew," Jonah said grimly.

"And . . . even before Second got involved . . . JB wouldn't have sent us back with Andrea if she was just supposed to have a happy little family reunion," Katherine said. "There's still something we'll have to rescue her from."

"Well, yeah," Jonah said. "And then who's going to rescue us from Second?"

THIRTY-FOUR

Jonah woke the next morning to the smell of cooking fish. He groaned and rolled over.

Andrea was sitting in the sand right beside him, leafing through one of John White's sketchbooks. She must have been waiting for him to wake up, because she looked up immediately.

"I was mean to you yesterday," she said. "I'm sorry."

"It's okay," Jonah said.

"No," Andrea shook her head, her hair whipping side to side. "It's not. I— Do you ever feel like you just have to really, really care about something—or someone—or else you might as well be dead?" She didn't give Jonah much of a chance to answer. Which was good, because Jonah didn't know what to say.

Andrea stared down at the sketchbook and kept talking.

"Ever since my parents died, I just latch on to things . . . and I forget . . . other people have feelings too."

Was there any way Jonah could say something like, *Oh, I do have feelings—I have feelings for you?* Without having it sound completely cheesy?

Jonah decided that was impossible.

"It's okay," he said again. "It's just . . . why do you care so much about your grandfather? You don't even know him!"

"I feel like I do," Andrea said quietly. "What I read about him, what he wrote about trying to get back to his family, it's kind of how I feel about . . . you know." She didn't have to say, *my parents.* "And just looking at the pictures he drew—they're so real."

She tilted the sketchbook toward Jonah. He sat up so he could get a better look at the picture she was gazing at. It showed another Native American village, but from a different perspective than the other drawing Jonah had seen. It was as if John White had stood in the village square and looked all around: at dogs sleeping in the sunlight, at little boys guarding the cornfield, at women braiding their daughters' hair.

"He really was a good artist," Jonah said, though he didn't really know anything about art. "That picture makes you feel like you're right there, and all those people are still alive."

And, Jonah realized, they might be.

"I'm telling myself this is what Croatoan Island is going to be like," Andrea said. "Except there's a big group of extra people who came from England right over here"— she pointed to the empty section of paper, off to the side—"who fit right in. And a grandfather/governor/artist who's totally awake and ready to draw them all. . . ."

"Andrea," Jonah began.

"Just let me have some hope, okay?" Andrea said.

They set off as soon as they'd cleaned up from their all-fish breakfast. It turned out that Katherine and Andrea had figured out a rhythm to hanging out in the canoe all day. No matter what, everyone had to keep out of the way of Brendan and Antonio, who had to stay with their tracers to paddle, so the real canoe and the tracer canoe stayed precisely together as one—all so John White wouldn't get separated from *his* tracer. But sometimes Brendan and Antonio's tracers would take breaks from paddling, and then the two boys could come out of the tracers enough to talk.

Jonah decided it was a good time to test Brendan's and Antonio's memories, or at least find out a little more information. He'd missed a lot when he was sleeping.

"Okay," he said, when the two boys were taking their first break, as the canoe drifted in the gentle current. "I know you said your tracers aren't letting you know any-thing about Croatoan Island—"

"They're just not thinking about it," Brendan corrected lazily, stretching in the back of the canoe. "That's all."

"Oh, yeah, that's right," Jonah said. "But do they know anything about what happened to the Roanoke Colony? I mean, they were right there!"

"Antonio and I have heard rumors in our tribe," Brendan said, "that there might be a boy with yellow hair living two tribes away. That he might be one of the people-who-look-like-ghosts who came across the waters to Roanoke, many moons ago."

"'Many moons ago?'" Antonio snorted. "Don't talk like that around them. They'll laugh."

"No we won't," Andrea said softly.

Antonio glowered, but didn't say anything else.

"So that means you weren't on Roanoke Island just waiting for Andrea's grandfather to show up," Jonah said, feeling disappointed.

"No, but"—Brendan shot a glance at Antonio, who was reclining at the front of the canoe—"we were there kind of waiting for white men."

"What?" Jonah said. In his surprise, he jolted back against John White's leg. The old man moaned in his sleep. Dare, who was sleeping beside him, opened one eye, seemed to decide that Jonah wasn't a threat, and went back to snoring.

"White men came to Roanoke Island in the waning months of summer—er, August, I guess—every year for several years," Brendan said. "Several times they killed Indians and burned their villages nearby. Even when they only visited local tribes, *acting* like they were friendly, they left behind, um—"

"Do not say, *invisible evil spirits!*" Antonio commanded. "Or *invisible bullets!* That's not what it was!"

"Really, we're not going to laugh, no matter what," Katherine said.

Antonio ignored her.

"We were on Roanoke Island as sentries, all right?" Antonio finished for Brendan. "Our tribe sends someone every August. We were watching, so we could alert our tribe if anyone came. They trusted us!"

"But you saved his life," Jonah said, touching John White's leg. "Why did you do that if you thought his people were dangerous?"

"It's our tribe's code," Brendan said. "He was alone and in trouble, so we saved him. Just like the tribe saved us."

"Brendan was a slave when the tribe took him in," Katherine said in a hushed voice.

"So you were right, thinking that he was a runaway," Jonah said.

"Oh, no," Brendan said, and for the first time, he sounded even more bitter and angry than Antonio. "I was just a baby, on a ship carrying slaves. Sir Francis Drake— remember him from Social Studies class? He stopped by Roanoke Island when there were just some English soldiers there, before they sent the colonists. The soldiers were starving—"

"And the Indians were getting sick of them stealing their food—" Antonio interrupted.

"So Sir Francis Drake became the big hero," Brendan said mockingly. "He dumped out hundreds of slaves to make room to take the soldiers home to England."

Jonah looked at Katherine.

"Is this something else I missed hearing about in fifth-grade Social Studies?" he asked.

"Wasn't mentioned," Katherine said, biting off her words.

"But it's true!" Brendan said. "Hundreds of slaves, stolen from a Spanish colony, used to being slaves, yes, but also used to being fed—suddenly they're dumped out on an empty island with no food, no boats to use to get to the mainland. . . . If our tribe hadn't taken us in, everyone would have died."

"Your tribe took in hundreds of people?" Jonah asked. He wondered why *that* wasn't something he'd studied at school. These people sounded like saints.

"No. A lot of the slaves died before the tribe found them," Brendan said, "including my parents."

Now he was glowering every bit as angrily as Antonio. Jonah wanted to say, *Look, I'm not related to Sir Francis Drake! I didn't have anything to do with this!*

Except maybe he did. He didn't have any idea who he was related to or what time period he'd originally lived in.

"Sir Francis Drake didn't even see the slaves as people," Brendan said bitterly.

"It's not just slaves who are treated like that," Antonio said. "Did Katherine or Andrea tell you *my* story?" he asked Jonah.

Jonah shook his head.

"I was a cabin boy on a Spanish ship," Antonio said. "Not such a bad life—there are worse places for orphans to live—as long as you're good at dodging fists. So then, a couple years ago, the captain decided he might make more money trading with tribes way north of Saint Augustine. Only problem was, none of those tribes spoke Spanish. No one on the ship spoke the Indians' languages. So—leave a little kid behind, come back a year or two later—you, captain, have got yourself a translator." Antonio seemed to be straining harder and harder to sound as if he didn't care. "If the kid's still alive."

"You mean, they dropped you off alone?" Jonah asked. "Someplace you didn't know anyone, where you didn't even know the language, when you were . . . how old?" He squinted at Antonio. The boy and his tracer were almost exactly the same size, which made the tracer about thirteen too. And Antonio had said before that he'd come to America three years ago. That meant he'd been . . . "Only ten?" Jonah asked.

"Yeah. But, hey, I survived," Antonio said, and now there was pride in his voice. "Next year, the ship came back and, baby, I hid. I knew a good thing when I had it. I knew where people treated me like a human being."

The lower half of his body was reaching for his paddle again.

"Back to work," Antonio said, though he didn't sound sorry about it. He slid his head back, rejoining his tracer completely. Then he froze.

"Oh, no," he moaned.

At the back of the canoe, Brendan gasped.

"What?" Jonah asked.

"So *that's* why our tracers didn't want to think about Croatoan Island," Antonio muttered.

"You know now?" Katherine asked excitedly.

But Antonio didn't look excited. He—and his tracer— were just sitting there, stunned, staring off into the distance.

"The evil spirits," Antonio whispered. "The invisible bullets."

"Germs," Brendan corrected.

"You're talking about—what? Bacteria? Some kind of virus?" Jonah asked, looking from one boy to the other. He couldn't understand why they both looked so horrified. "That doesn't sound so terrible."

Then Antonio pointed.

And Jonah saw the skulls.

THIRTY-FIVE

They were strewn about on the shore of a nearby island. It looked as if so many deaths had occurred there that nobody had been left to pick up the bodies.

"Our tracers didn't know we'd drifted so close to Croatoan while we were talking," Brendan whispered. "And they were trying so hard not to think about it. . . . They blocked it from their minds."

"Because it's too awful," Antonio agreed.

"Did Second do this?" Jonah asked, his outrage building. "This massacre—"

"No, no," Brendan began.

Katherine let out a huge gasp of air, as if she'd been holding her breath.

"They're not human," she said. "I thought they were human!"

Jonah blinked. He could see why Katherine had

thought that. He had almost thought it himself. But he didn't feel any relief as his eyes assured him that there were just animal skeletons before him—skulls and rib cages that must belong to deer, foxes, wolves, beavers . . . not humans. The bones were so numerous that they seemed to whisper, *Death, death, everyone died. . . .*

"This is so wrong," Brendan said in a tight voice. "An abomination."

"A desecration," Antonio said.

Jonah thought that they'd slipped into Algonquian to say that, as if the English words weren't quite strong enough.

"I don't understand," Katherine said. "You've killed animals. I mean—your tracers did. And not just fish. We saw the tracers back on Roanoke shooting that deer. They . . . slaughtered it."

"After asking the deer's permission," Brendan said.

"Stop trying to explain," Antonio said harshly. "They're not going to understand!"

"No—I have to explain," Brendan said. He looked directly at Katherine. "Our tribe sees itself in balance with nature. When we take a life, we do it with respect. We treat the animal with respect, even in death." He made a rueful face. "No matter how it might have looked to you, we're not savages."

"The white men are the savages!" Antonio said. "The way they kill—without respect—"

"Antonio, you're white too!" Jonah said, because he couldn't take any more of this.

"I gave that up," Antonio said, his face utterly serious. "I am a tribesman now."

And then Jonah couldn't argue with that. He could tell that Antonio wasn't talking about skin color, but a mind-set, a way of seeing the world.

"So Europeans did this?" Katherine asked in a puzzled voice. She waved her hand toward the skeletons lining the shore. "Was it the English? The Spanish? Or—"

"Yes and no," Brendan said.

"It was because of my people," Andrea said in a haunted voice. "The Roanoke colonists. We brought death when we came here. Plagues. I read all about the diseases, but I didn't understand. . . ."

Jonah had been so focused on the scene before him that he'd almost forgotten about Andrea. She'd been sitting there so silently. Even now she looked like a statue, her face gone pale beneath the sunburn, her eyes glittering with pain. Jonah knew nothing about art, and didn't often think about it, but he could imagine someone making a sculpture of Andrea right now.

The title of the sculpture would be *Devastated*.

"You mean, the Roanoke colonists brought some plague, some disease, that killed all these animals?" Katherine asked, still sounding baffled.

"No, their diseases killed people," Brendan said. "Lots and lots of people. In some villages, so many people died that the survivors just fled, leaving the bodies where they fell."

"And to us, to tribesmen—that's a terrible sin," Antonio said. "Sacrilege."

"Our tracers know to avoid those villages," Brendan said. "They believe the evil spirits linger."

Jonah noticed that Antonio didn't correct Brendan this time about calling the germs *evil spirits*.

"But here, at Croatoan, this is the worst place," Brendan said. "As people were dying, they put out animal carcasses on the shore, to warn travelers away, to warn of the evil. Because this is evil too, treating dead animals this way."

He gestured at the skeletons, the rows and rows of the dead.

"And all the people died, so their bones are still here too?" Katherine asked, horrified.

Brendan shrugged helplessly.

"That's what our tracers think," he said.

"Don't show my grandfather this," Andrea burst out.

"Please, I'm begging you, don't let your tracers show my grandfather what happened here."

Jonah had stopped thinking about the tracers. It had completely slipped his mind why they'd come here—because John White had asked Walks with Pride and One Who Survives Much to take him to Croatoan Island. Because John White thought he would find his family and friends there.

Jonah forced himself to look past the skeletons littering the shore. Just beyond the shoreline, rows of native huts were falling in on themselves, clearly abandoned. They looked so much worse than the Indian village back at Roanoke. So much sadder.

This would not be the scene of the happy family reunion that John White—and Andrea—were longing for.

"Andrea," Brendan said apologetically. "We can't control our tracers. We don't know how to stop them."

Andrea bent down and hugged John White's shoulders.

"Oh, Grandfather, I'm so glad you're not conscious for real!" she said. "I'm so glad you're going to miss this!"

For the moment, he was completely joined with his tracer, the tracer's eyes closed just as tightly as the real man's.

"Didn't the tracer boys tell John White what he'd see here?" Katherine asked. "Didn't they warn him?"

Antonio shook his head.

"They tried, but—they're not communicating very well," he said. "Our tracers can't speak English, and John White doesn't know much Algonquian."

Jonah realized that the whole time Antonio and Brendan had been with their tracers, he really hadn't heard them say much back and forth with John White.

"But back on Roanoke, all the tracers seemed to be talking to each other," Jonah said. "Making sense. When John White asked the tracer boys to get his treasure chest . . . When he asked to come to Croatoan . . ."

Jonah remembered the slow, deliberate way the tracer boys had nodded. Had they said something before or after that, trying to explain? Jonah hadn't really been paying attention, because he and Katherine and Andrea had gotten so excited about going to Croatoan Island themselves.

"Everything John White said, he said in both Algonquian and English," Brendan explained.

"Oh! That's why I could understand!" Andrea said, as if this was something she'd been wondering about.

"Even though his Algonquian's like baby talk, our tracers can follow some of it," Antonio said. "But no matter how much they tried to use easy words, he couldn't understand much of what they said. So . . . they thought they'd just have to show him."

Jonah was kind of hoping they'd just keep talking about translations or some other boring, useless topics. But Brendan and Antonio's tracers had stopped staring silently at the skeletons on Croatoan Island. The two tracer boys set their jaws and clenched their teeth—tiny, almost imperceptible signs that they were bracing themselves for an unpleasant task—and got into position to paddle toward the Croatoan shore.

Brendan and Antonio themselves didn't move.

"We don't have to stay with our tracers for this," Brendan said softly. "They're not planning to be on Croatoan long. We can just stay in the canoe and wait for them."

Everyone turned to Andrea, as if they all silently agreed that she deserved to make this decision.

"No, no," she said in a strangled voice. "We should . . . I should see this. The rest of you can wait with the canoe, but I have to go. . . ."

Without another word, Antonio spun around. With a few deft movements, he'd caught up with his tracer. In the back of the canoe, Jonah could hear Brendan's paddle dipping quietly into the water.

They reached the shore too quickly, Antonio and Brendan tying the canoe to a tree too efficiently.

I'm not ready to see this, Jonah thought.

"John White wouldn't be able to tell any difference between Croatoan skeletons and English skeletons, would he?" Andrea asked faintly.

"I don't . . . think so," Katherine said, with none of her usual confidence.

"I just wouldn't want him to look at the skeletons and be able to know, *This was my daughter, this was my son-in-law, this was . . . ,*" Andrea's voice shook, but she made herself finish, "*. . . this was my granddaughter.*"

"Andrea, your skeleton won't be here," Jonah said. "Remember? You feel good in this time period, so you're still alive; Virginia Dare is still alive. Your tracer's still out there somewhere."

It was hard thinking ahead, past this island of death. But they were still going to have to look for Andrea's tracer . . . somewhere.

Even if they were out of clues.

Andrea winced.

"I'm not . . . exactly . . . feeling so good right now," she said, and made a brave attempt at a smile.

Andrea stepped out of the canoe right behind Brendan and Antonio. Dare jumped out beside her and rubbed against her leg, whimpering, as if he understood that she was facing something awful.

Meanwhile, Antonio bent over and started to pick up John White. Then he stepped back, so it was only his tracer picking up the tracer of John White.

"We'll leave the real man safe and asleep in the canoe," he mumbled, and Jonah felt a little guilty for having thought that Antonio was nothing but a jerk.

Antonio rejoined his tracer as soon as the tracer straightened up. Jonah and Katherine climbed out of the canoe too.

"Really, you don't all have to see this," Andrea said. "It could just be me and the tracers."

"We're all in this together," Katherine said, and for once Jonah agreed with his sister wholeheartedly. He even forgot to be annoyed that he hadn't thought to say that himself.

Antonio carried John White's tracer very gingerly past the animal bones littering the shoreline. The others all stayed close by, picking their way around the bones. Antonio stepped so carefully—and gracefully—that John White's tracer stayed asleep, snoring gently. *No,* Jonah corrected himself. *Antonio can't affect the tracer. Antonio couldn't wake him up if he tried!* But Antonio was moving completely in concert with his own tracer, so it looked like the boy really was interacting with the old man's tracer. Once they reached the row of collapsing huts, Antonio crouched down with the tracer man, seeming to shake him awake and place him in a seated position, facing away from the bones on the shore.

"He's being so kind," Andrea marveled. "He's trying to keep John White from seeing the worst of it!"

No, Jonah wanted to correct Andrea, too. *It's Antonio's tracer being kind.* But right now Antonio and his tracer were one, so it was impossible to think of them separately.

And then Jonah forgot everything else, watching the drama before him. Brendan, also completely joined with his tracer, crouched on the other side of John White's tracer.

"This Croatoan Island," Brendan said softly, speaking in his tracer's voice. Jonah could tell how hard he was trying to speak slowly and simply for the sake of John White's limited Algonquian skills. "Understand? Everyone gone. Maybe all dead. Maybe just left."

"Dead?" John White's tracer repeated numbly. His expression was so stark that, for once, Jonah thought he could read lips accurately. "Dead means . . ."

John White's tracer struggled to stand up. For a moment it looked like Antonio was going to try to hold him back, but then Brendan said, with his tracer, "He'll want to see for himself. He won't believe us otherwise."

Antonio began helping the old man's tracer up. He kept his arm around the tracer's shoulder. Brendan braced the tracer from the other side, and the two boys led him to the nearest hut.

Jonah couldn't help admiring the way they guided John White's tracer, keeping him from seeing the animal skeletons. But what good did that do if the tracer was just going to see human skeletons in the hut?

Nervously, Jonah crept up behind Antonio and Brendan and the tracer, trying to see past them into the hut.

"Oh!" Brendan exclaimed, whirling around, away from his tracer. "There aren't any skeletons here!"

Jonah peeked in—it was just an empty hut.

The next hut was empty, too, as was the third and the fourth. . . . Then they came to a different kind of a building, its walls lined with a sort of wooden scaffolding. Elongated lumps wrapped in animal skins lay on each level of the scaffolding—could the lumps be skeletons?

John White's tracer nodded, as if he understood. But he didn't look upset. He opened his mouth and spoke. Jonah wished so badly that he could hear what the tracer was saying. But of course, separated from the real John White, the tracer was completely silent.

"Oh, this is weird—he's speaking English right now, and my tracer doesn't understand. But I can understand what my tracer is hearing," Brendan said. "John White is saying he knows this is the Croatoans' temple, where the bodies of their important leaders are kept after death. He saw this in other villages, on his previous trips to America. He's saying it's like what they do in England, putting their honored dead in crypts in cathedrals."

Jonah had actually been in one of those crypts, back in the 1400s, on his last trip through time. This village's temple didn't seem any creepier than that.

They stepped out of the temple, Jonah and Katherine and Andrea scurrying ahead so they didn't keep Antonio and Brendan from staying with their tracers. The two boys walked John White's tracer toward an open field.

"This is the burial ground for all the other dead," Antonio said, speaking with his tracer.

John White spoke, and Brendan translated: "He's asking us, 'Many, many generations?'"

"No," Antonio said. "Many died all at once."

Jonah could tell that John White's tracer understood, because sorrow crept over his face.

"But some survived," Antonio said. "Some survived to bury their dead before they left."

John White's tracer spoke again, and Jonah could guess at his meaning even without Brendan's translation: "Where did they go?"

Antonio shrugged.

"We don't know," he said softly. "Nobody knows until now, we didn't know that anybody lived."

John White's tracer turned away, his expression sad and thoughtful—but not hopeless. He spoke.

"He's saying, 'My search goes on. I knew it would not be easy,'" Brendan whispered.

Andrea let out a gasp. She had tears in her eyes, but she was nodding.

She was still hopeful too.

The others turned back toward the rest of the village. But Jonah walked a little farther into the field.

No different than a cemetery, he thought. *Just without creepy tombstones with the names and all. Maybe the Indians weren't so concerned about how they'd be remembered?*

Sunlight streamed down on Jonah's head; tall grasses waved in the hot summer breeze. Without the piles of human skeletons Jonah had been expecting, this part of Croatoan Island wasn't horrifying. It was . . . peaceful. Jonah knew there'd been death here—lots of it—but that was a long time ago. The bodies buried beneath this ground had been resting in peace for years.

Hadn't they?

Jonah noticed a mound toward the back of the field. The soil here was more sand than dirt, and whoever had built this mound had had to pack the soil together tightly to get it to stay in place.

Jonah thought of sand castles on a beach, the way the ones you built at the beginning of a vacation always wore

away by the end of the week. How could the sandy soil of this mound still look so tightly packed if it'd been built years ago?

It couldn't have, Jonah thought.

He stared down at the mound, trying to read messages in grains of sand. They *were* tightly pressed. Nothing had worn away.

Didn't that mean this grave, at least, was . . . fresh?

THIRTY-SIX

Jonah whirled around and raced back toward the others.

"Hey, guys!" he said. "Come look at this!"

He decided he wouldn't tell them what he'd figured out—he'd let them look first and see what they concluded.

"Shh," Katherine hissed at him. "Antonio and Brendan—er, their tracers—they're trying to decide how to get off the island without letting John White see all the animal bones."

"We should protect him from knowing the evil that was here," Antonio was saying, as his tracer would have. "Since it wasn't as bad as we thought, since he still believes he will find his family, since he's such an old man . . ."

"But he's a ghost-man," Brendan replied, in his tracer's voice. "Ghost-men don't know that it is evil to treat our brother animals that way, in death. It will not matter to him."

Jonah barely listened, because all he could think about was the fresh grave. Who was in it? Who had dug it? Brendan and Antonio had said Indians were afraid to come to Croatoan Island, so it probably wasn't anyone native. Andrea had said the English never went to Croatoan to look for the Roanoke colonists.

Well, not that history recorded, Jonah corrected himself. *John White's here right now. And that's not even a change we can blame on Second, because the tracer's here. . . .*

Second! What if Second had killed someone and buried him on Croatoan Island?

Jonah was feeling a little bit dizzy, and it wasn't just because of the heat.

"Maybe it would worry the old man more to have us cover his eyes than it would to see the desecrated animal bones," Antonio was concluding. "Let us just leave then and be done with this place."

"No, wait!" Jonah shouted. "There's something I have to show you before we go!"

Katherine and Andrea turned toward Jonah—even the dog turned toward Jonah. But Antonio and Brendan were still locked in place with their tracers.

Then the boys' tracers stiffened. They jerked their

heads around, side to side, their faces masks of fear.

"We'll leave quickly," Antonio snapped, and Brendan's tracer nodded.

Brendan pulled back from his tracer to report to the others, "That was so weird! My tracer thinks he heard a ghost, but I didn't hear a thing."

It was something that happened in original time, that didn't happen now? Jonah thought. *Because of something time travelers changed? Was it us who did that? Or . . . Second?*

Jonah didn't have time to try these theories on the others—or to show them the grave. Brendan and Antonio were pulling John White's tracer out of yet another empty hut.

"We go," Antonio was saying, his tracer slipping back into the simple words he used with John White. "Must leave now. Danger."

Dazedly John White's tracer nodded and stepped forward. But Antonio and Brendan were rushing him along too fast.

"Wait—before—shouldn't—" Jonah couldn't decide what to tell the others.

Antonio and Brendan and John White's tracer were already at the edge of the village. John White caught his first glimpse of the piles of animal bones. He turned toward Antonio, horror and disbelief painted across his entire expression.

"He understands exactly what this means," Andrea whispered. "But they're in such a hurry they don't see— Brendan! Antonio! Watch out!"

Brendan and Antonio slowed down and looked around. But their tracers plowed forward, shoving John White's tracer on.

John White's tracer stumbled, wobbled—and then plunged straight down to the ground.

THIRTY-SEVEN

Antonio and Brendan immediately rejoined their tracers to huddle over the fallen man.

"Old man! Old man!" Antonio called out, gently shaking John White's tracer shoulders. "Wake up!"

"Did he faint?" Andrea asked, crouching down with the two boys.

"I think so. And then—" Brendan broke off, because Antonio's tracer was turning John White's head side to side, then pushing him to the left, revealing the point of a rock right where his head had been.

"He hit his head!" Katherine cried.

Andrea reached out, as if she'd forgotten that she wouldn't be able to touch the tracer. She pointed instead, to a gash beneath the man's hair.

"It's in the same place," she whispered, her voice a mix

of awe and fear. "It's exactly where the real man hit his head when he almost drowned. It's just not . . . bleeding."

"Get ready—get ready," Brendan separated from his tracer to tell the others. Then he rejoined his tracer to tell Antonio, "I knew there were still evil spirits here. Make haste!"

Antonio scooped up John White's tracer and practically ran toward the canoe. Brendan was right behind him. He broke away from his tracer to call back over his shoulder, "Our tracers aren't going to mess around getting away from here! Get in the canoe as fast as you can!"

Jonah began running through the bones, alongside Katherine and Andrea and Dare.

We'll just have to come back later to look at that grave, he thought. *There's no way I can tell them about it now!*

Antonio reached the canoe and gingerly placed John White's tracer inside, right on top of the real man. The real man rolled to the side, fitting precisely into the tracer, linking completely. When John White turned his head, Jonah could see that Andrea had been right about the location of the tracer's injury: The real and tracer wounds matched exactly.

But the tracer's injury must not be as bad, Jonah thought. *Because it matches the other wound after it's had two days to heal. . . .*

Should Jonah tell Andrea that now or wait until they were out on the water again?

Just then Dare reached the side of the canoe. But he didn't leap in, the way he always had before. He stopped, then spun around to face the woods that lay beyond the village. He pricked his ears up and seemed to be staring intently at . . . something. And then, barking furiously, he began racing toward the woods.

"No, boy!" Andrea cried, reaching down to stop him. "We're leaving!"

Dare slipped right through her grasp.

"I'll get him!" Jonah called.

He dashed off after the dog, but couldn't quite catch up. This time Jonah made no effort to pick his way around the animal skeletons. He cracked skulls beneath his feet; he splintered brittle bones with practically every step.

I bet I'm leaving a lot of tracers, Jonah thought.

That was hardly his biggest worry right now.

Some vague thought teased at his brain: *Tracers . . . tracers . . . were there any signs of tracer lights beside that fresh grave back by the temple? That would have helped me know if Second was the one who dug it. . . .*

But Jonah hadn't thought to look for any sign of tracers back at the burial ground; he didn't have time to think about it now. He lunged for Dare but the dog streaked away, still barking.

"No, boy!" Jonah called. "Come back!"

And then they were at the edge of the woods, Dare barking even more fervently. The dog plunged into the underbrush and Jonah lurched after him—dodging trees, ducking under branches.

"Jonah!" Katherine called from back at the canoe. "Hurry up!"

"Almost—got—" Jonah yelled. He decided to leap toward the dog rather than saying the last word. His fingers brushed Dare's fur, and then he grabbed on to the collar. There! He had him.

Dare whined and tried to pull away. He barked again, staring straight ahead, as if to say: *Look! Look! You've got to see this!*

"What? There's nothing there," Jonah said disgustedly. He gestured with his free hand, and his hand swiped through something pale and ethereal.

Pale. Ethereal. See-through. Ghostly.

Glowing.

It was another tracer.

Still clutching the dog's collar, Jonah took a step back. The dog whimpered.

"I see it, I see it," Jonah muttered.

The tracer was an Indian girl in a deerskin dress. She had long braids on either side of her head. And even though she was a tracer, Jonah could make out the light tone of her skin, the sad gray of her eyes.

Light skin. Gray eyes. This wasn't an Indian girl's tracer.

This was Andrea's.

THIRTY-EIGHT

The fresh grave, Jonah thought. *Is this tracer here because Second murdered Virginia Dare?*

Jonah realized he was so stunned, he wasn't even thinking about tracer rules right. Nobody could have murdered Virginia Dare—at least, not yet. Because *Andrea* was Virginia Dare. And Andrea was still alive, back at the canoe, right now calling out, "Jonah?"

Jonah didn't answer.

This tracer is here because of Gary and Hodge stealing Andrea— Virginia Dare—from history, Jonah was reminding himself. *And then because Second made sure that Andrea didn't come back to the right time or place . . .*

The tracer girl stood on her tiptoes, peering through the branches, straight out toward the canoe.

She sees them, Jonah thought. *She sees Walks with Pride and*

One Who Survives Much. Can she see her grandfather, too?

The tracer girl's mouth made a little O of surprise, and then she looked down—evidently she'd snapped a twig with her bare toes or made some other little noise with her movement.

Back at the canoe, Antonio cried out in his tracer's voice, "There it is again! The sound of an unsettled spirit! Let's go!"

That's why the tracer boys heard sounds that Antonio and Brendan didn't, Jonah thought. *Because it was this tracer walking around, moving through the woods.*

"Jonah!" Katherine called from behind him. "I'm serious! The tracers aren't going to wait for you! Get Dare and come on!"

But Jonah wanted to wait. He wanted to wait for Andrea's tracer to step forward, out of the woods. Then Brendan's tracer would see her, and Antonio's tracer would see her, and maybe even John White's tracer would be awake by now to see her too. And whatever was supposed to happen next—whatever had happened in original time—would happen.

Andrea's tracer didn't step forward. She shrank back.

"It's okay," Jonah whispered. "We're friendly."

But of course the tracer couldn't hear him. She slid farther back into the woods, deeper into the shadows.

She wasn't planning to go out and meet the other

tracers—Brendan's and Antonio's and her grandfather's. She was afraid of them. She was hiding.

"Jonah, what are you doing?" Katherine called again. "If you don't come now, you're going to have to swim!"

What was Jonah supposed to do? They'd come to the past to reunite Andrea with her tracer. It had been such a clear goal. But that was before they knew about Second, before Andrea changed the Elucidator code, before John White showed up, before Brendan and Antonio appeared out of nowhere—and before they'd discovered that Croatoan was an island of death. What difference did all those changes make? Could they change the need for Andrea to join with her tracer? What if this was the wrong time and the wrong place for it?

How could Jonah know?

"Just give me a minute!" Jonah yelled back to Katherine, even though he knew it wasn't just her choice whether to go or stay.

And how much choice do I have? Jonah thought. *How much choice* should *I have when it's Andrea's life, not mine?*

Jonah glanced back toward the canoe. Katherine had exaggerated a little—they weren't casting off quite yet. Brendan was still untying the canoe. There was still time. A minute or two.

Jonah took a deep breath.

"Andrea!" he called unsteadily. "Come quick! I found your tracer!"

"What?" Katherine yelled. "Now? Are you kidding?"

Brendan stopped in the middle of flipping the rope back into the canoe, though his tracer continued without him. Antonio almost dropped his paddle. And Andrea jumped out of the canoe.

"I knew we'd find her!" Andrea exulted. "I knew John White would find his granddaughter!"

Andrea raced toward Jonah and Dare and the tracer. She stopped only when she reached Jonah's side, directly facing her double. She gasped.

"You don't have a whole lot of time to stand there marveling at how weird all this is," Jonah muttered.

"How do I . . . ?" Andrea began. "Do I jump? Hold my breath? Close my eyes? Back in?"

Jonah pushed her. It wasn't his smoothest move, but he was acutely aware of the time ticking away.

Andrea jolted forward, her mouth still agog. She spun around, her features lining up with the tracer girl's features; her limbs lining up with the tracer girl's limbs: one arm bent around a tree trunk, one foot half off the ground, as if she was poised to run.

Andrea's face came back out of her tracer's face.

"She doesn't live on this island!" Andrea gasped. "She

came from far, away from the mainland—she came back to bury the skeletons she knew were here, to honor the Croatoans. . . . She didn't think anyone else would come to the island!"

"Okay," Jonah said impatiently. "And . . ."

Andrea's face toggled back into her tracer and out again. This time her entire expression had changed, so it was easy to tell her and the tracer apart. The tracer looked slightly apprehensive.

Andrea looked furious.

"No!" she screamed. "It's not fair! It can't happen like that!"

"Like what?" Jonah asked.

"She's just going to hide until the strangers leave," Andrea said. "She doesn't even know her grandfather's with them! To be this close and not meet—no! I won't let it happen that way!"

"Andrea," Jonah said, and her name came out sounding like an apology. "It's not your choice. You can't control your tracer. You only get to choose for yourself."

Jonah tried to decide how to spell out all the potential choices. Ideally, they'd all get to vote. Everyone could stay with their respective tracers, no matter what. Or everyone could stay on Croatoan, leaving the tracers of Brendan, Antonio, and John White to go on only as ghosts. Or all the kids could cast off in the canoe together, leaving Andrea's longed-for tracer behind. Only Jonah and Katherine didn't have a tracer here to choose or not choose, to weigh in the balance between friends and fate.

There wasn't time to say any of that. Andrea was screaming again.

"No! My tracer's never going to meet her grandfather! And my grandfather will never see me as myself! No! It can't be! You're—coming—with—me!"

Jonah could tell that Andrea wasn't talking to him.

Andrea had grabbed her tracer's hands, and was trying to tug her tracer away from behind the tree. It was a weird effect, like watching someone wrestle with her own shadow—from *inside* the shadow.

Dare whined and backed away, more freaked out than ever. Jonah tightened his grip on the dog's collar.

"Jonah! Andrea! Come on!" Brendan called from behind them. "My tracer's done! I'm getting into the canoe! We're leaving!"

"No—you're—not!" Andrea yelled.

The tracer-joined-with-Andrea took a step forward.

Optical illusion, Jonah thought. *Trick of the eye.*

Another step.

Andrea grinned.

Except, it wasn't just Andrea grinning. It was the tracer, too, the smile lines around her eyes radiating back toward her braids.

"Wait!" Andrea/Virginia called, and even though Jonah understood perfectly, he knew she wasn't speaking English. She was speaking another Algonquian dialect similar to the one Brendan's and Antonio's tracers used.

Andrea didn't know any Algonquian dialects. Did she?

"Do not depart in such haste," Andrea/Virginia continued, walking toward Brendan, out into the sunlight. "Do you have a ghost-man in your canoe? I am a ghost-girl, and he might be my kin."

Brendan turned around.

No—it was Brendan-joined-with-his-tracer who turned around. The tracer turned too.

Can't be, Jonah thought. *I know that didn't happen. Andrea's tracer wouldn't have called out. Brendan's tracer wouldn't have looked back.*

"Are you a lost spirit of the dead?" Brendan's tracer asked. His knees knocked together slightly, and Jonah decided the tracer was brave not to run if he was that afraid.

"No," Andrea/Virginia said. "I am alive. But my grandfather is lost."

Brendan's tracer hesitated. Then he swept his hand toward the canoe.

"Come and find him," he said.

THIRTY-NINE

Andrea/Virginia raced forward, across the shoreline littered with bones. Jonah whipped his head around in disbelief. Out of the corner of his eye he caught a glimpse of something pale in the spot where Andrea's tracer had been standing only a moment before. Jonah turned his head—a tracer still stood there. But this one was even dimmer, even less substantial, fading away even as Jonah watched. Jonah looked from this tracer back to Andrea: Yes, Andrea was still wearing the deerskin dress and braids. She was still joined with her tracer.

A tracer in the wrong place, the other tracer disappearing . . . I thought tracers couldn't change, Jonah marveled. *Does that mean . . . Andrea completely changed time? Even original time? Is that possible?*

Out on the water, an equally ghostly tracer canoe

slipped silently away from the island, paddled by barely visible tracers of Walks with Pride and One Who Survives Much. Squinting, Jonah could just make out the translucent hand of John White's tracer clutching the side of the canoe.

And then the entire tracer canoe vanished too.

Yet, when Jonah stepped forward a bit and shifted his view back to the shoreline, he could see Antonio/ Walks with Pride and Brendan/One Who Survives Much—both in loincloths—standing by the real canoe. The Brendan figure bent down and crouched beside John White.

"He is hurt and sick and does not wake," Brendan said.

"He has seen many troubles," Andrea said. "It is written on his face."

Jonah had stopped thinking of her as Andrea/Virginia. She still looked like the tracer—and was still completely joined. But Andrea was in control.

She bent down and stroked her grandfather's forehead, smoothed back his hair.

"Your troubles are over now," she said.

Jonah could see John White's eyelids flutter—his real eyelids.

"Grandfather?" Andrea whispered. She had called him

that before, but it sounded different now. Jonah could hear a trace of an accent in her voice—not English, but Algonquian. It sounded . . . right.

John White's eyelids weren't just fluttering now. They were blinking.

And then the eyelids stopped moving and his eyes focused. Even at this distance, Jonah could tell that John White's eyes were focused on Andrea's face.

"Oh, my child," he whispered, "My child. You look just like my daughter, Eleanor."

"Eleanor was my mother," Andrea said. She touched her grandfather's cheek. "She always said that you would come back."

Jonah saw Katherine stumble out of the canoe. At first Jonah thought she was just making room for Andrea and her grandfather to talk, now that he could actually see her, now that he wasn't just talking in his sleep. But Katherine kept walking, past the litter of bones, toward Jonah.

She seemed to run out of energy a few steps away. She clutched a tree as if she needed the help to stand up.

"What just happened?" she asked. "What was that?"

Jonah opened his mouth, even though he didn't have the slightest idea what to tell her.

"Excellent question, my dear," a voice said from behind

Jonah. "I would call that a second chance. Which also happens—not so coincidentally—to be my name."

Katherine gaped; her eyes seemed to double in size.

"Then, you're . . . Second?" she whispered.

FORTY

Jonah whirled around.

A strange man stood behind him. If they'd been in the twenty-first century, Jonah would have described the man as a standard-issue computer nerd. He had pasty-white skin, as if he'd spent too much time indoors. His blond hair stood out in all directions, as if, like Einstein, he had other things to think about than using a comb. And he had one side of his shirt tucked into his pants and the other hanging out loose—though for all Jonah knew, maybe that was the fashion in some far-off future.

"Second Chance, at your service," the man said, bowing slightly. He cut off the ending of the bow and jerked back up hastily, to peer straight at Jonah. "But I'm forgetting myself . . . given that you were ready to punch Antonio just on the *suspicion* that he might be working for me, perhaps you'll forgive me if I don't want to place myself in such a vulnerable position." He tilted his head to the side, thinking. "Of course, I believe flabbergasted would be a more predictable emotion than furious for the two of you right now."

"I—you—" Jonah could barely speak, let alone throw any punches.

"See?" the man said. "Just as I predicted."

Jonah still didn't understand what was going on, but he didn't like proving Second right.

"So . . . ," Jonah tried again, struggling to gather his wits enough to ask a complete question. "This is what you were aiming for all along?" He gestured weakly toward Andrea, still bent over her grandfather back at the canoe. "This? Andrea and her grandfather—I mean, Virginia Dare and John White—finding each other?"

"Exactly," Second said, beaming.

Jonah squinted, no less confused. He'd gotten so used to thinking of Second as someone bad, someone to fight against. To resist.

"You want Andrea to be happy?" Jonah asked.

"Don't you?" Second replied.

"Sure, but . . . that's not how things went in original time, was it?" Katherine said. "This wasn't supposed to happen."

Second sighed. He glanced at something in his pocket.

"It took you three minutes and forty-one seconds to reach that conclusion," he said. "That's about what I predicted—I was just two seconds off. Still, it's a bit disappointing, when you've just witnessed the biggest scientific advance since humanity discovered time travel in the first place, and all you can say is, 'This wasn't supposed to happen'?"

The way he mimicked Katherine's voice was cruel, making her sound childish and stupid.

"As your friend Andrea pointed out, original time wasn't some priceless, perfect jewel," Second said. "Isn't it better to make an old man and a little girl happy?"

Jonah didn't like Second calling Andrea little.

"But . . . but . . . if you change time, you might cause a dangerous paradox," Jonah said. "Make it so that your own parents are never born. Or you might make other things change—so that, I don't know, hundreds of years from now, the South wins the Civil War. Nobody ever abolishes slavery. Hitler wins World War II. Or . . ."

Jonah was casting about for other examples of how history could go terribly wrong. But he couldn't think clearly because Second had begun grinning in such a mocking way—almost chortling, even.

"What if we make it so that Hitler never *starts* World War II?" Second asked gleefully. "Or that slavery never catches on in the United States, and there's no Civil War because there's no slavery to fight over? So there's no racism, because there's no heritage of slavery . . . Martin Luther King is never shot, the Trail of Tears never happens, the Bay of Pigs never happens, the *Maine* doesn't sink—"

"All that's going to happen just because of Andrea and her grandfather?" Jonah asked incredulously.

"No," Second said. "I am 99.9998 percent certain that none of that will change because of Andrea and her grandfather. But don't you see? We start small, almost invisibly—one girl and her grandfather, on an out-of-the-way island—and then, who knows? Maybe everything else is possible too."

He was back to beaming again.

Jonah remembered something Katherine had said way back when they'd first learned that Jonah and his friend Chip had a connection to time travel: *If you're going to go back in time, you save Abraham Lincoln from being assassinated. Or John F. Kennedy. Or, you keep the Titanic from sinking. Or you stop September 11. Or—I know—you assassinate Hitler before he has a chance to start World War II.*

Maybe Second had heard her say that.

"So you're trying to create alternative dimensions," Jonah said, proud of himself for figuring this out. "Ones with all sorts of different possibilities."

"No," Second said. "Not *alternative*. You didn't enter an alternative dimension when Andrea forced her tracer to step forward. Time itself changed. There's only one time stream, only one history. Time travel just makes it look like more."

"But tracers show 'original time,' and then there's the way time really goes, what we see when we come back in time . . . ," Jonah interrupted. "So there's two versions, right there."

"You're wrong," Second said. "Tracers only live through time once, no more than anyone else. It was just that they always drew everyone and everything toward what seemed to be a preordained path. Toward their destinies, you might say. But tracers themselves could never change. Until now." Jonah wouldn't have said it was possible, but Second's grin got even bigger. "You two just witnessed the first time shift in history. The first time destiny itself was derailed. The *end* of destiny. It's like . . . you are Watson, and I am Alexander Graham Bell. You are the little boy who watched the first airplane flight, and I am Orville Wright. You are lizards in the New Mexico desert, and I am Robert Oppenheimer."

Jonah didn't have the slightest idea who Robert
Oppenheimer was, but he thought it was a little insulting
to be called a lizard.

"Hold on," Katherine said, stamping her foot. "You
want us to think this is like you just created the atomic
bomb?"

Oh, Jonah thought. *That must be what Robert Oppenheimer
did.*

"I'm not comparing the morality of it," Second said.
"I'm just saying—this is that monumental. Its repercus-
sions will reverberate forever."

Katherine glared at him.

"You're crazy," she said. "And conceited."

"Now, now," Second said. "Do you *like* the way time
was supposed to go?"

Jonah opened his mouth. Then he shut it. He noticed
that Katherine didn't say anything either.

"In original time, Virginia Dare and her grandfather
were never to be reunited," Second said, a tinge of sad-
ness entering his voice for the first time. "It was what we
call a near miss. Time is rubbed so thin at the site of a
near miss. . . . Virginia Dare was standing here and her
grandfather was just a few yards away, and they would
never know it. They were destined to go to their graves
without ever knowing the fate of the other. And, believe

me, their graves were coming for both of them, very soon. Wouldn't you call that a mistake on time's part? Didn't it need to be corrected?"

The question hung in the air. Jonah saw doubt flutter over his sister's face.

"You're manipulating us again," Jonah accused Second. "You've been manipulating us all along!"

Second raised an eyebrow.

"Perhaps," he said. "Though perhaps not as much as you think."

"You lied to Andrea to get her to change the Elucidator!" Katherine said.

"True," Second said. "That was necessary, though I do regret the pain it caused her."

"You wanted us to lose the Elucidator!" Jonah charged.

"Of course," Second agreed.

"Didn't you know we'd be scared?" Jonah asked.

"I had every reason to believe you'd be okay," Second said.

"Then . . . somehow . . . you arranged it so Walks with Pride and One Who Survives Much weren't there to save John White," Katherine said.

Second shrugged.

"I just delayed Brendan and Antonio's return to their

proper time by a few days," he said. "Just as I changed Andrea's return to time only slightly—placing her on Roanoke Island instead of Croatoan."

"You did that so we would rescue John White, right?" Jonah said. "And so Andrea would get attached to him?"

"Bingo!" Second said, his grin back.

"What if we hadn't saved him?" Katherine challenged. "What if he'd drowned?"

"Well, I did have to bribe Dare with some dog treats, to get him to bark at the right time," Second admitted. "That was a little dicey. But once you were there on the beach, watching, there was virtually no chance that you wouldn't try to help."

"Andrea could have drowned!" Jonah said. "I could have drowned!"

"Nope," Second said, shaking his head. "Not even statistically possible. You were both too strong and determined for that."

Jonah frowned. Something was still nagging at him.

"How'd you know we'd have Dare with us anyhow?" he asked. "That's not even something JB planned for. He just sent Dare with us because his projectionist said . . ."

Jonah stopped, because Second was pulling some sort of timepiece out of his pocket.

"Hmm," he said. "I really had projected that you

would figure out this part by now. You're eleven seconds off. Perhaps a small clue is in order. As you might have guessed, Second Chance isn't the name my parents gave me at birth. I adopted that appellation only very recently, to go along with my quest to change history. You might actually have heard of me previously, by another name—Sam, perhaps? Sam Chase?"

Sam, Jonah thought. *Sam Chase.* Back home, Jonah knew two Sams and a Samuel at school, and a Sammy on his soccer team. But all that seemed so far away, so long ago—or long *ahead.* Even the most recent time he'd heard the name Sam seemed distant. It had been JB speaking, JB saying, *Sam is the most brilliant projectionist I've ever worked with. . . .*

Jonah's jaw dropped. He felt his eyes bugging out.

"You're JB's projectionist?" he gasped.

FORTY-ONE

Second clicked his thumb against the object in his hand—maybe it was a stopwatch.

"Wow," he said. "Thirty-six seconds off. I'm really slipping. Or, the two of you are."

"It's true, then?" Katherine asked. "You work for JB?"

"JB signs my paychecks," Second said, his cocky grin back.

"Then . . . then he knew what was happening to us along?" Jonah asked. He was having trouble believing this. "He knew from the beginning that Andrea was going to change the Elucidator, that we were going to lose all contact, that we were going to rescue John White, that . . . that *this* was what we were moving toward?" Without looking, he gestured toward the other kids and Andrea's grandfather, still back at the canoe.

"Let's just say that JB can be a bit hands-off as a boss," Second said. "All about the big picture, not so concerned about the tiny details along the way. Looks at the forest, not the individual trees. Leaves it to me to understand the trees."

Jonah didn't have a clue what any of that meant. He couldn't stop thinking about how certain he'd been, back in the hut on Roanoke Island, that JB had lost them completely. Hadn't JB assured them, back at the beginning when he was shaking their hands, that they were all on the same team? That there wouldn't be any secrets on this trip?

No, Jonah realized. *That wasn't what JB said. He said no one would keep any secrets "unnecessarily."*

Jonah felt betrayed. He wanted to scream out, like Andrea's grandfather in the midst of one of his nightmares, "Treachery! Betrayal! Deceit!"

"But . . . but . . . the big picture here is that Andrea changed history," Katherine said. "JB's big picture isn't about changing history. He just wants to put kids back where they belong so history will go the way it's supposed to."

"You think JB is still the same time purist he was when you first met him?" Second asked. "Do you think, if he'd stayed like that, he would have let you rescue Chip and

Alex from the fifteenth century?" Second smirked. "Don't you know how people's hearts go soft around orphans and dogs?"

He pointed toward Andrea and Dare, but Jonah just kept staring at Second.

"JB would never have let you give Andrea steroids in her food," Jonah said.

"There *weren't* any steroids in her food pellet. It was just food," Second said.

"But the way she paddled," Jonah argued, "when she was trying to catch up with the tracer canoe—"

"She was just determined. Very, very stubborn and full of resolve," Second said. "Like you were full of resolve when the food pellets showed up—you were so determined that you were going to spite me by not eating them, that you forgot to think about being hungry. And that carried you through until you could eat the fish."

Jonah winced. Second was exactly right—that was how Jonah had felt.

"I will admit that I tampered a bit with the food pellet I knew Andrea would give to John White," Second said. "It had a sedative in it, to make sure that he didn't wake up too soon. And, although the medicine in the pellet helped him heal, it made him *look* like he was getting worse."

Jonah's jaw dropped.

"Why would you do that? Andrea was so worried about her grandfather!" he protested.

"*And* so convinced that she had to keep him with his tracer," Second said. He smirked again. "Ultimately, it was for her own good."

Jonah scowled at him.

"What about the paint jars you left in that hut?" Katherine said. "What was that all about?"

"Well . . . John White can use the paint, because some of his was damaged by the seawater," Second said. "But, mostly, the way those showed up made Jonah so mad at me that he was determined to get off Roanoke Island, no matter what, even if he had to carve a canoe himself." Second chuckled, not very kindly. "Teenage boys really are very easy to manipulate."

This made Jonah even angrier. If it hadn't been for the paint jars, he would have thought more about whether or not it really mattered to keep John White with his tracer. He would have thought more about the big picture, himself.

Second probably predicted that I'd be mad now, Jonah seethed.

He forced himself to at least try to appear calm.

"There's still something weird about all this," Katherine muttered.

"Yeah. . . . What about the way Antonio came back

in time?" Jonah said. "When he . . . fell on me. I bet *that* wasn't something JB knew about, or approved, or wanted to happen. That was wrong, wasn't it?"

"Not wrong, exactly," Second said. For the first time, his gaze seemed shifty; he wouldn't look Jonah in the eye. "It was a bit unconventional . . . just a little risky. . . . Okay, that kind of re-entry had never been tried before. It's called a time smack. And it was the only way to stretch time just enough for the shift, to loosen the connection between Brendan and Antonio and their tracers . . ."

I don't trust their tracers, Katherine had said, only the night before. She'd been right. They weren't trustworthy. But it really wasn't their fault.

"So I caused one little time smack, along with the time shift. Why does that give you the right to put me on trial?" Second asked. "This is all good! John White gets to meet his granddaughter! It's a happy ending!"

"Is it an ending or—just the beginning?" Katherine asked.

"Oh, very good!" Second was beaming again. "You are so right. There are so many possibilities, even from this one little change . . . With his granddaughter at his side, John White has a reason to live now. To heal. And he'll keep drawing pictures. In just seven years, English settlers are going to try again, at Jamestown. What if

John White's new drawings get to Jamestown and then back to England? What if that changes how everyone in England views the Americas? What if John White and Virginia Dare go and help out at Jamestown, bridging the gap between the English and the natives much better than a bunch of trigger-happy, starving soldiers? What if there's finally some respect between the two sides?"

Jonah glanced toward Andrea and the others once again. He gasped.

"And what if your wonderful time shift ruins everything?" he asked.

He pointed.

Andrea was still bent over her grandfather, her hand gently touching his face. Brendan and Antonio still hovered nearby, staring solemnly at the reunited pair. This wasn't so odd. The four of them might have been so awed by the moment that they wanted to stay in the same position, without moving, for a long time. But it wasn't just them staying so still. Dare's body arced above the canoe, frozen mid-leap. A bird flying overhead was suspended in mid-air, its wings outstretched but unmoving. Even the waves beyond the canoe had stopped lapping against the sand, the crests and valleys of water locked in place, unchanging. It was impossible, but true: Except for the little cluster of Jonah, Katherine, and Second, the entire world had stopped.

FORTY-TWO

"Oh, that," Second said. "It's temporary. See?"

He rubbed the surface of the thing Jonah had thought was a stopwatch. Once again Jonah heard the pounding of the surf against the sand. The bird soared out of sight. Dare landed on the sand at Andrea's side and brushed his head against her leg. The dog looked up at her as if he expected to be petted.

Brendan, Antonio, and John White laughed.

"Our canine friend admires you," John White said.

Jonah turned his attention back to Second.

"That's an Elucidator you're holding, isn't it?" Jonah asked, gesturing toward the watchlike object. "You can stop time with an Elucidator?"

"Not *really*," Second said. "That's just how it looks to the uneducated eye. In reality, I pulled the three of us out of time. It's like—you've gone into time hollows with JB, haven't you? And the time cave? This is the same kind of thing, except easier. Not so much travel and wear and tear. We just hide in between the nanoseconds."

Jonah was only half-listening. He was keeping his eye—educated or not—on the Elucidator. After a moment, Second slipped it back into his pocket without pressing it again. He shrugged.

"We might as well watch what happens next," he said.

In the canoe, John White was shaking his head at Andrea.

"I have been confused these many days," he said. "I have dreamed of you, my child, dreamed of your voice. . . ."

Andrea did not say, *You mean, because I've been talking to you for two days, but you've been too out of it to really listen? Or to open your eyes and see me?* Instead, she flipped her braids over her shoulder and said, "I've dreamed of you, too, Grandfather. My mother used to tell me stories of you. She promised you would do everything you could to come back."

"I did," her grandfather murmured. "I have."

"Amazing," Second whispered beside Jonah. "Even with the time shift, time can still adjust itself. The human mind can adjust itself. John White will never again wonder why he sort of remembers hearing Andrea before—he'll always think that was just a dream. Because time would never have allowed him to see and hear her for real, to *recognize* her without her tracer. . . ."

"I thought he was unconscious and couldn't see or hear her because you put a sedative in his food," Jonah said. "*And* because of his head injury."

"You don't think time could have caused his head injury?" Second asked.

"Time's not a person," Jonah objected. "Time can't make someone hurt his head."

"Can't it?" Second asked.

"But—" Jonah began.

"Shh," Katherine interrupted. "Argue later. I'm trying to hear."

In the canoe, John White was clearing his throat, peering down awkwardly at his hands, then back up at Andrea.

"I fear to ask," he began. "Your mother, my Eleanor. And Ananias, your father. Are they . . ."

Andrea was already shaking her head.

"Their spirits took flight," she said. "Five summers ago, when the sickness came. . . ."

John White had tears glistening in his eyes, but he spoke gently.

"And you, child. Who takes care of you?"

"The Croatoan tribe is kind, those few who are left,"

Andrea said. "They count me as one of their own. We have moved in with distant relatives. . . ."

"Kind?" Antonio interrupted. "They sent you, a girl, alone, to an evil island? You call that kind?"

Andrea frowned.

"That is not their fault," Andrea said. "The sickness has come back, and many are weak again. I chose this myself, as a way to make peace with the evil spirits. I thought if I could bury the dead, bury the animal bones, it would show that the Croatoans are worthy people . . . worthy to live on, not die, not all die out. . . ."

Her voice was thick with grief.

The fresh grave, Jonah thought with a jolt. That's the explanation! It was Andrea—or, Virginia Dare, rather—she was burying all the skeletons of the dead Croatoans from some plague from years ago. Maybe she put them all in one grave, or maybe there were other fresh graves I didn't see. . . .

Katherine turned her head to whisper in Jonah's ear.

"Doesn't it seem like they've forgotten we're even here?" she asked. She waved her arms and raised her voice. "Hey, Andrea! Remember us?"

Second immediately clamped his hand over Katherine's mouth.

"Shh! Stop interfering!" he hissed, which Jonah thought was a little funny, given what Second had done.

A flicker of irritation appeared on Andrea's face, but she didn't turn her head. Brendan and Antonio didn't look up either. John White, however, squinted toward the woods.

"Do my eyes and ears betray me?" he muttered. "Or do I see more figments from my dreams, come terrifyingly to life?" He blinked—maybe his vision wasn't the clearest. He looked back at Andrea. "Perhaps I was mistaken—are you but a figment too? Do I dream and think I am awake?"

"I'm real," Andrea insisted. "You're not dreaming. But lie back, Grandfather, and rest."

Obediently, he slid back down in the canoe. It seemed barely a second before Jonah could hear the old man snoring.

A moment later, Andrea came stomping toward Jonah and Katherine and Second.

"Don't ruin it!" she ordered Katherine. "When my grandfather sees or hears something he doesn't understand, he gets confused. He has to fall asleep again. And you and Jonah don't fit for him. You—"

"What, you're saying we don't belong here?" Katherine asked indignantly. "After all we've done for you? The help we've given you?"

Impatience played over Andrea's face.

"That's not it," she said. "I'm grateful. I appreciate everything you've done. But can't you feel how fragile this is? One wrong move, and time could snatch me back. I'll be running toward the woods"—she pointed into the trees, and for an instant, Jonah thought he could see the other ghostly tracer again—"and my grandfather will be floating away. Out of reach."

"Really?" Second said, as if Andrea had just provided him with an amazing detail. "You still feel the pull of the original tracer?"

"Less and less with each moment that passes," Andrea said. "But still . . ."

Second frowned.

"But I was so sure," he muttered.

Jonah decided it was time to take control of the conversation.

"Don't worry, Andrea," Jonah said. "Remember, this is all just temporary. We're going to fix time—well, whatever that means *now*—and then we're all going back to the twenty-first century and have our normal lives."

Normal was sounding especially good to Jonah right now. Even the most boring moments of his ordinary twenty-first-century life seemed achingly precious. The time he'd spent brushing his teeth. Opening the refrigerator to look for a snack. Flipping through the TV channels with the remote control. Waiting for the computer to fire up. Sitting through Social Studies class at school and feeling like none of it really mattered—it was all history and dead and gone and past. . . .

"Oh, Jonah," Andrea said, shaking her head sadly. A hint of tears glittered in her eyes once again. But, oddly, this time it seemed as if she was about to cry over *Jonah*. She was staring straight at him, just as intently as she'd always stared at her grandfather. "You never give up, do you? I just hope . . ."

She broke off, because something strange was happening to Second. He let out a strangled cry: "Erp—" It sounded like he was having trouble swallowing.

No. It was more like he was *being* swallowed.

In the next moment, Second seemed to age several years at once. His blond hair suddenly looked blond and brown, all at once. His face seemed to unravel and reknit itself into a completely different form.

And then Second pitched forward, looking like himself again. But he left behind someone else in the space he'd occupied a moment earlier. Someone taller and older, with darker hair.

JB.

JB glared down at Second on the ground before him.

"Traitor," JB said.

FORTY-THREE

The next thing JB did was surprising: He reached out and grabbed Katherine with one arm and Jonah with the other, so he could draw them both into a tight hug.

"I was so worried about you," he murmured. "Are you all right?"

Jonah pushed away, because he wanted to show JB he could stand on his own two feet.

"We're fine," he said. He couldn't stop himself from adding the rest: "Now that you're here."

It was such a relief to know that JB would fix the mess that Second had made of time. It was such a relief to see the smug look wiped from Second's face. He seemed almost harmless now, lying stunned in the sand.

"I'm sorry," Jonah told JB. "We let him manipulate us."

"You did the best you could, under the circumstances,"

JB said. "Nobody could expect any more than that."

Katherine surprised Jonah by pulling away from JB and kicking Second's shoulder.

"You lied to us!" She cried. "You were working for Gary and Hodge the whole time, weren't you? You were going to steal Andrea and Brendan and Antonio—and, and Jonah—and take them off to be adopted in the future . . . and you probably would have left me here alone. . . ."

She would have kicked him again, except that JB pulled her back.

"Katherine," he said warningly. "He actually didn't tell you any lies. A few evasions, yes, a few partial truths, but no actual lies."

Katherine stopped in confusion.

"But—he said he worked for you! He said he was your projectionist!"

"That's true," JB said grimly. "Or—it was." He narrowed his eyes, peering down at Second. "You're fired."

"Wh-what?" Second moaned.

"You heard me," JB said. "Would you like to hear my reasons? Number one, for sabotaging a crucial time mission, completely subverting the purpose of sending these kids back in time. Number two, for repeatedly endangering six lives—all the kids', plus John White's. No, make that seven lives. I'll count the dog, too. Number three, for double-crossing my every effort to find Jonah and Katherine and Andrea after they disappeared from contact."

Jonah felt oddly cheered by this item on the list. He *knew* JB wouldn't have left them stranded and scared on Roanoke.

"Weren't you looking for Brendan and me?" Antonio interrupted. Jonah was surprised—he hadn't even noticed when the other two boys and Dare had shown up beside them.

JB glanced sympathetically at Antonio and broke off his list making.

"To the best of my knowledge—which, obviously, wasn't very good—I thought the two of you were still safely in the twenty-first century," JB said. "You were supposed to be going on with your lives, waiting your turn to go back in time. And"—JB glared at Second again—"it wasn't their turn yet."

"But—but—Andrea and us," Brendan said. "We're connected."

"Not really," JB said. "Only because Gary and Hodge were supremely lazy and sloppy in the way they pulled the three of you out of time in the first place." He sighed heavily. "This was all so unnecessary."

"How can you say that?" Andrea asked wildly. Her voice was thick with emotion. "My grandfather—"

"Was a remarkable man," JB said. "History has never given him the respect he deserved. But neither did time." He sighed again. "His best efforts were doomed to fail. His connection to you—except as a fairy tale, a pleasant story your mother told you—all of that was supposed to end when you were a baby. You truly were never supposed to see him again."

"That's so wrong!" Andrea complained, and this time she made no effort to hide the tears brimming in her eyes.

"You of all people know that things go wrong all the time," JB said gently. "And I know it's no comfort, but as a time traveler, I've seen so many ways that wrong things can turn out to be right after all, that bad can lead to good, that no one can get the good without the bad coming first. . . ."

"You're right," Andrea said, snipping off the ends of her words. "It's no comfort."

JB shrugged helplessly.

"I'm sorry," he said.

"What *was* supposed to happen to Andrea and Brendan and Antonio?" Katherine asked. "What were they supposed to do when they came back in time?"

JB nodded, as if he thought this would be easier to talk about.

"Gary and Hodge kidnapped Andrea from Croatoan Island while she was in the midst of burying all the skeletons and corpses," he said. "She actually would have been a good candidate for them to take to the future, if they'd just waited a few extra days, until she'd finished."

"Only the animal bones were left," Andrea murmured.

It took Jonah a minute to grasp this.

"Hold on," Jonah interrupted. "That's all you wanted me and Katherine to do when we came back with Andrea? Help her bury some bones?"

"Not even that," JB said, shaking his head. "You just needed to be there. My brilliant projectionist said you and the dog would provide the 'emotional support' she'd need during her task, which would be too 'traumatic' otherwise," JB's tone cast doubt on every word. He snorted scornfully. "And I fell for it!" He nudged Second's shoulder with his foot. "You must have thought I was a complete fool! Trusting you!"

"Wasn't complete lie," Second muttered. "Jonah . . . gaga . . . over Andrea . . . Romance always . . . distracting . . ."

Now Jonah felt like kicking Second too. He didn't quite dare to look at Andrea—or anyone else—to see how they took this news. He was grateful when JB ignored Second and kept explaining.

"You wouldn't think a scattering of animal skeletons

would matter so much in the grand sweep of history," JB continued. "But if Virginia Dare hadn't moved them, Croatoan Island would have kept its reputation as an evil island. The memory of the plague spread by the Roanoke colonists would have lingered, setting off massacres when the next wave of English colonists arrived. . . ."

"So Virginia Dare did do something crucial to history," Katherine said. "It wasn't just that she was famous for being born."

Andrea ducked her head. Jonah couldn't tell if she was being modest or if she was still annoyed with JB.

"Which was the reason I was kidnapped?" Andrea asked. "Because I did something important or just because I was born?"

There was bitterness in her voice—Jonah decided she was still upset.

"It's hard to know for sure," JB said gently. "For generations you were known only as the first English child born in the Americas. Before time travel, that's all there was *to* know about you. That was enough for Gary and Hodge to want you for their baby-smuggling operation. But one of their customers also specified that they wanted a famous child who was capable of being brave and loyal, who was willing to take risks in desperate times. So we know Gary and Hodge planned to charge more for you, because they knew more of your story." He swept his hands out helplessly. "Who can say how much that affects time and history?"

"That's why you thought it had to be Andrea who came back to bury the bones," Jonah said, catching on. "That's why it had to be her and not me or Katherine or just some random time traveler. . . ."

JB nodded.

"Authenticity matters," he said. "We can never know all the consequences of any action, so we were trying to err on the side of caution and restore everything we could."

Jonah looked down at Second, who had not erred on the side of caution, who'd been gleeful about changing time, rather than restoring it. Everyone was quiet for a minute.

"What about Brendan and me?" Antonio asked. "The ex-slave and the Spanish orphan turned tribesmen? What made us famous and worth being kidnapped?"

"Your artwork," JB said.

"Yeah, right," Brendan said, laughing. "Very funny. Tell us the truth—were we in some famous battle? How brave were we? Don't worry—I won't brag too much about it when I find out."

Antonio just stood there.

"Dude," he said. "I think he's serious."

"Huh?" Brendan said.

"My tracer—he's been thinking a lot about the drawings John White showed them," Antonio said. "He's been wondering if the old man could show him how to draw like that. . . ."

JB nodded.

"It's true," he said. "After you two rescued John White, he got well enough, temporarily, to give you a few art lessons. And then—art's not my specialty—but I think the proper term is that you *fused* the various traditions, English art and Native American art and African art and Spanish art, and the two of you came up with something completely new, far ahead of your time. You were like twin Leonardo da Vincis—except that Leonardo's work survived, and yours was all destroyed in a fire that blew through your village . . . also killing you."

"That's seriously twisted!" Brendan said.

"That you died with your work?" Andrea asked softly.

"No—that I'm supposed to be some famous artist," he said, shaking his head in disbelief. "I almost flunked art last year!" He stopped, a thoughtful expression on his face. "Because . . . I thought the teacher was wrong, always wanting to have separate categories of art. . . . You say we were famous for mixing things up?"

JB nodded.

"But . . . we weren't *really* famous," Antonio said, "not

if everything was destroyed, and nobody ever knew what we did."

He already looked sad at the thought that artwork he hadn't created yet would never be seen.

"But time travelers saw the work, right?" Katherine asked. "They're the ones who would have made you famous."

"Right," JB said. "There was a strong—and illegal, I might add—art-smuggling effort, where renegade time travelers managed to rescue all your work, right before it burned. It made for some very dramatic time-travel stories."

"Wow," Antonio said, puffing up his chest. "Famous artist! Worth having his work stolen!"

"But then Gary and Hodge decided, why steal the art when you can steal the artists instead?" JB said. "So they yanked you out of time right when they pulled Virginia Dare out, while they were in the neighborhood. Before you'd rescued John White. Before you'd done any of your art."

"So that created a paradox, didn't it?" Jonah asked.

"Exactly," JB said. "If there's no artwork, there's no reason Brendan and Antonio are famous, so there's no reason Gary and Hodge would kidnap them."

"Not . . . paradox. If ripple . . . stopped," Second murmured, from his position on the ground. He'd managed to roll to his side, but it looked painful.

"Ah, yes," JB agreed, frowning. "As my *former* projectionist reminds me, there isn't a paradox, or isn't one yet, because we put up a time barrier to prevent the results of your kidnappings from rippling on into the future. So there's still time to fix things."

"So you still want me to move all these bones?" Andrea asked, looking down at the skeletons strewn along the sand.

"And we have to do all that artwork?" Brendan asked. His words made it sound as if he didn't want to, but he had a faraway, dreamy look in his eye.

"We'll help as much as possible," JB said, looking toward Andrea. "And . . . I will make sure I get you out of this time period before your village burns, Brendan and Antonio. And before you drown, leaving Croatoan, Andrea."

His voice was soft, saying Andrea's name.

"What about my grandfather?" Andrea challenged.

JB sighed.

"I'll see what we can do about him," he said.

Jonah wasn't quite sure what that meant. But he remembered what Second had said about JB, implying that he wasn't such a time purist anymore, that he'd gone softhearted.

And JB said that Second didn't lie to us, Jonah thought. Still, something nagged at him, something he'd missed.

He remembered what it was.

"Are you sure you've told us everything we need to know?" He asked JB, a bitter twist to his words. "Or are you still working on not keeping secrets *unnecessarily?*"

JB's face flushed.

"Sam—Second—*he* told me I had to say it like that," JB said. "To make Andrea feel like it was okay not to tell you about her parents from the beginning. I swear, I wasn't saying it for my own benefit!"

Jonah believed him.

"Add that to . . . the list," Second muttered.

"The list?" JB said blankly.

"Of reasons I'm . . . being fired," Second whispered from the ground. "Tell me all of them."

"Got a couple centuries?" JB joked. "There's the time smack, of course, with Antonio coming into 1600 in the same space as Jonah. Though, actually, I'm grateful for that, because that was the clue that helped me find you. You camouflaged all your other tracks, but you couldn't hide that. So maybe the time judge won't charge you for that one. But I don't think anyone will forgive you for forcing *me* to do a time smack, hitting you, because it was the only way I could get in to rescue these kids. . . ."

Second gulped.

"*That* was a time smack then too?" he asked. "An

authentic one? Not just a very, very close call?"

"Perfectly planned, perfectly executed," JB bragged. A hard look came into his eyes. "I did all the calculations myself."

Second's face went pale.

"But there was only a 38 percent chance that you would find us, only a 20 percent chance that you would take such a huge risk . . . ," he whispered.

"Obviously you underestimated me," JB said.

Second looked up at Jonah.

"That day in the canoe," Second murmured. "Yesterday. After your . . . time smack. Did you *have* to sleep the rest of the day? Or were you just being lazy?"

"It just happened," Jonah said. "I couldn't help myself."

Second's face turned even paler.

"Then I don't have much time," he said. "I didn't want to have to work things this way, but . . ."

With great effort, he forced himself up from the ground. He staggered toward Andrea, reaching his hand toward hers.

"You take . . . Elucidator," he whispered. "You have the most interest . . . in seeing this through. Just press . . . No, wait, I can do that. . . . My one last . . ."

He collapsed to the ground at her feet. A hearty snore escaped from his mouth.

"He's out," JB said, sounding relieved. "He'll sleep for hours. Except—Andrea, did he hit that button?"

Andrea was staring down at the Elucidator that Second had dropped into her hand.

"I don't—" she began.

Just then, something like a movie screen appeared in the trees behind them.

"He did," JB muttered. "But why? What's he trying to do?"

Second's face appeared on the screen, beaming and confident.

"I can answer that," he said.

FORTY-FOUR

Jonah stared in confusion back and forth between the sleeping man on the ground and the grinning, triumphant-looking man on the screen.

"He knew ahead of time what JB was going to ask?" Katherine muttered.

Oh—it's pre-recorded, Jonah thought. *Video, or something like that.*

"Actually, I'm only 94 percent certain that you would ask, 'What's he trying to do?'" Second continued, speaking from the screen. "And only 88 percent certain that Andrea would press the button, if I couldn't. But, as you can see, I prepare for every eventuality. It's what JB's been paying me top dollar for, all these years."

He cleared his throat.

"Speaking of dollars, I want to be clear—I am not in

this for the money. I am not like those greedy bumblers, Gary and Hodge. Then, why did I do this, you ask?" He stroked his chin, like an actor trying to look deep and thoughtful. "The short answer is: hope."

"Oh, please!" JB erupted. "You know better than that!"

"Hope, and . . . I have to admit . . . a bit of boredom," Second continued. "In my job, I watch the same bit of history again and again, sometimes hundreds of times. Can you blame me for getting a little tired of it all? For wanting to do something besides always making sure everything turns out the same way? For wanting something . . . better?"

"How can you be so sure your changes would be better?" JB yelled at the screen.

"You doubt my certainty?" Second asked, as if he'd anticipated JB's outburst. "Never mind. I am done with all that. I am finished with projections and predictions and everything we were always so sure about. Let the changes begin! Because . . ." He smiled sweetly. "I have released the ripple."

"No-o-o-o-o!" JB wailed, diving toward the Elucidator in Andrea's hand. He fell short, landing on Second's unconscious form. "No," he moaned again.

"Too late," Second taunted from the screen. "It's already happening."

JB dug an Elucidator out of his own pocket and began frantically pushing buttons.

"What does he mean, he 'released the ripple'?" Andrea asked. "And *what's* already happening?"

"He broke down our time barrier, to allow the ripples of change to spread forward from you and Brendan and Antonio being kidnapped, and from all of you being incorrectly returned to time," JB said, without looking up from his Elucidator. "The ripples are already flowing. . . ."

Jonah shivered. Nothing looked any different around him—he was still standing in sand near skeletons and trees. The sun still beat down on his head; the heat was still thick around him. Only Dare acted like something had changed: The dog whimpered and moved close to JB.

Then the ground began to shake.

"What's that?" Katherine screamed.

"Time's reacting. Too much change all at once," JB said curtly. "Here." He held out his Elucidator. "We've got to get you kids to safety. Everyone grab on. I can only send you as far as the site of the next time barrier, but as soon as I fix things here, I'll come and get you. Or"—he seemed to very carefully avoid looking directly at any-one—"somebody will."

None of the kids made the slightest move toward JB's Elucidator.

"But this is our time period," Andrea said stubbornly. "You need us to fix it. And to take care of my grandfather."

"And Katherine and me, we came to help Andrea," Jonah said, just as stubbornly. "We aren't finished yet!"

"I was pretty sure you'd feel that way," JB muttered. "Fortunately, I don't need your cooperation."

He hit something on the Elucidator. Jonah caught one last glimpse of JB standing on sand, with Dare huddled against his leg.

And then everything went black.

FORTY-FIVE

Jonah could feel the time speeding past him: seconds, minutes, hours, days, months, years. . . . He was aware of the time passing before he could draw in a single breath, before he could open his mouth to complain, "No, wait, JB, don't send us away. . . ."

He could hear the other kids protesting too.

"No!"

"Stop!"

"Don't!"

"Please!"

Jonah blinked. They weren't actually in total darkness: A dim light glowed off to his left. It was just bright enough that he could make out shadowed figures nearby—four of them.

So just us kids, Jonah thought. *Not JB. Not Dare. JB and the dog stayed behind.*

Jonah and the other kids were all zooming forward in time together, in a loose circle around the light.

The light must be coming from the Elucidator.

Jonah reached toward it.

"JB, I'm going to reprogram the Elucidator," he threatened. "If you don't tell me the right code, I'll just hit numbers at random, and who knows where we'll end up!"

"I thought you might try that." JB's voice came from the Elucidator. "So I locked out any changes."

"Why?" Jonah asked. "You probably just ruined time, sending us away!"

"But I'm keeping you safe," JB said.

Jonah remembered way back at the beginning, when he'd wondered what JB would do if he had to make a choice between saving kids and saving history. This was his answer.

Who would have thought that Jonah would disagree?

"It gets harder and harder to care only about abstract issues like history when you get to know the people involved," JB continued.

"Right, and this is about my grandfather, too," Andrea yelled. "Please . . ."

"Don't worry, Andrea," another voice said.

This voice also had the tinny, slightly distorted sound of an Elucidator transmission, but it wasn't JB speaking.

"Second?" Andrea whispered.

It *was* Second's voice. Jonah saw Andrea looking down; he saw the surprise register on her face as she realized that she was still holding Second's Elucidator.

"I planned for this, too," Second continued. "This is a pre-recorded message, set to be triggered if you were sent forward in time. I knew what JB would do. If you hold on to your friends' hands and press the glowing button, you can all go back to 1600."

"Yes!" Andrea cheered.

"Can we trust him?" Katherine asked.

Jonah leaned closer to the Elucidator that JB had programmed.

"Do you hear that, JB?" he yelled. "If you don't bring us back, Second will."

JB didn't answer.

"JB?" Jonah yelled.

The Elucidator made a whirring noise and clicked out an automated-sounding voice: "Subject you are attempting to reach has been knocked unconscious. Danger! Danger! Alert! Rescue mission needed!"

"That's it," Andrea muttered. "I'll take my chances with Second's plan. Brendan? Antonio?"

"I'm in," Antonio said, grabbing Andrea's hand. "I miss my tracer already."

"I'm all for saving the world with art," Brendan said,

grabbing for Second's Elucidator as well, his hand landing right on top of Andrea's and Antonio's.

"Me, too!" Jonah said, reaching forward. He hesitated. "But maybe Katherine shouldn't—"

"Oh, no, you don't!" Katherine screamed in his ear. She clutched her brother's arm. "You're not going to protect me! I'm going back too!"

Jonah's fingers brushed Andrea's, but at the last moment she yanked her hand away.

"What are you doing?" he yelled.

Andrea stared at him, her eyes sad in the dim light from the Elucidator.

"I don't know if I can save my grandfather," she said. "Or myself. But I know I can save you."

"What? No!" Jonah screamed. He was dizzy suddenly. Did Andrea really mean that she was willing to take chances with her own life, but not his and Katherine's? Was *she* protecting *him*?

"It's supposed to be the other way around!" He yelled at Andrea. "Katherine and me, we're supposed to be saving you!"

Andrea gave him a wistful half smile.

"If you really care about somebody, it works in both directions," she said.

And then she was gone.

FORTY-SIX

"No!" Jonah screamed. "No!"

"Wait!" Katherine screamed. "Andrea? Brendan? Antonio?"

All of them had vanished.

Jonah grabbed the Elucidator that JB had programmed.

"JB?" he yelled into it. "Andrea?"

Silence. They kept zooming through the darkness.

"At least you got what you wanted," Katherine said after a few moments.

"What are you talking about?" Jonah asked. "We're floating through time! We don't know where we're going! We don't know what's happening to Andrea and the others! I don't have anything I want!"

"You got to hear Andrea say she cares about you," Katherine said.

"She didn't—" Jonah began. Then he stopped. He remembered Andrea's last words: *If you really care about somebody, it works in both directions.* And then she'd protected him, just as he'd been trying all along to protect her. Was that like saying she cared?

"But that's not how I thought it'd work!" Jonah complained. "When you and Chip had your big boyfriend-girlfriend talk, he ended up coming home with us. It fixed everything!"

"Yeah, well, it's different this time," Katherine said. "And—aaahhh!"

Something hit Jonah just then, a force powerful enough to spin him around and somersault him head over heels. He clutched the Elucidator with one hand; with the other, he grabbed Katherine's arm while she held his.

"Wh-what was that?" Katherine asked when they'd both stopped spinning.

The Elucidator clicked and whirred.

"That would be the ripple," a voice said from the Elucidator. "Flowing from all the changes in 1600. It's come this far."

"Is that Second *again*?" Jonah asked incredulously.

"On JB's Elucidator?" Katherine added.

"If you've reached this point, you know I prepare for every possibility," the voice continued. It was definitely Second's. "I don't want to brag, but I preloaded 6,582 different messages onto JB's Elucidator, and I covered my tracks so thoroughly that I'm 99.994 percent certain that he didn't find any of them. Although, if it's you hearing this message, JB, I apologize for underestimating you again."

Second paused.

"Still with me, Jonah and Katherine? I thought so." Jonah could hear the smirk in Second's voice, the overconfidence. "This message was triggered by a very exact set of circumstances, some of which may leave you a bit anxious about your friends' fate."

"No, duh," Jonah muttered.

"Oops, did I say *fate*? That's not really the right word anymore," Second continued. "I can't offer anyone as much certainty as I once could, but it's most *likely* that your friends' nobility and self-sacrifice and talent and, well, sheer goodness, have paid off. I believe you're passing the year 1602 right about now, and by then, odds are that Brendan and Antonio have already finished their first major masterpiece, and Andrea has nursed her grandfather back to health. Everyone's doing great. Even JB."

"Then let us stop in and see for ourselves!" Katherine hollered at the Elucidator.

"Now, now," Second said. "I'm sure you're clamoring for some proof of this, but the fact is, I can't do everything. And, well, there are a few teensy problems I sort of created when I released the ripple in 1600. Some would even accuse me of being reckless but, let me just say, I have every confidence that the two of you are going to be able to fix my mistakes. Or, at least, as much confidence as possible, given this new uncertainty."

"Wait a minute—what? What are you talking about? What are we supposed to do?" Jonah sputtered.

He began spinning again: up, down, left to right, right to left, head over heels, heels over head.

"No-o-o-o-o," Katherine moaned.

"Sorry about that," Second said. "You'll be leap-frogging back and forth through the ripple for a while. It will be a race, to see who gets to 1611 first. The two of you, on your mission to fix time? Or the ripple, changing everything?"

Jonah began spinning again.

"I did check, and it appears that neither of you are particularly susceptible to motion sickness," Second said. "Which is a very, very good thing."

More spinning.

"I will never go to an amusement park again!" Katherine screamed.

"Isn't this fun?" Second asked, his voice entirely too cheerful. "I've never been a betting man—what was the point of betting when I always knew the outcome? But now, when anything could happen . . ."

Jonah missed the rest of Second's sentence, because the spinning started all over again.

"So I was thinking a little bet is in order," Second was saying when the spinning stopped. "You succeed in cleaning up the problems in 1611, and I'll guarantee your friends get safely out of the 1600s and back to the twenty-first century. Safely *and* happily, even in Andrea's case."

"And . . . JB's," Jonah mumbled, fighting back dizziness. He couldn't tell if the spinning had begun again or if it all was in his head. "Save JB, too."

"What's that you say?" Second asked. "You say you count JB as your friend now too? Aw, how sweet. I can throw him and the dog in as a bonus. So the bet is, you succeed, and everyone's safe. You fail and—well, anything could happen then! Time itself could end!"

"Jonah," Katherine whispered, tugging on his arm. She pointed.

Jonah had been too focused on the spinning to notice, but there were lights directly ahead of them, zooming closer and closer, faster and faster.

"We're about to land," Katherine whispered.

"My message can only last the duration of your trip through time," Second was saying. "So I'll leave you with this final thought: How many times did you cross the ripple?"

"Five?" Jonah said. "Six?"

"I wasn't counting!" Katherine fumed.

"The actual number doesn't matter as much as whether it's even or odd," Second said cheerfully. "Even numbers mean you'll beat the ripple to 1611; odd means you're starting out behind."

"But we don't know!" Jonah screamed.

"Either way, best of luck!" Second continued. "I'll be waiting for you after 1611!"

"He can't be sure of that," Katherine complained. "He passed out, remember? By now, JB will have him in time prison!"

"Don't you think—" Jonah began, but they hit the last part of their journey just then, the part where everything sped up and it felt like they were being torn to pieces, down to each individual atom. The re-entry into time was harder than ever because they kept hitting the ripple. Spin, stop, spin, stop, spin, stop . . .

Even if Jonah had had an accurate count before, he would have lost it through all that spinning and tumbling.

And then everything stopped for good.

"Numb," Jonah mumbled. "Can't see. Can't hear."

Or maybe Jonah couldn't speak, either, and he only imagined that his mouth was moving. Could he *feel* anything? It took a moment or two, but he could tell that the Elucidator was still in his right hand; he could feel Katherine's hand still clutched around his right arm; he could tell he was lying flat on his back on some hard surface. And then something hit him in the face. Something light—a feather? A leaf?

Remembering how he'd had to brush away pine needles when he'd first arrived on Roanoke Island, Jonah clumsily groped his left hand up toward his face. It took three tries, but he managed to grab on to something: a piece of paper. There was a ripping sound. Jonah didn't really have enough energy even to rip paper, so he froze, clutching the paper.

"Jonah? Katherine? Please answer! Please!"

Absently, Jonah noticed that this was JB's voice again, coming from JB's Elucidator.

Good, Jonah thought. *That's how it's supposed to be. Not Second on JB's Elucidator. That's too confusing.*

"Please answer! Are you there? Can you hear me?"

"—uh?" Jonah said.

He'd been trying for *Huh?* but evidently that was beyond him right now.

"We're on emergency backup power—I don't know how much longer I'm going to be able to talk to you," JB continued. "This is what I have to tell you. Second escaped—"

"Escaped?" Katherine repeated. She was apparently recovering more quickly than Jonah, if she was able to say a whole two-syllable word. And sound outraged, all at once.

"Yes . . . I don't know how he did it—he must have been prepared for me to hit him with that time smack. He must have just been faking it, when he passed out," JB said. "And then he knocked me out and vanished. I should have been prepared for that, just in case. . . ."

Jonah blanked out for a moment. He wasn't worried about Second just then. There was something else . . . someone else. . . .

"Andrea?" he whispered, with great effort. "How's Andrea?"

"Jonah, she's fine for now," JB said. "We're all fine. She's buried the bones; Brendan and Antonio are doing their artwork. . . . We're coping. But listen—" The urgency was back in his voice. "Everything depends on you and Katherine."

Jonah couldn't hear what JB said after that. Maybe the Elucidator shorted out for a few minutes.

"Feel like . . . John White," he muttered to Katherine.

"What are you talking about?" Katherine asked.

"Him, us . . . had to leave everyone . . . go . . . help . . . "
Jonah had it worked out much better in his mind,

better than what he could say. He meant that now he could understand how John White felt, how heart-wrenching it must have been for the old man to sail away from the people he loved, thinking that their very survival depended on him.

Katherine slugged Jonah's arm. She was definitely recovering faster than he was.

"How can you say that?" she asked. "Look what happened to John White!"

"He made it back," Jonah protested. "Found . . . granddaughter, at least."

"*Did* he?" Katherine asked. "How can we know which version of history really happened?"

Jonah waved his arm warningly at her. He was trying to look threatening, trying to keep her from slugging him again. But he'd forgotten that he was still clutching the paper that had blown against his face. Moving the paper back a little meant that his eyes could focus on it now.

It was a page torn from a book. The top of the page had the words NEW VIEWS OF THE NEW WORLD printed in old-fashioned type. Below that was a drawing of a girl in a deerskin dress and a white-haired man standing in the midst of a crowd of Native Americans. The old man was shaking hands with a dark-skinned boy who was wearing a loincloth.

Below the drawing was the caption: *John White and Virginia Dare joining a native tribe, welcomed by One Who Survives Much. Drawn by Walks with Pride.*

"This happened," Jonah whispered.

Katherine stared at the paper.

"Then—the ripple," she said. "It's here."

Jonah thought about that. He thought about how he'd landed and then the paper had come fluttering down onto his face.

"We got here first," he said confidently. "That's good, don't you think?"

The Elucidator crackled to life again.

"Jonah, Katherine, I have to tell you what to do," JB shouted.

Jonah was still looking at the drawing on the page before him. He saw the way Virginia Dare/Andrea held her grandfather's arm, the peacefulness that shone from her face.

"Not if it means undoing 1600," Jonah said. "I won't do that to Andrea."

Time travel was so confusing—making it hard to see what was right and what was wrong, who was a friend and who was an enemy, even which events followed which, and which led to something else. But this was one fact Jonah was sure of: He didn't want to do anything to erase the joy on Andrea's face in this picture.

"You don't have to worry about that," JB said grimly. "Believe me, nobody can undo anything about 1600 now."

Katherine gasped.

"Then you're all stuck there?" she asked. "You, Brendan, Antonio, Andrea—none of you can ever get back to the twenty-first century? None of you will ever see your families again, ever—"

"I didn't say that," JB said, his voice tense. "The year 1600 is sealed off now, all but carved in stone. But we're living *through* it. We're not in any imminent danger, and there are still some possible escape routes up ahead."

"Then why can't we just come back and get you?" Jonah asked. "Meet you at one of those escape routes, maybe. At the bottom of the exit ramp, or whatever you'd call it for time travel."

"Because those escape routes will work only if you and Katherine fix things in 1611," JB said. "Everything's connected."

"That kind of sounds like what Second told us," Katherine whispered.

"You have to keep 1611 stable!" JB yelled, speaking quickly now, as if he was running out of time. "You're our only hope! You're time's only hope! Or else—"

The Elucidator went dead again.

Jonah didn't mind too much. He wasn't quite ready

to think about *or else's*. He went back to staring at the drawing of Andrea, soaking in the peace and joy in her expression.

I did help her, he thought. *And she helped me. It worked in both directions.*

"I can see why some old people just want to think about their pasts," Jonah muttered. "Where they know how things turned out."

"We know some things about the future, too," Katherine reminded him. "We know, no matter what, that we're going to do everything we can to fix time and rescue our friends. Second was wrong—some things are always predictable."

Second was wrong, Jonah thought. *He was wrong about a lot of things.*

It was dizzying to think about how much Second had manipulated them—had manipulated even JB. And though the projectionist had made Andrea happy, Jonah knew that Second had been too reckless, too dangerous, too much of a threat to time.

There would be consequences.

Jonah lowered the picture of Andrea and squinted out toward the world beyond. It was all still just a big gray blur, but he knew that everything would come into focus soon.

Maybe they hadn't exactly outsmarted Second in 1600. But they'd held their own: Everyone was still safe for now. And 1611 wasn't just another dangerous year.

It was also another chance.

AUTHOR'S NOTE

If you go to Roanoke Island in North Carolina right now, in the twenty-first century, you can get there by driving across Virginia Dare Memorial Bridge. And, when you arrive, you'll be in Dare County. Go a little farther east, to the islands that make up the Outer Banks, and you can drive along Virginia Dare Trail. Go north, to Smith Mountain Lake in Virginia, and you can take a cruise on a ship called the *Virginia Dare*. Or, if you just want to stay home, you could bake a cake using Virginia Dare vanilla or listen to music by a band called Virginia Dare.

Virginia Dare is incredibly famous for someone we know so little about. History records only two events from her actual life: She was born to Ananias and Eleanor Dare on August 18, 1587. And she was baptized six days later, on August 24, 1587. And that's it. That's all we know for sure. Both of those details come from accounts written by Virginia's grandfather, John White, who was the governor of the Roanoke Colony. And he left Roanoke on August 27, when Virginia was only nine days old. After that, Virginia's life is a complete unknown. Everything else about her is speculation, myth, and mystery.

I first became intrigued by the Roanoke Colony story when I was a kid. I can even remember reading a biography of Virginia Dare—*Virginia Dare: Mystery Girl*—in the Childhood of Famous Americans series. (You would think that that would have been a really, really short book, but it wasn't.) When I first began thinking about The Missing series, I knew right away that I wanted to include Virginia Dare as one of the missing kids from history. But when I began doing research about the Roanoke Colony, I discovered a much more complicated story than the one I thought I knew.

As far as anyone can tell, Virginia Dare truly was the first English child born in the Western Hemisphere. But even the Roanoke Colony's claim to being the first English settlement in the Americas is a little suspect. As early as 1583, a group of Englishmen tried to start a settlement in Newfoundland. But they gave up after just a few weeks because of a lack of supplies.

When I was a kid thinking about the early Europeans coming to the Americas, I pictured it as being comparable to people in the late twentieth century landing on the moon. But that really isn't the best comparison. First of all, unlike the moon, the Americas already had people living there. Secondly, in a forty-year time span, humans have made exactly nine manned trips to the moon. During the 1500s, Europeans made hundreds of trips back and forth from the Americas. English fishermen, along with those of other nationalities, were routinely sailing to the waters off

Newfoundland, fishing during the warmer months, and then taking their catch home to sell. The Spanish, who had gotten a huge head start and already had numerous settlements in the Western Hemisphere, were routinely crossing the Atlantic with ships full of treasure from Central and South America.

When the English looked at that imbalance—we're getting fish; they're getting gold—they didn't like it. They considered the Spanish their enemies, anyhow, for a variety of reasons, including religion. (Spain was a Catholic country; by the late 1500s, England was Protestant.) Spain seemed to have all the power and was expanding its influence across Europe as well as in the Americas. One of England's main ways of fighting back was to have English ships attack Spanish ships and steal everything they could. This sounds like piracy—or outright acts of war—but the English had another name for it: privateering. All that meant is that the English didn't feel they were doing anything wrong. The English government and its leaders not only allowed the theft of Spanish treasure—they encouraged it. And Queen Elizabeth got a cut of the profits.

Sir Walter Raleigh, one of the queen's favorite courtiers, was also one of the men most heavily involved with privateering. (You probably remember Raleigh's name from some Social Studies class, if you were paying more attention than Jonah.) Raleigh thought that starting a colony in North America would be a way to counter Spain's power in the Western Hemisphere—especially if it served as a base and hiding place for English privateers.

Raleigh himself didn't plan to go to the new colony he envisioned; he stayed in England and sent others out on his behalf. It's hard to know what motivated the actual Roanoke colonists to leave everything they knew and try to set up new homes in an unfamiliar place. Some historians think some or all of the colonists might have wanted to separate from the Church of England and practice their own religion, like the Pilgrims who settled in Massachusetts thirty-three years later. Other historians think the financial incentives might have been more important: Each male colonist was supposed to receive five hundred acres of land.

One of the things I didn't remember about the Roanoke Colony—or had never known—was that there were a few trials runs before John White, the Dares, and more than a hundred other men, women, and children showed up on Roanoke Island at the end of July 1587. Various all-male groups of English explorers and soldiers inhabited the island on and off beginning in 1584. In many ways, these trial runs were disasters and planted the seeds of more disaster. The Englishmen expected the local people to supply them with food—never mind that there was a drought and the natives had barely enough food for themselves. And never mind that the English acted almost schizophrenic, alternately befriending and killing their new neighbors. When the English thought an Indian might have stolen a silver communion cup, they burned an entire Indian village and destroyed the villagers' corn. Later, they stole and ate dogs belonging to other Indians. They also kidnapped a prominent Indian leader's young son. None of this could have endeared the English to the natives. When Virginia Dare's parents and their fellow Roanoke colonists arrived in the summer of 1587, they expected to find fifteen soldiers who had been left to guard an English fort. Instead, they found a skeleton, presumably belonging to a soldier who'd been killed by Indians. Nobody knows what happened to the other fourteen soldiers.

That first discovery must have been disheartening, but there was plenty of bad news to come. Six days after they arrived, one of the colonists, George Howe, was killed by Indians while he was out alone looking for crabs. He left behind his young son, now an orphan. When the colonists decided to retaliate for Howe's murder and attack a nearby Indian village, they discovered partway into the attack that they'd made a huge mistake: The village was occupied by Native Americans who were friendly toward the English, not the enemies they expected to find.

Amazingly, those Indians seem to have been willing to look past that error. But the Roanoke colonists still had plenty of other problems. For a variety of reasons, they'd failed to load up on necessary supplies—including food—on their way to America. And because the captains of the ships bringing them to America had wanted to spend as much of the sailing season as they could privateering (a common theme in the history of the English on Roanoke Island), the colonists didn't arrive until late summer, when it was too late to plant any crops. Finally, one of the things the English had learned from their previous trial runs was that Roanoke Island was actually a *lousy* place for the English to try to settle. This time around, the colonists intended to settle farther north, in the Chesapeake Bay area. But Simon Fernandez, the pilot leading their fleet of ships, reportedly refused to take them anywhere else. Much of the speculation about the Roanoke Colony's fate has been directed at Simon Fernandez. Was he intentionally sabotaging the colony? If so, who told him to do that? And why? Was he secretly working for Spain? Or was he taking bribes from some enemy of Raleigh's within the English court?

Or have Fernandez's intentions simply been misinterpreted because his side of the story is lost to history?

Regardless, Simon Fernandez did agree to let one person go back to England to plead for more supplies: John White. According to his own account, White was very reluctant to leave Roanoke, but the other colonists persuaded him that his word would carry the most clout—he would be the one most likely to be able to get help.

Once he got back to England, White faced obstacle after obstacle. The English were worried about a naval attack from Spain, so Queen Elizabeth ordered English ships to stay in port, to be ready to defend their country. At one point, White had permission to sail, but then the permission was revoked before he could actually leave. Another time, White managed to leave in a small ship with supplies and fifteen new colonists, but they never made it to America. Instead, the ship did a lot of privateering and then came under attack by French privateers. White himself was injured twice during the ensuing fight, and the ship was so badly damaged that it had to return to England. A few months later, the Spanish Armada attacked. But even after England defeated Spain in that epic battle, the Roanoke Colony investors were apparently too distracted to put together another rescue attempt right away.

White finally set sail for America on March 20, 1590, nearly three years after he'd left his colony behind. And he was able to sail then only because he agreed not to take any new colonists. He complained in his writings that he wasn't even allowed to take a boy to act as his servant during the trip. The ship's captain wanted as much room as possible to store the treasures he expected to gain through privateering. And he took a very leisurely path toward Roanoke, detouring to help capture a Spanish ship. As White himself described the situation, "both Governors, Masters, and sailers, regard(ed) very smally the good of their countreymen" in the Roanoke Colony.

The ship White was on, the *Hopewell*, finally neared Roanoke Island in mid-August 1590. The first evening, White was encouraged when he saw smoke rising from the area where he'd left the colony. The next morning, seeing smoke rising from another island nearby, White and others from the *Hopewell* decided to search there first. But this turned out to be a wild goose chase: No humans were in sight, and the fire evidently had natural causes. The second morning, two boats rowed toward Roanoke, but one capsized in the dangerous waters, and seven men drowned. By the time the survivors had dealt with this disaster, they decided it was too late and getting too dark to go to Roanoke. Anchored nearby, in sight of a fire on Roanoke Island, White and the others called out and played the trumpet and sang familiar English songs, in an effort to get the colonists' attention. White heard no reply, and in the morning when he and the sailors were able to land on Roanoke, they discovered that the fire was only from dry grass and dead trees. On their way to the colony site, they saw footprints in the sand that White concluded belonged to Indians, but they met no one.

The rest of the story is as Andrea and Katherine told it: White and the men with him found the colony site deserted and mostly destroyed, but with CRO carved on an nearby tree and CROATOAN carved on a post of the wooden fort (which the kids in this book refer to as a fence, though White would have called it a palisade). White was upset to find that some of his own possessions—including a suit of armor—had been dug up from their hiding places in trunks and left to rot and rust and spoil. He blamed enemy natives for this. But he was overjoyed by the carved CROATOAN, especially since there was no cross carved along with the word. A cross was the sign he and the other colonists had agreed upon to mean that they had left the island in distress. White concluded that his colonists were safe with the friendly Croatoan tribe on nearby Croatoan Island (probably the island now known as Hatteras).

White intended to go to Croatoan Island the very next day. But a storm blew up in the night, and a series of disasters caused the *Hopewell* to lose three of its four anchors. At first, the plan was to go to Trinidad to make repairs and get supplies before coming back to search for the colonists on Croatoan. But continued violent weather blew the *Hopewell* far off course, and it ended up in the Azores, in the mid-Atlantic. From there, the ship's captain decided to return to England.

And that was the end of the *Hopewell's* efforts to find the Roanoke colonists.

In 1593, White wrote a letter to a man named Richard Hakluyt describing his 1590 voyage. By then—six years after he'd last seen his daughter, son-in-law, and grand-daughter; three years after he'd made it back across the ocean to search for them—he seemed to have a philo-sophical attitude toward his losses. But he was still pray-ing for the safety of those he had left behind at Roanoke.

After that 1593 letter, John White vanished from his-tory almost as completely as the rest of his family. Some believe that, since he wrote that last letter from Ireland, he must have lived out his days there, on land belong-ing to Sir Walter Raleigh. Others point to records of a Brigit White appointed to administer the estate of her late brother, John White, in 1606. They say this means

Governor John White must have died that year—even though it's impossible to know if this is the right John White. Still others believe that White might have returned to America yet again to look for his family, just on a voyage that wasn't very well documented. (This is the theory that I would want to believe, even if it didn't help the plot of my book.)

Regardless of what happens to them in life, artists can hope to live on through their work after they die. Woodcuts of White's drawings were published in 1590, but for many years his original work was lost. Some of his drawings showed up in 1788, and they were eventually purchased by the British Museum. Because of growing interest in his work, *The American Drawings of John White* was published in 1964, as a joint project between the museum and the University of North Carolina Press. As Andrea boasts, White's work really is praised for his sensitivity and his depiction of Native Americans as human beings, not completely alien creatures.

For the past four hundred years, Virginia Dare and the other people John White left behind on Roanoke Island have been referred to as the Lost Colonists. What constantly amazed me, researching this book, was how poorly that term fits. It's not exactly that the colonists were lost; it's more that looking for them just wasn't a very high priority for anyone besides John White. In more modern times, if we'd been forced to leave astronauts behind on the moon, I'm sure we would have done everything we could to rescue them. But again, I'm making the mistake of trying to look at the past as if it's the same as the present.

After Roanoke, the English waited twenty years before they tried again to start a settlement in the Americas. This time they targeted a site a little farther north, on the James River in Virginia. The Jamestown settlers heard rumors about sightings of people nearby who had fair skin and blond hair—or people who wore English clothing or spoke English or lived in English-style houses. And there were suggestions that some of those people might have been the remnants of the Roanoke Colony. But the Jamestown residents put very little effort into searching for them. This is frustrating for historians, but understandable. The Jamestown settlers were struggling just to survive. In their first year, all but 38 of the 104 original Jamestown settlers died.

So what really happened to Virginia Dare and the rest of the Roanoke Colony in "original" history? The most depressing possibility is that everyone died not long after John White left. Maybe some of their Indian enemies killed them all. Maybe a Spanish raiding party murdered them. Maybe everyone starved to death.

What John White found in 1590—particularly the lack of a cross alongside the word *CROATOAN*—would seem to indicate that, if nothing else, the colonists did manage to get safely off Roanoke Island. Some historians theorize that the colonists might have split into two groups: One group could have gone to the Chesapeake area as originally planned, while a smaller group stayed with the Croatoans, close enough to Roanoke to watch for White's return. A modern Indian tribe in North Carolina known as the Lumbee claims that the Roanoke colonists intermarried with Native Americans and became their ancestors. One study of these Indians in the late nineteenth century found that 41 of the 95 surnames represented among the Roanoke colonists were carried by members of this tribe.

Others tell different stories about the colonists. Captain John Smith said that Powhatan, the powerful Indian leader near Jamestown, claimed at one point that *he* had killed all the Roanoke colonists. (Powhatan was also Pocahantas's father, as you might remember if you were paying attention in Social Studies and/or watched the Disney movie.) Another sad possibility is that some of the Roanoke colonists might have become slaves of a rather cruel tribe farther inland from the coast. There were reports of unusually light-skinned people working for that

tribe, along with the reports of light-skinned people living more happily alongside other natives.

Of course, the Roanoke colonists of 1587 weren't the
only ones with light skin who might have been wandering
around North America in the late 1500s and early 1600s.
Besides the Spanish and the English, other Europeans
such as the French and the Dutch were exploring North
America. And the history Antonio describes really did
occur: European sea captains did leave behind cabin boys
to learn native languages, so they could eventually serve
as translators. If the European ships then sank or just didn't
bother coming back, the European kids who managed to
survive would have blended in with the native cultures. Or
maybe, like Antonio, some of them might have decided
they liked life as adopted Indians better than life as lowly
cabin boys. Apparently, many of the Native Americans
were quite open-minded about welcoming outsiders into
their tribes.

Even before the official "Lost Colonists," the trial-run
settlements on Roanoke Island provided several missing
persons who might also have accounted for some of the
reports of people who looked or acted like Europeans,
residing in various places along the Atlantic coast. Virginia
Dare may be the most famous person to have vanished
from Roanoke Island, but she had a lot of company. There

were the fourteen soldiers who vanished from the island sometime between the summer of 1586 and August 1587. There were also three men abandoned in June 1586 when their fellow soldier/explorers took Sir Francis Drake's offer of a free ride back to England.

I had never known the story of Drake's rescue effort before, and, like Brendan, I was horrified by his choices. Drake really did abandon hundreds of slaves (both of Indian and African origin) on Roanoke Island to make room to rescue the English soldiers. And he undoubtedly thought he was being heroic and generous, doing this. The slaves immediately vanish from the historical record—nobody knows what happened to them.

It is hard to read the history of this time period without feeling appalled: by how slaves were treated, by how Native Americans were treated, by how the common (nonnoble) English people were treated. And so many of their stories are lost to history because their voices weren't considered important either. I do think time travel would show us many, many fascinating individuals and perspectives and events that have been completely overlooked by history.

Even without time travel, history is constantly reevaluated. Historians have a much better understanding now of how devastating it was for Native Americans to be exposed to European diseases. It is true that entire villages vanished; entire tribes were reduced to a handful of survivors. It's impossible to know exactly how many people died, but early European accounts of travel to the Americas tell again and again of explorers meeting teeming communities of natives at first contact and then, when Europeans came back later, finding nothing but a vast empty wilderness.

If I were a time traveler, I would want very badly to sneak vaccines into the past.

In the absence of any verifiable accounts of what really happened to Virginia Dare and the other Roanoke colonists, numerous stories and fables and myths have grown up during the past four hundred years. Sometimes the stories are passed off as truth: In the late 1930s, people across Georgia and the Carolinas found 48 carved stones allegedly left by Eleanor Dare to tell her family's story. A 1941 magazine article discredited the stones and revealed them as elaborate hoaxes. But as recently as 1991 a book called *A Witness for Eleanor Dare* argued that the stones were authentic.

Even more fancifully, a woman named Sallie Southall Cotten wrote a book in 1901 claiming to retell an "Indian fable" in a long narrative poem: Virginia Dare spurns the advances of an evil Indian magician so, in revenge, he turns her into a white doe. Her true love, an Indian warrior, tries to rescue her by shooting her with a magic arrow, but a rival is hunting her as well. Struck by two arrows at once, she turns back into a human just in time to die.

Maybe if we'd known what really happened to Virginia Dare from the beginning, nobody would remember her or care. Maybe it's just the mystery that makes her so interesting.

Or maybe the truth is an even better story than anyone can imagine. We just don't know what it is.

PEACHTREE